THE NIG
OF TH
STOR

THE NIGHT OF THE STORM

A NOVEL

NISHITA PAREKH

DUTTON

DUTTON

An imprint of Penguin Random House LLC
penguinrandomhouse.com

LIBRARY OF CONGRESS CATALOGING-IN-PUBLICATION DATA
Names: Parekh, Nishita, author.
Title: The night of the storm: a novel / Nishita Parekh.
Description: New York : Dutton, [2024]
Identifiers: LCCN 2023020088 (print) | LCCN 2023020089 (ebook) |
ISBN 9780593473375 (hardcover) | ISBN 9780593473382 (ebook)
Subjects: LCGFT: Thrillers (Fiction) | Novels.
Classification: LCC PR9499.4.P3746 N54 2024 (print) | LCC PR9499.4.P3746 (ebook) |
DDC 823/.92—dc23/eng/20230606
LC record available at https://lccn.loc.gov/2023020088
LC ebook record available at https://lccn.loc.gov/2023020089

Printed in the United States of America

1st Printing

BOOK DESIGN BY DANIEL BROUNT

For Kushal and Avi.
My everything.

THE NIGHT

OF THE

STORM

ONE

The world was ending. The instant meteorologists upgraded Harvey to a Category 2 hurricane, Houston residents stopped dismissing weather advisories and promptly dialed their fears up to apocalyptic levels. Rows of barren shelves gaped in supermarket aisles, muddy footprints streaked the floor, and cash registers beeped like heart rate monitors.

"Honestly, ma'am," the young cashier said, "you will not find drinking water anywhere in the city today."

Jia Shah's shoulders slumped. "Can you please check again?" Her damp hands were clamped around the handle of a steel cart, empty but for a soaked umbrella. While the HEB store clerk clacked away on his keyboard, Jia held her breath, waiting for the *tap-tap* of his fingers to conjure an aisle number with the last case of bottled water.

When he shook his head without looking up, she sighed. "Do you know when you'll get restocked?"

He shrugged and looked past her, exhaustion etched on his boyish face.

"Lady, if you ain't buying, move!" someone chided from the rear of the line.

"Ma'am, please," the cashier implored, his expression equal parts exasperation and pity.

"Yes, yes, I'll get out of the way," Jia said, cheeks warming.

Jia did not blame the cashier. She must cut a pathetic figure—a frazzled Indian woman dressed in a sweat-stained flannel shirt and mom jeans. Her curly hair, grayer than warranted by her thirty-six years of age, was tied in a frayed scrunchie. Six months postdivorce, her signature look was of a woman barely holding it together.

She jostled her way to the back of the store, the cart's rusty wheels squeaking like a faulty air conditioner. She *needed* that case of water.

Spotting a mis-shelved bottled water pack tucked behind canned beans, she felt elated, and pushed past another shopper to grab the case. The woman glowered, and Jia was about to issue a hurried apology when a solitaire diamond snug on the woman's ring finger caught her eye.

Jia's remorse evaporated.

This irate shopper had a partner to commiserate with over her encounter with the rude woman at the store, someone who would *tsk-tsk* at all the right moments in her story. All Jia had was an ex-husband hovering like a vulture over the carcass of her deteriorating relationship with her preteen son.

Earlier that day, Jia had been sitting at her desk, busy copying numbers into a spreadsheet, when she noticed the new email waiting in her inbox like a stealth bomb, ready to detonate her life with one mouse click.

Subject: Re: Case #9950 Custody evaluation.

Dear Ms. Jia Shah,

Based on the recent events at his son's school, my client Dev Banerjee has no choice but to revisit your custody arrangement. It is evident that my client's son is not being provided the best care by his mother. Given the circumstances, it is in the child's best interests to request a thorough custody evaluation.

Custody evaluation. A bolt of anxiety shot through Jia thinking about these two words. It was just like her ex-husband to use her son's suspension as leverage to take him away from her.

The move to Houston was supposed to be a fresh start for her and Ishaan. Jia had wanted to divorce Dev in order to keep Ishaan away from his father's malignant influence, so Ishaan's suspension, after less than a year in her sole care, felt like a slap in the face.

Her ex's name, "Dev," was aspirational. His parents, zealous believers of Hindu astrology, who would refrain from emptying their bowels at inauspicious times were it possible, had consulted a Brahmin priest to find out the Sanskrit characters associated with their baby's moon sign before choosing the name "Dev," a Hindu synonym for "god." Yet for all their efforts, their choice was anything but felicitous. For much of his adult life, Dev had acted in decidedly ungodly ways.

He'd spied on her in the past when they'd both still lived in Chicago, using ostensibly friendly drop-in visits from their common friends to keep tabs on her, but how, Jia wondered, had he found out about the suspension from all the way across the country?

Her phone buzzed. "Seema" flashed on the cracked screen. Jia's chest constricted. She swiped left, shoving her sister's call to voice-mail.

Seema, a Houstonian for over a decade, likely had crates of water stowed away in her kitchen pantry. Normally, in a situation like this, Jia would be camped in her sister's well-lit, well-stocked house in the Sugar Land suburb, lounging on a handcrafted wood swing, royal-red cushions soft on her back, warm hands cupped around a steaming mug of chai. Instead, she was canvassing every grocery store within a ten-mile radius and ignoring her sister's calls.

But the specter of facing her brother-in-law, Vipul, chilled her. Regret curdled in her stomach. The cover-up was worse than the crime, and even worse were *multiple* cover-ups, every missed opportunity to come clean to Seema another brick of guilt erecting a wall between them. Now, given the choice, hunkering down on Galveston Beach, staring into the eye of the storm, was a more appealing option than a night under Vipul's roof.

She was crossing the dairy aisle, nose scrunched at the funk of sulfury stress sweat mixed with rainwater dripping from the shoppers' clothes, when her phone vibrated again with another call from Seema. Seema Joshi was nothing if not persistent. She would keep calling till Jia picked up. On the fourth ring, Jia answered.

"Where are you? I've been calling you since *forever*," Seema intoned. Her sister often had a teenager's grasp of time.

"Sorry, my phone was on silent," Jia said, surprised by the way the lie slipped out easily, plucked from a panoply of her usual excuses: busy at work, lost track of time, poor network at the apartment. She lied on autopilot, but there was no getting used to the uneasy feeling that rose in her throat on deceiving her sister.

"You must come stay with us tonight, okay?" Seema's orders often masqueraded as questions.

"I don't think that's necessary." Jia fidgeted with the sleeve of her rumpled shirt.

Seema was only a year older than Jia, yet Jia was used to playing the role of a dutiful soldier. Even now that they were both adults, Jia had to fight the instinct to comply with Seema.

"You're all aloooone." Seema's inflection turned ghoulish on the last word.

For Seema, married for over a decade, the lives of single mothers were filled with unfathomable horrors. Like first world residents rage-tweeting about the plight of refugees, she had plenty of sympathy to dispense but not an ounce of empathy, because Seema sure as hell was not walking in a single mother's shoes.

"I'm not alone, I have Ishaan," Jia said, checking her watch. She had to get home fast to pick him up from Ms. Nikki's house.

"Okay, fine, I mean you and my dear nephew are both alone."

Isn't everyone alone by that logic? Jia pursed her lips. She stepped aside as a child zoomed past her, knocking down boxes of Froot Loops.

Seema continued, "Vipul says it's the storm of the century. He suggested I call you immediately."

"Did he now? That's very kind of him." Jia said, keeping her tone measured, even as her mind churned, scrambling to decipher the subtext of his words. "Thanks for the offer, but we'll be all right."

"Okay, fine," Seema said, her gruff tone suggesting the opposite.

Acquiescing to Seema was a dynamic easy to fall back on, like slipping into a pair of old, well-worn yet comfortable jeans.

But this time Jia had good reasons to stand her ground.

"Did you fill your bathtub?" Seema asked.

"What? Why?"

"You'll need water to flush the toilet if you're stranded in your apartment without running water."

"Please tell me you're joking." Jia pinched her nose. The exigencies of a hurricane baffled her. The clamor for stocking up on water with the entire city under the threat of submersion seemed counterintuitive.

"You're not taking this seriously enough. You will be safe in our house. It's dangerous out there."

"Umm, yeah, I'll definitely think about it."

"So basically, you'll come up with a last-minute excuse." A loud exhale on the other end. "Listen, if you decide to come, have dinner with us."

Ending the call, Jia exited the store and stopped mid-stride, sucking in her breath. Although it was only five in the evening, complete darkness greeted her. Thick billowing clouds eclipsed the sun. The last vestiges of daylight had dispelled hours earlier than usual for August. The air was thick with dewy petrichor. The light drizzle of the morning had progressed to steady rain, fat waterdrops falling en masse to the ground, bursting into diamonds.

As she dashed toward her parked car, a violent gust whipped her curls and turned her umbrella inside out.

She plugged her key into the ignition, bringing the car's radio to life: "Folks, we have an important update. Hurricane Harvey has now strengthened to a Category 3 hurricane, with winds up to one hundred twenty miles per hour. Oil refineries have been shut down. It is anticipated that schools will stay closed for weeks. Stay tuned for more details . . ."

A slew of incoming messages from Seema buzzed her phone like a vibrating restaurant beeper.

It's a Cat 3 hurricane now! They've started
canceling flights from Corpus Christi. Come
here ASAP.

And in perfect Seema fashion, she followed the alarming warnings with a sanguine Boomerang clip: Seema in her living room, two fingers V-shaped, expansive glass windows behind her reflecting a silver blur of rain, a single tree rocking sideways in the wind. The video's caption: "#glamping."

Jia swallowed, tossed the phone on the passenger seat, and tuned in to Radio Mirchi station. An upbeat RJ ran through a playlist of rainfall-themed Bollywood songs. Jia increased the volume as the singer crooned, earnestly thanking God for blessing the barren lands with rain.

But the throbbing beats were not enough to distract her from Seema's warning.

It's dangerous out there.

Her phone pinged with an email notification.

Her throat turned dry.

Mandatory Evacuation

Per the latest guidance issued by the governor of Texas, we hereby require all residents of Shadowland Apartments to evacuate the premises immediately. Gather your loved ones, pets, and emergency necessities and leave the evacuation zone as soon as possible. Please note that Shadowland Apartments will not be liable for trapped tenants who choose to ignore this order.

Heat crawled up her neck like a bout of fever. Scrolling through her contacts list, she reached the end in two pathetic thumb strokes. Then again, she had never needed to go past her sister's name in the favorites tab. Seema was truly her emergency contact, her first call when a driver scratched her car in the parking lot of Patel Brothers store or when she and Ishaan needed a place to crash after Texas's electric grid failures stripped their apartment of power.

Seema's offer bubbled to the surface like suppressed vomit.

Like a radio station tuned to the frequency of Jia's lowest vulnerability, her ex-husband's words broadcast in her mind.

You cannot raise Ishaan by yourself. When you screw up, I'll be there to take him away.

He had said "when," not "if," as though her failure was an inevitability. Jia's body tensed. The custody evaluation was a storm cloud hovering above her. Every decision she made tonight was crucial. A single mistake could lead to the worst outcome, she and Ishaan trapped alone in darkness, the stench of rotting vegetables filling the air, rationing water while they waited for rescue.

She could imagine the follow-up email from Dev's attorney.

It is evident that the mother's poor judgment led to her son being trapped in a flooded apartment for days.

Jia straightened her spine. If Dev wanted to take Ishaan away, she was not going to make it easy for him.

Her options whittled down; a decision was made.

She would pick up her son from Ms. Nikki's house and go to stay with Seema.

Even if that meant coming face-to-face with Vipul.

TWO

Her nose inches from the steering wheel, Jia squinted at the windshield that remained stubbornly blurry despite the urgent *swish-swish* of the wipers set at full speed. Blinking red sockets of malfunctioning traffic signals seesawed under the pressure of fierce winds. Jia's sedan trundled along Highway 6, in her best estimation of the middle lane, cutting a path through floodwater. The car jerked as if a malevolent spirit were pushing it into a ditch. Currents of churning waves swelled from all directions.

Incessant flash flood warnings made her phone jump in the cupholder like a frog in boiling water.

DON'T DROWN, TURN AROUND.

A glance at her son in the passenger seat instantly calmed her nerves. His lanky frame angled sideways, he peered out the window, shoulders slouched under phantom backpack handles.

Loving Ishaan was a lesson in perception. He bore a striking resemblance to Dev, with his sharp aquiline nose and messy hair, but the same features she had come to revile in her ex, she adored in her son.

When Jia gently nudged the accelerator, a tidal wave of water splashed against the bonnet. The car sputtered for a second. She licked her dry lips. *Damn it.* If the engine flooded and stalled, she and Ishaan would be stranded on this dark street as the car slowly filled up with water. That is, if the rising waves did not sweep them away first. Thanks to his Sunday lessons at the YMCA, Ishaan was a good swimmer, but Jia's mom, in a misguided attempt to keep her daughters away from water, had never taught Seema and Jia how to swim.

Jia pictured herself flailing in the murky depths of the flooding road, silt entering her lungs, desperately trying to come up for air, trying to get Ishaan to safety as all remnants of life deserted her body. He would claim not only the last minutes of her life but also her death, for a young mother's obituary elicited sympathy in readers for a life cut short, but the real sadness, that pang in the heart, was reserved for the children left motherless.

Get a grip on yourself. Jia herded in her spiraling thoughts.

Suddenly, Ishaan yelled, "Mom, watch out!"

Jia gasped. Farther ahead was a street she had taken countless times, but now there was no road.

The street was a river.

Her jaw dropped.

A sliver of a car's roof bobbed in the water. Angry waves splashed against a half-submerged stop sign. A downed tree connected the opposite footpaths.

Her knuckles ghost white, Jia swerved the car in a sharp U-turn and scrambled to find alternate directions on her phone.

Ishaan said, "Mom, listen, let me help you. If you take a left on the next light, it connects to the same street."

He pushed his red-framed glasses up his nose, eyes wide and

alert as he scanned the dark roads, his determined and anxious expression alien on a young boy. He guided her through two more turns, and when they entered Seema's community, he pumped his fists in the air. "I told you I'd get us here, we did it, Mom!"

Jia felt a twinge of guilt.

Were they tripping into each other trying to fill Dev's shoes? She'd informed him that they were going to Seema Auntie's house for a sleepover, bracing herself for an argument—*I want to finish the TV show, why do I need to pack for just one night*—but instead, Ishaan jumped to his feet and said, "We shouldn't have waited this long. It's getting dark, and, Mom, I've seen how you drive when it's raining."

Lately, with Ishaan teetering on the precipice of teenage life, she'd noticed a subtle change in their dynamic. She no longer had to nag him to finish his school assignments, and if she had pronounced under-eye circles, he asked whether her boss was giving her a hard time at work. Jia blamed his hormones for random growth spurts and a burgeoning field of acne on his cheeks, but when it came to an increase in his emotional maturity, she had only herself to blame.

During the darkest times of the divorce proceedings, Jia had been parked on the couch all day, skipping showers and lunches, crying so hard and so often, her eyes puffed up and her cheeks burned from the salt in her tears. One evening Ishaan placed a bowl of soggy, lumpy Maggi noodles on the table, begging her to eat something. It was only when she touched his arm and felt the burning fever raging through his body that she snapped out of her fugue state. She was a mother first, and it was her job to take care of Ishaan, not the other way around.

But now she feared it was too late. After all the times Jia had sobbed into his arms, he had internalized this feeling: It was the two of them together against the world.

After a left on Lolarie Street, she drove past a sign:

HERITAGE WOODS. WONDERFUL LAKEFRONT COMMUNITY!
GRAND NEW HOMES STARTING FROM LOW $700K.

A massive iron gate slid sideways, opening the entrance to a fortress.

Jia drove along a winding trail parallel to a row of small artificial ponds on either side. Jia's trepidation increased with each passing body of water, swelling with rainfall every second, windy rain thrashing the lake upward into an erratic aquatic show.

Even though she had been here many times, Jia's breath still caught a little as she came closer to the house.

Seema's two-story house loomed large on the cul-de-sac. The biggest model in the community, it sat at a higher elevation, as if looking down on all the other houses. The front stucco elevation had a facade of pale brown and cream stones reminiscent of a giraffe's coat.

In the center of the sloping roof, a set of rectangular skylights sat flush with the roofline, meant to stream natural daylight into the house, but tonight, the only light the sky had to spare were the flashes of lightning, and the glass panes were yet another reflection of the storm.

Palm trees, imported from Florida for Seema's "tropical" vibe, struggled to stay upright against the strength of the violent gale-force winds, leaves and branches swaying like a woman's unruly tresses on a beach.

Jia revved the engine to climb the steep European-style cobble-stone driveway, coming to a halt outside an expansive four-car garage, a security camera mounted at the top of each corner. A huge wrought iron door towered in the center of the house, and adjoining it, to the far right, sat the study, shuttered blinds bathed in fluorescent yellow. Was Vipul at his desk at this very moment? Pretending to work, but secretly waiting for the sound of Jia's car? If he flipped the blinds, he would have a clear view of her Toyota.

Ishaan exclaimed, "Mom, look, this is almost like going up the Batman roller coaster."

Jia put the car in park and glanced over at him. He flashed a grin. She smiled. "It's like we're up one of those mountains in Big Bend Park, isn't it?" she said. When he lifted his palms in the air, the way he did on his favorite ride at Six Flags, a different image intruded unbidden into her mind. The same hands pushing another kid. His classmate upright one second, knocked down the next, blood congealing on the cafeteria floor.

Jia's breathing hitched, and she shook her head. She could not let the school's sinister portrait of her son pollute her mind. Ishaan was a normal kid who loved playing *Fortnite* with his friends and begged her to get a puppy. He was not a nascent bully. But in the absence of a partner who knew Ishaan as well as she did, her fears festered in the dark corners of her brain.

Single parent. Pair-ent. It was the cruelest oxymoron in the English language. How unfair it was, traveling the path of parenthood alone, a journey impossible to embark upon without the participation of *two* people.

Jia squashed the worrying knot in her chest and let her gaze travel over the massive structure of Seema's house to boost her confidence. Ishaan would be safe here, and that was what was most important.

There was no room for mistakes.

Within an hour of getting the custody evaluation notice, Jia had met with her attorney, an appointment for thirty minutes that lasted well over an hour as Hanna, a divorcée herself, paused several times to press a glass of chilled water in Jia's hands, asking her to stop panicking and take a sip. Although both parents had equal rights under the law, courts tended to favor mothers as primary caregivers to protect the best interests of the child. Hanna covered the basics of a custody evaluation: The court would appoint a licensed social worker to conduct home visits, review Ishaan's school and medical records, and interview her, Dev, and Ishaan separately before compiling a report with recommendations on the best parenting arrangement.

Hanna's directive was clear: "There is no margin for error." In order to bolster his case, Dev had already started looking for apartments in Houston, demonstrating how far he was willing to go to stay in Ishaan's life. The best course of action, Hanna advised, was to counter with compelling documentation of Ishaan's well-being.

Being legally mandated to prove her worth as a mother was a fitting coda to her downward trajectory since the divorce, but she was willing to do whatever it took to keep Ishaan in her life. A paper was folded in the bowels of her purse, a draft written in the feeble light of her bedside lamp once Ishaan drifted off to sleep in his bedroom, gently snoring, his mouth partly open.

It is my pleasure to write a statement on behalf of Jia for her child custody request. As her sister, I have known her and Ishaan for all their lives, and from the day of his birth, when I saw my sister swaddling my nephew, I knew she'd be a dedicated mother who always puts Ishaan first. I strongly support Jia's request for primary child custody because Ishaan is adjusting well to his new school, and he loves spending time with my daughter, Asha . . .

Some of it was fiction because Ishaan had little in common with Seema's nineteen-month-old toddler. The document went on for two pages, a blank space at the end for Seema's initials, a thousand-word draft that fell far short of conveying the love Jia felt for Ishaan with every fiber of her being, their unbreakable bond. When she was more than forty weeks pregnant and had never felt any contractions, the doctor tried to induce labor, and when that failed, he cut her open with a scalpel to pull out Ishaan, an organ capable of living outside her body. How could a judge be the arbiter of her creation? The flesh on his bones was stitched with her body's sacrifices, but somehow, she wasn't worthy of raising him.

Hanna said, not unkindly, "We cannot have any more missteps. Especially given . . ." She was referring to the suspension of course. She did not know about the incident at the store. Not only did Jia have to be on her best behavior, but Ishaan did too, because behind every misbehaving child was a negligent mother.

They agreed to meet the following week, once the hurricane had passed, to review the documentation and discuss next steps. But in many ways, the damage was already done.

In a country where the government had unchecked powers to separate children from their biological parents without notice, a lot of Jia's mothering was performative, whether refraining from yelling at Ishaan in the supermarket, or arriving extra early to his pediatrician appointments, but the threat of an invisible evaluator watching over her shoulder had especially curdled her relationship with her son.

After taking him to volunteer at a local food bank, Jia wondered on the drive back, did she do it because she wanted him to care about the less privileged or because she hoped it would slip into his interview with the social worker?

A gust of wind slammed into the car, breaking her reverie.

The car shook. Ishaan's hand pressed against the dashboard.

A broken tree branch went flying past the windshield. Jia gasped. Ferocious winds decapitated the security camera mounted above the garage. The frayed end of a white cable dangled in the air.

Dread roiled in her stomach. She swiveled in her seat and craned her neck, frowning at the empty streets.

At first glance, she spotted not a single car.

An eerie feeling slithered up her spine.

Then she noticed that in the house facing Seema's home, a Jeep was parked in the driveway. Where was Mr. Sharma's Tesla? Usually his zero-emission car sat in the driveway, both it and the solar-paneled roof were paid for by his six-figure salary as a tech consultant for the oil and gas industry. He had moved from California with his wife and four children, magnetically drawn to the affordable real estate and absence of state income tax in Texas. Sugar Land was the mecca for Indian immigrants fleeing New York and California. The last time it had rained, Mr. Sharma was out on the streets, teaching his boys how to make paper boats float on water, a feeble attempt to re-create the India he'd left behind.

But tonight, the house was cloaked in darkness.

The hair on the back of her neck prickled. The deserted streets struck her as odd. Seema had said her neighborhood was supposed to be a safe refuge from the floodwaters. Why had everyone left?

Jia tried to reason away the spooky feeling in her belly.

As she stared, a light turned on in one of the rooms. A gap in the blinds emerged. A shape formed in the window. A dark silhouette.

Jia sucked in a breath.

What kind of a person felt comfortable sitting in the dark in this situation?

She flinched—the presence of another human should have assuaged her fears, but something about the person made her nerve endings feel raw.

It was the utter stillness of the figure.

The rain blurred her vision, but Jia knew this in her gut.

The person in the house was watching her intently.

Ishaan pressed on the button to release the seat belt, and as the belt snapped back into place, so did Jia's focus. She groped the backseat for an umbrella and sneezed three times in a row.

"Grandma says sneezing is an evil omen," piped in Ishaan.

"Not everything Grandma says is true."

"It is true!" said Ishaan. "This one time a crow pooped on my scalp, and she said it would bring me good luck and she was right. I aced my math test that day."

Jia pressed her fingers to her temples. Trust Mom to convince a child that getting crapped upon was a good thing.

Mom flung her superstitions at people with the enthusiasm of a saleswoman failing to meet her quotas. *Hanging lemon and green chilies on a thread outside a home's front door wards off evil eye. Eating a spoonful of curd before starting a trip ensures a safe and sound journey. Wearing a black dress to a wedding henna ceremony? Tsk-tsk. Do you want the couple to get divorced?*

According to her, the universe constantly sent signals; people merely had to pay attention to the signs. Jia made a mental note to have a word with Mom before Ishaan's next summer trip to India. She had to limit her son's dips in the pool of Mom's infinite wisdom. "Coincidences don't make luck. Also, doesn't Grandma say rainfall is a positive omen?" Jia motioned to the windows. "It's pouring right now. Shouldn't the good and bad omens cancel each other out?" She smiled.

Ishaan frowned and stared out the window, and she could only assume he was mulling over the lapses in Grandma's logic, of which there were many.

Caw. Caw. Jia jerked. A crow was perched on the rocking chair on the porch of Seema's house, claws digging into the wood, its harsh strident note an unsettling accompaniment to the rain.

The sight filled her with anxiety, and she shut her eyes.

Because though she was loath to admit it, Mom's proclamations sometimes came true.

A crow was an omen of death. Was someone in the house going to die?

The next instant, staccato-sharp knocks burst on her car window.

THREE

Jia jumped.

Seema tapped on the car window, swiping a hand across her wet chin. A tent-sized umbrella in hand, she wore skin-tight jeans and a black T-shirt contoured to her curves. Her hair was tied in a "messy bun"—a misnomer, because this was artfully done, with just a few strands of hair flying loose around her face.

They scurried into a regal limestone foyer, where white marble tiles gleamed under a crystal chandelier, and Jia blinked as her eyes adjusted to the sudden brightness.

On the wall by the entryway, an idol of Ganesh on a metallic leaf observed the proceedings. The idol had plenty of divine company, with framed images of goddess Laxmi and Saraswathi in different nooks, in keeping with a Hindu household's requirement of ten gods per resident.

On her left, a grand spiral staircase trimmed with a red runner led to the second floor, and on her right was the study, its massive French doors closed, no light filtering through the bottom gap. If Vipul was here before, he certainly was not in now.

Phew. Jia followed Seema, feeling a lightness in her legs.

When Ishaan greeted Seema, she pulled him into a strong hug, the kind of fierce embrace that coming from Jia would have made him squirm and protest, but Ishaan wrapped his arms around his aunt, making Jia feel both warm and jealous.

On hearing about the damaged camera, Seema said that the security system had been installed recently, but it hadn't been working properly since the afternoon due to spotty Wi-Fi, and sheepishly admitted that in any case, most of the cameras were actually decoys put up by Vipul. In response to Jia's horrified expression, she added, in a reassuring tone, "Vipul says *we* know they don't work, but no one outside the house does and that's the most important thing."

Uneasiness enveloped Jia. That man across the street, what was he doing right at this moment? Was his gaze pinned to this house and its occupants?

She needed actual safety, not just an illusion of safety. Seema might have sensed some of her anxiety because she shuffled back to the main door and fastened the double-bolt lock.

Seema ruffled Ishaan's hair. "Excited that school is canceled? All your classmates must be thrilled."

A glint of irritation flashed in Ishaan's eyes. He shrugged. "How would I know . . . I've been home—"

Jia coughed loudly, blathering about the weather, and asked Ishaan to dry himself off and change his clothes. She couldn't let Ishaan reveal he had been home all week, his suspension tossed on the growing pile of secrets between her and Seema. But at least for this deception, there was a noble reason. Seema loved her nephew so much; it would break Jia's heart to see that pure affection marred by a wariness or worry. What if Seema was no longer comfortable having him near Asha? It was bad enough he didn't have his father around; she would hate for him to lose his favorite aunt too.

Ishaan ignored Jia's request and whizzed down the hallway toward the living room with the giant television, abandoning his bag on the floor. "Wait, dry up," Jia called out, cringing as his pants left a trail of water, sullying the tiled floor. "Sorry," she mouthed to Seema, but Seema waved a hand. Ishaan had become such a master at ignoring her lately, Jia had considered taking him to a doctor to get his hearing checked out.

"Ugh, the weather's getting worse, isn't it?" Seema said, nude eyeshadow glinting under the recess lights. She had gone for the "effortless" no-makeup look, which likely took her a solid fifteen minutes. Seema looked better on a night staying in than Jia did going out.

Although Seema was only three years shy of forty, her skin was as taut as a college student's thanks to the charcoal masks and eye creams, samples of which she fervently urged Jia to try.

"So, we also invited my brother-in-law Raj and his wife, Lisa. Their apartment is in Clear Lake, and I've been running around trying to get the rooms ready." Seema paused for breath, sounding like a stressed-out party host. "You're lucky you don't have a husband." Her hands flew to her mouth. "I'm sorry, that came out wrong."

"It's okay." Jia gave a strained smile. She glanced askance at Seema and frowned. Lately, these slips had become frequent, as if Seema were trying to feel better about her own marriage—a little dose of schadenfreude to cure the blues. Had Seema lifted the floorboards of her marriage and seen the signs of rot? The back of Jia's throat ached. If Seema knew about Vipul's clandestine visits to Jia's house, would she see Jia as an innocuous victim or a termite eating away at her marital bliss?

Jia had procrastinated herself into a corner, and now she would have to either lie to her sister to her face or blow up her marriage.

It was time to rip off the Band-Aid.

"Listen, I need to talk—" Jia started.

She smelled him before she saw him. Her heartbeats sped up as the earthy, spicy odor of his deodorant wafted through the air. Vipul descended the left staircase, one hand lazily tracing the wooden banister. His red T-shirt stretched over his protruding belly, and a fat gold chain snaked around his neck. A pendant with the letter *V* peeked out amid the clump of wiry chest hair.

Vipul's face lit up, mustached lips breaking into a smile.

A chill hit Jia's core. His last text message hovered between them, the message so potent that Jia was sure if she didn't break eye contact, the words would magically appear in the air, clear for Seema to read.

> The ball is in your court, Jia. I won't contact
> you again. I'll wait as long as it takes. I'll
> wait for you to give me a sign.

And what was a better sign than spending a night in his house?

This was what she was afraid of, that he might see her desperation as an invitation.

"Jia, it's been ages since I saw you."

"Yes," Jia replied. Her heart throbbed. The game had begun. By coming here, she'd ensured he wouldn't see her as a victim of unwelcome advances but as a willing participant. Did he enjoy this, forcing her to lie in front of Seema? She had turned into the kind of person she herself abhorred: a liar.

He smiled again, his teeth dispelling any hopes he felt contrition.

As if they shared a dirty secret. The shame of his actions, her burden.

He pointedly glanced at the wall clock above the foyer.

Seema startled. "Gosh, I forgot. I'll get started on your tea."

"And don't skimp on the ginger," he said, dismissing his wife with the flourish of a busy customer.

He headed back upstairs while Seema and Jia walked down the tiled hallway.

Jia purposely trailed behind, and with Seema's back turned to her, Jia surreptitiously pulled up her phone. When she opened Vipul's chat, her thumb moved on its own accord, like a nail tearing through a scab even after it started bleeding.

My lonely heart was desolate, lacking in love.
Your company bloomed flowers in my barren soul.
I confided to my love but was spurned again.
Oh heart, how do I heal you now?

She selected all the messages and hit delete.

/ / / / / /

AN EN SUITE BATHROOM ABUTTED THE STUDY, AND A LITTLE FARTHER down the hallway was Jia's guest room. A pale blue comforter was tucked hotel-room tight, and a sealed bottle of water waited on the side table.

"I know you tend to feel thirsty at night," Seema said. They were as familiar with each other's quirks as with the stretch marks on their own bodies.

Seema scanned Jia's empty hands. "Where's the rest of your stuff?"

Jia clapped her palm on her forehead. "I had packed an overnight bag for myself, but I left it near the shoe rack back at my place," she said, deflated.

Seema tapped a manicured finger on her lips as her gaze hovered over Jia's curves. "Obviously, none of my clothes will fit you. Maybe my loose flowy dresses I wore when I was having Asha might work." She clapped her hands together. "Ooh. I have this designer collection that's been sitting in my closet forever."

Seema was practically salivating at the prospect of upgrading Jia's "flannel factory," as she called it, and if Jia didn't stop this runaway train, soon she would find herself standing in front of the vanity mirror in the main bedroom, swiveling around on Seema's instructions while she *oohed* and *aahed* at her own clothes. Borrowing Seema's dresses had been fun in college, but there was something pathetic about raiding Seema's maternity wardrobe in her mid-thirties.

"Don't worry about it," Jia said quickly.

"Are you sure you don't want something softer on your skin?" Seema said.

"Yes, I'm very comfortable," Jia said as she concentrated on keeping her teeth from chattering, fighting the chill of her soaked jeans clinging to her skin. "But since I forgot my charger, can I borrow yours?"

Seema cocked her head. "We're an Apple family, remember? But you can use my phone and we have a landline. You don't need to worry about anything when you are with us."

Jia's phone still had a nearly full battery. It was enough.

The room had a single square window with a view of the side street. Jia remembered the creepy neighbor and wondered if he was still silently watching the house. She thought back to her drive here, the row of unoccupied houses, solar landscape-lighting fitted on walkways dimming away like trapped fireflies. "Where are your neighbors?"

Seema made a noncommittal noise. "I'm just glad you're here

with us and not staying in some overpriced hotel. Ishaan can sleep in Asha's room upstairs, and hey, before I forget, there's a gift for his birthday. An Xbox." Seema put her hands up. "I know, I know, I went overboard. But you know he's been through a lot this year, what with your divorce and everything."

Jia was stunned. "I don't know what to say, Seema, that's so sweet of you."

Seema waved a hand. "Don't tell Vipul, though. I told him I'm regifting one of Asha's unopened gifts from her birthday last month."

Asha had so many friends. Jia hoped Ishaan would too after they'd been here awhile. But her sister's words gave Jia an idea. "Do you think we can invite Asha's friends for a birthday party for Ishaan? Especially ones with older siblings. It's just that he doesn't know that many people."

"Of course," Seema said. She counted on her hands a list of all of Asha's friends with siblings around Ishaan's age. As she ticked off each name, Jia's heart swelled with happiness. She could supply Hanna with photographs of Ishaan smiling, gorging on cake, surrounded by wrapped gift boxes.

"Thanks," Jia said softly, overwhelmed with gratitude.

Seema smiled. "What are sisters for?"

"I honestly don't know what I'd do if you didn't have my back."

Seema clasped Jia's hands tight, and when she locked her gaze on Jia's face, her eyes shone with such a discomforting intensity that Jia wanted to look away. Then Seema said, "When were you planning on telling me?"

Jia's stomach dropped. Of course Seema knew. She knew everything. This was what she would do if she knew, plan an ambush.

She pressed her lips together to stifle a whimper. Scrambling, Jia's mind groped and landed on flat-out denial. "I have no idea what you are talking about."

"Still trying to hide from me?" Seema tipped her head sideways. Panic bubbled in her stomach.

Jia's limbs felt weak, and she gripped the dresser edge. She stood perfectly still.

It was like they were teenagers again. Jia had committed the grave offense of meeting up for coffee with a girl with whom Seema had had a falling-out. Seema had waited in the sun all day to accost her, her skin burned from hours of standing in the sweltering heat.

That day, Jia learned that Seema would go to any lengths for revenge, even destroying herself in the process.

"Your ex," Seema said. "He called asking about you. Said you have blocked all communications with him and requested to talk through official channels only. Asked where you were staying during the storm."

"What?" Jia reeled. *Dev?* Her relief that Seema did not know about Vipul was eclipsed by the horror at this revelation.

She felt like a car driver avoiding a collision, only to fall off a cliff.

"Did you tell him where I was?"

Seema cocked her head. "Obviously I told him I wasn't letting my sister stay alone. He sounded really worried, you know."

Dev is in touch with Seema? Jia had kept the reasons for her divorce close to her chest, so for Seema, Dev was still a mild-mannered accountant who could not hurt a fly. They had always been on friendly terms because Dev was talented at cementing himself as an easygoing person with a cheeky sense of humor.

On one visit to Houston, both couples had gone to Jimmy Changas for lunch, where Dev offered his beer and said, "Care for a sip, Jianna?" Seema looked quizzically at Jia, and Dev joked that her three-lettered name didn't leave much room for nicknames, so he'd decided to extend it instead. It amused him to address her that way in front of company, prompting "Oh, is that what Jia is short for," and Seema had found this downright charming, side-eyeing Vipul, who was working on an enormous plate of enchiladas. Her expression was dour, as if wondering why he couldn't come up with inside jokes like this. Eventually, "Jianna" became Dev's nickname for Jia.

In hindsight, Dev contacting Seema should not have surprised Jia. Although Dev had cousins in Louisiana, he didn't personally know anyone else in Texas, and Seema, with her insatiable need to gossip, was the next best option for him to get updates on Ishaan. In a fleeting moment of panic, Jia wondered, *Was Seema the one who told Dev about Ishaan's suspension?* But then she remembered that Seema didn't know about the suspension.

Maybe Dev wanted to check if Jia had chosen to ignore her apartment's evacuation orders. Build an ironclad case against her. Ammunition for the next week. He was leaving no stone unturned.

Seema straightened the already crisp bedsheet. "Look, I think it's best you make up with him. I mean, he gave you full custody and you got to move across the country with his only son. Now I have friends who are divorced, and you should see the amount of stress they go through just to make holiday travel plans. Either you had the greatest lawyer in the world, or he obviously still cares about you."

Jia looked away. Her sole custody was not a result of legal jujitsu or generosity on her ex's part.

She had finagled her escape with Ishaan using something much simpler and more primal, and it still filled her with shame: blackmail.

"But wasn't he always good with Ishaan?" Seema pressed.

Jia sighed. Yes. He was a good father. But he was also a good husband, until he wasn't. From waking up for Ishaan's midnight formula feedings to driving him to swimming lessons, Dev took care of Ishaan with genuine love. While Jia was still scrambling to reconcile the kicking lump in her belly with the mewling creature in her hands, Dev rocked Ishaan with natural ease.

When her friends complained that their husbands made excuses for not feeding the kids, stayed late at work on purpose, called ten minutes of playing with their kids "pitching in," and pretended to sleep through their babies crying, Jia had nothing to offer. In fact, the only point of contention she had was that Dev cared too much, was a natural at parenting, leaving Jia stranded on the island of incompetent first-time parents. But this strong bond was exactly why she could not risk Ishaan being with Dev. Ishaan idolized Dev. He would absorb Dev's flaws like a sponge, and what kind of a man would he turn into? What if Dev betrayed Ishaan the way he had betrayed Jia? She couldn't let Ishaan experience the whiplash she had felt struggling to accept that she hadn't truly known the person she'd trusted more than anyone.

"Please don't talk to him," Jia begged Seema. She explained the upcoming custody evaluation and showed her the witness statement draft.

Seema eyed the document, and after a momentary pause, she said, "I'd be happy to. Who, after all, is a better witness than me of your *good character*?"

Did her sister's tone turn ominous at the end? A frisson of fear went through Jia, but the moment passed, and Seema was already pulling out the top dresser drawer for a pen. She made room for the paper by nudging a photo frame aside, laid it flat on the wooden surface, scanned the document again, and was about to sign it, but then she looked up, the pen's tip pressed against her pink lips.

"You know what," Seema said. "Why don't I read this carefully and see if I can make it shine."

"Shine?"

"Yeah. This is good, but we can make it more personal." Seema said. "I'll pepper this with anecdotes about times when you have put Ishaan's interests above yours. I'll talk about how Ishaan is always respectful and honest, and he gets that from his mother."

Jia thanked Seema again, but an alarming thought came to her.

If Seema knew about Vipul, what would she do? Would she still sign the statement attesting to Jia's good character? No, instead, she would hop on the phone and tell Dev about the time Ishaan waited alone on the school grounds because Jia was late picking him up, or the chats in which Jia shared her worries that Ishaan didn't have any positive male role models, or her guilty admissions of the times she happily dropped him off at school and then took the day off from work to spend the day alone in peace.

Jia made up her mind then and there. She wouldn't tell Seema anything.

Hot shame filled her. Didn't her sister have a right to know? As a wife, Seema deserved to see the cracks in the foundation of her marriage, but Jia was a mother first.

When Ishaan was born, Jia's mom had served up clichés like "A mother is reborn when a child is born."

But the mystical platitude really meant this: Most parts of her would die after giving birth. Not an instant annihilation, but a gradual stripping, like metal corroding, reducing other roles to ghosts of their former selves, till only one remained. A mother.

As Seema nipped to the kitchen to get started on Vipul's tea, Jia flopped on the bed and stared out the window.

Fat drops speckled the glass panes, and only then Jia did realize that Seema had never answered her question.

Where were all the neighbors?

/ / / / / /

JIA PADDED DOWN THE HALLWAY, KEEPING HER EYES PEELED FOR Vipul. Next to her room was Asha's playroom, and farther ahead, next to a powder room, lay a narrow corridor, at the end of which was Seema's mother-in-law's bedroom. Shrill background tunes of a Hindi soap opera drifted from the room. Grandma spent her free time, of which she had plenty, glued to a stable of regressive television shows starring mothers-in-law in garish makeup scheming against their daughters-in-law. It was a war between women, with the kitchen as the battleground, and weapons of war were food, petty insults, and fabricated misunderstandings. The grand prize was the honor of being the vilest human. The shows encouraged their audiences to one-up machinations against their own family members, and as executive producers, spurred by the ratings, churned out more and more material, it created such a toxic feedback loop that it was hard to tell if the actors inspired the audiences or vice versa.

Jia kept going, coming to the family room at the far end of the house, which had a lofty ceiling redolent of a cathedral. Once a quick scan confirmed Vipul's absence, Jia flopped in relief onto an immaculate beige leather love seat.

A giant wall-mounted flat-screen television showed a news channel, and the media, never letting a tragedy go to waste, had wall-to-wall coverage of the hurricane, the rainfall and winds already wreaking horrific damage: houses reduced to rubble, flooded highways with the tops of the exit markers the only indicators of formerly bustling roadways underneath.

Ishaan watched the news, plonked on a recliner opposite her, crossing and uncrossing his long legs on the extended footrest, fingers tapping on the armrests, a ball of restless energy with no outlet.

A chyron appeared at the bottom of the screen:

HURRICANE HARVEY HAS NOW BEEN UPGRADED TO A
CATEGORY 4 HURRICANE.

A buttoned-up host grimly explained that while a Category 3 was a major hurricane, a Category 4 hurricane was catastrophic. Irreparable damage to houses and trees was inevitable. They were looking at possibly weeks with no water and no electric supply.

"Simply put," the host said morbidly, "this is an unprecedented event. The next eight hours are critical."

Jia gulped. Eight hours to avoid Vipul. Eight hours to get Seema's signature.

A sofa and a hard-backed armchair completed the seating area, all arrayed around a long rectangular glass coffee table on top of a white Persian rug. The furniture pieces exuded luxury, looked fantastic, but were fragile and high-maintenance, right on brand for Seema.

An Italian-style fireplace with imported Tuscan stones sat on the far back wall, because Seema was a fan of all things European.

Ishaan was eyeing the coffee table, and Jia followed his gaze to a small metallic turtle in the center.

Pinpricks of anxiety broke out on Jia's skin.

She quickly inventoried the items in Ishaan's proximity, anything that could be discreetly slipped into a pants pocket or tucked inside a shirt pocket. She committed to memory the set of coasters, a Rubik's cube, and an antique elephant candleholder on the coffee table.

Nothing from the house would be nicked on her watch; she would make sure of it.

Heavenly scents of cinnamon mixed with ginger permeated the air.

The house was open concept and had a combo living-room-and-kitchen design, giving Jia a clear view of the granite island in the center where Seema stood, pouring tea into a ceramic cup. Along with an irrational love of cricket and a reverence for white skin, an addiction to tea was one of the enduring legacies of the British Empire. Making chai was practically an art form.

Jia called to Seema, "How bad can a Category 4 hurricane get?"

Seema fiddled with her bracelet, mulling over the question. "Category 4? I don't know." She bit her lips in worry. "We've never lived through that before. I think the last one that big to hit Texas was in the '70s."

The uncertainty in Houston veteran Seema's tone worried Jia more than the anchor's predictions.

Suddenly, there was a loud clap of thunder outside. Ishaan jumped. He had always hated storms, especially thunder, calling it "earthquakes in the sky," and if they were in their apartment, he would have rushed to Jia, but tonight, when she reached out to place a reassuring hand on his knee, he recoiled as if Jia were trying to kiss him. "Mom, I'm not a baby."

The oversized bay windows reflected the raging storm, sheets of rain splashing at slanted angles. Jia had an urge to pull the extra-high curtains closed. She had come here to escape the storm, but the house's transparency made her feel like she was right in the middle of it.

Lightning struck with the fast *flash, flash, flash* of excited paparazzi. The sheer length of the glass lent the house a naked aura.

Nothing to hide here.

Glass sliding doors in the kitchen area led to a lush green backyard decked with mini trees, and the only sore spot in the grand oasis was an ugly utility pole, wires crisscrossing it in the far corner. Seema frequently bemoaned how they'd learned about that addition too late in the home-building process to thwart its placement, and her attempts to cover it up by planting flower beds around it had backfired by drawing even more attention to the thirty feet of wood rising from a riot of colors.

"Mom, can we please watch something else?" Ishaan bellyached.

When Jia shushed him, he muttered under his breath, "This is so dumb."

Ishaan, boy of few words, had anointed "dumb" as word of the month, replacing last month's winner, "whatever." A lot of things were included under the umbrella of dumb stuff, things that irked him or annoyed him, but Jia had yet to see him use the term for something objectively stupid.

The doorbell rang, its *ding ding* echoing twice inside the house. Ishaan bounced from his seat, making his way to the fridge, where the digital screen on the stainless steel surface came to life, showing a live view of the door outside. "Cool," he said, suitably impressed, habituated as he was to the old appliance at their apartment, which acted more like a white noise machine than a refrigerator, requiring him to sniff-test the milk.

An attractive couple in their thirties were silhouetted on the screen, faces wet.

Seema smoothed her T-shirt, gave her hair a twirl, and answered the door, trailed by Ishaan with a spring in his step, likely welcoming the break in monotony. She ushered in her brother-in-law, Rajendra, and his wife, Lisa. They strolled inside holding hands, clad in matching black rain jackets.

They looked like the leads of a Hollywood rom-com with a diversity mandate: Rajendra with his almond-hued skin, an easygoing dimpled smile, damp hair stuck pleasantly to his forehead; Lisa with dewy white skin, radiating youth, her marigold hair tied in a French twist, a simple brown leather satchel slung on her shoulder. Their fragrances too were complimentary, his spicy musk aftershave to her floral rose perfume.

Rajendra set a case of beer on the kitchen island, muttering, "It's crazy out there."

"Hi, Rajendra . . ." Jia said.

"I go by Raj now. It has been my writing pseudonym for a while, and I've recently started using it IRL too."

Seema nodded vigorously, approving the abbreviated name, easier on American tongues.

Lisa smiled at Jia, rubbing a toe on the carpet, nails painted in unassuming nude shades, apparently following the Hindu custom of walking barefoot in a home. "Haven't seen you since . . ." She trailed off, a flush rising in her neck.

The corners of Ishaan's mouth turned down. Jia felt her own cheeks warm.

They had met last on Lisa's wedding day, an event at which Dev too was in attendance. Lisa had been clad in a heavy red saree for hours, dutifully repeating chants in a language she did not understand, throwing grains of rice in a fire when instructed by the priest and discreetly rubbing the spots where the itchy fabric had chafed against her skin.

While Ishaan had proceeded to rip the flowers festooned on the mandap, Dev had good-naturedly laughed, and when Jia had admonished him, he'd said, "Lighten up, he's a boy. That's how boys are . . ." Then he had playfully punched Ishaan's arm and said, "Just don't get caught, okay, that's the main thing." He had winked and Jia couldn't help but smile, only later seeing the words for the ominous warning they were. Ishaan and Dev had their own language of play-

THE NIGHT OF THE STORM

ful shoves and shoulder squeezes, and he'd always had a comfort level with Ishaan that made Jia feel like a third wheel. Now one of the wheels had been pulled off—no wonder their life felt so off balance.

"Hope Houston is treating you well," Raj said, coming to Lisa's rescue, and she shot him a quick grateful glance for the change of topic.

One arm looped around Lisa's waist, Raj pulled Seema into a one-sided hug.

"Bhabhi," he said. The Indian endearment for a sister-in-law rolled off his tongue with affection. He gave her a once-over. "You've lost weight."

Seema blushed like a beetroot. "I've been trying this new diet, actually."

While Seema explained the ins and outs of intermittent fasting, Raj and Lisa removed their jackets, and though Raj had on a comfortable cotton T-shirt, Lisa was clad in a long-sleeved, high-necked white tunic, the modest V-neck embroidered with diamond-shaped crystals that had not been in fashion in India since the late '90s.

They grabbed beers and settled on the couch, all without letting go of each other's hands for more than five seconds.

What initially seemed romantic was starting to look ridiculous, like the ungainly actions of a couple on a game show challenged to complete tasks one-handed.

On the television, the newscaster declared solemnly, "No other way to put it. We are expecting a number of casualties tonight."

"That's a grim way to put it," Raj said. His fingers traced lazy circles on Lisa's shoulder.

A prickle of disquiet crested inside Jia. Raj's love language could best be categorized as physical touch because he held onto Lisa with the dedication of a child gripping a balloon string, warned that if this one was lost, another was not on its way, but Jia could not help but wonder, did Lisa find the constant physical affection reassuring or stifling?

Shivering slightly, Lisa tucked her feet inside a soft throw.

"Nice outfit," Seema said to Lisa, suppressing a smile.

She glanced in Jia's direction, an invitation to partake in her pettiness.

Jia refused to take the bait. "If you love wearing Indian clothes, there are great stores in Hillcroft that sell these things. They might even have jewelry that would go well with your dress. Perhaps a pair of silver hoop earrings."

Lisa nodded eagerly, her smile radiant enough to power a house, and although Jia felt the burn of Seema's indignant gaze and knew she would pay for this infraction later, she did not care.

She had a fiercely protective motherly urge around Lisa.

It hurt her to see Lisa bear the brunt of Seema's meanness. Seema's cattiness hovered at a tolerable level around Jia, tempered by the thirty-pound difference in their weight. In the proximity of someone naturally beautiful, however, a PSA had to be issued: *Woman with a flair for toxic passive aggression nearby.*

In many ways, Jia saw a reflection of her own immigrant experience in Lisa's assimilation into Raj's family. The challenges of juggling two cultures, starting life afresh and the inevitable missteps in that journey.

When Lisa bit into sweet after sweet force-fed by Indian aunties, not knowing exactly what she was eating except it was some combination of milk and sugar, did she miss the steak barbecues of her home?

One time, Jia, craving the spicy flatbread loaded with Amul cheese from her hometown, had bitten into a pepperoni pizza, her vegetarian palate gagging at the first taste of meat. She'd assumed at a glance that the even circles were tomatoes. She'd never make that mistake again.

Lisa had sat politely as a flurry of Gujarati words flew around her, learned to ask "How are you?" in a staple Guajarati phrase, "*Kem cho?*"—even as Raj's Indian-born cousins stifled giggles at her accent.

Just like Jia had to rework her English after coming to America, forcing her "zeds" into "zees," rewiring her brain to calculate weight in pounds instead of the British metric system of kilograms, trading one system designed by white men for another designed by a different set of white men. She learned that the quintessential American questions "How's it going? How are you doing?" had only one right answer—"I'm good, how about you?"—because the questioner had not an iota of interest in how you were actually doing.

When Raj asked about the whereabouts of Grandma, Seema waved away his inquiry.

"Oh," she said dismissively. "She's sleeping and she doesn't want to be disturbed, tired bones, you know. We shouldn't wake her up. She'll be out soon."

Seema wanting her mother-in-law to get rest was highly suspect, and more than likely, Seema simply wanted to reduce the amount of time she spent with Grandma.

A cough. Jia pivoted to see Vipul swaggering into the room, Asha waddling next to him.

In her plump clutches was a ragged doll, cotton stuffing peeking out from its holes, rapid wear and tear the toll of a child's favorite toy.

Asha grinned, revealing tiny teeth in her small mouth.

While Seema had a healthy tan, Asha had the pasty white skin of a melanin-deficient European. Seema's mother-in-law had hobbled into the hospital ward, peeked at her first grandchild, and sighed. "A boy would've been nice, but at least she is fair."

Apart from the difference in complexions, Asha was Seema's photocopy, right down to the lustrous thick hair and brown eyes.

This was fortunate because she had dodged a bullet by not inheriting her father's bulbous nose. As if the embryo had glanced once at the set of genes from her father's side and said, *No, thank you.*

When Seema held out her hands, Asha promptly abandoned the doll on the floor for the pasture of her mother's arms. Vipul's gaze traveled the room, and when their eyes met, Jia's blood pressure skyrocketed. Her palms and skin turned sticky and clammy.

Bile crept up her throat as the memories came rushing back. The midnight dings on her mobile from the flurry of Vipul's messages. Her skin turning sticky with sweat in a Pavlovian response to the white blinking dot on her phone.

> You lit up a single light and
> brought me back to life.

How could she escape?

Feigning a headache to hole up in her bedroom until the storm passed was an appealing option, but who would keep an eye on Ishaan?

Jia held her breath as Vipul's eyes swept the room, but in a miracle of miracles, they bypassed Jia as though she were invisible.

It confused Jia, but once she looked around the room, a weight lifted off her chest.

Three other adults occupied the room, all related to Vipul, one by blood.

Of course. Vipul had a lot more to lose than she did. He wasn't going to do anything inappropriate with his brother's family and his wife in proximity.

This gave Jia an idea for how to survive the night. She didn't need to avoid Vipul. She just had to make sure to stick close to the others.

Vipul wrinkled his nose as he looked at the beer bottles.

Raj winked. "Bhai, this wasn't my first preference either. Usually when I'm holed up in a place, I go for something stronger, if you know what I mean." He mimed taking a drag on a joint. "But you wouldn't let me in the house."

As if on cue, Lisa burst out laughing, and reaching across him, she picked up his beer can and left to get a refill.

Jia frowned in concern. Lisa's deferential attitude, her quest to always be a perfect wife, anticipating Raj's every need, set off alarm bells. Instead of changing the mindset of the family she had married into, she had taken her cues from Seema and thought the quickest way to ingratiate herself was by making sure her husband was most taken care of. But Seema's fulfillment of Vipul's demands held a "wouldn't do it if I had a choice" resignation, whereas Lisa's subservience had an undercurrent of fear.

What was she afraid of?

When Asha wriggled away from Seema, Raj covered his eyes and exclaimed, "Peekaboo!" He nudged Lisa. "She looks so big since we last saw her. Isn't she just off-the-charts adorable?"

Lisa's smile was a touch too enthusiastic to be considered authentic. She touched her earlobe where baby Asha had grabbed her long jhumka earrings at their wedding reception, turning her ears puce.

With a guarded expression, Lisa approached Asha and pinched her cheek.

Asha looked puzzled. "Noo," she yelled, pushing Lisa away with both her hands. Her bottom lip wobbled for a second before she burst into tears, both cheeks an angry red.

"I'm so sorry, honey," Lisa said, her ears scarlet. She glanced at Raj, face scrunched up.

Jia felt sorry for Lisa. While her shoulders slumped in disappointment, there was also resignation on her face, and she reminded Jia of the times Ishaan came home with poorly scored geography tests, exams he couldn't seem to ace even when he worked hard.

Asha's wails reached a fever pitch. The sound was trilling, grating enough for Jia to be ready to give up a kidney to make it stop.

"Don't worry, love," Raj said. "She'll get around to you, I promise." He lifted Asha in the air, and everyone seemed to exhale in relief as her cries dissolved into yelps of laughter.

When Lisa sagged back into her seat, relief flashed on her face, and as she let her head fall back, Jia wondered.

Was Lisa relieved because Asha had stopped crying?

Or was it because finally, finally she was free from Raj's clutches?

FOUR

Raj passed Asha to Vipul, who scooped her up in his pudgy arms and pinched her chubby cheeks. She was his "miracle baby," a surprise pregnancy after a decade's attempts at conception.

"*Qué pasa*," blurted Asha.

"What? Is that Spanish?" Raj asked, a bemused smile on his face.

"*Sí*," Asha replied instantly, and the room erupted in laughter.

Seema cleared her throat. "She's going to these preschool Spanish classes."

Vipul frowned. "Since when?"

"It's very important for kids to be multilingual. I told you last week," snapped Seema. "Which you would remember if you paid more attention when I was talking." She turned to Jia. "You can enroll Ishaan too if you want."

Jia pursed her lips. She had gone to the BAPS temple, clutching a rolled-up pamphlet with a schedule for kids' activities and Gujarati language-learning courses, hoping for Ishaan to learn his mother tongue and make new friends.

In lieu of small talk, a well-meaning devotee had asked her about the whereabouts of Ishaan's father, and after Jia saw Ishaan's crestfallen face, she ended up taking him for ice cream instead.

Seema's family was all they had in this city.

Now Jia turned to Ishaan. "Go play with your cousin. Maybe you'll pick up some Spanish."

He looked utterly baffled. "Play with her? She's a baby."

Asha abandoned her plastic ice cream cone and grabbed Ishaan's leg.

"Pweese . . ." Asha said, adorably patting his knee, and Jia quickly took out her phone to take a photo, recognizing an opportunity to document Ishaan's family ties. A picture showing him happy next to his cousin was worth more than a thousand words.

She clicked a snap, but looking at the picture, Jia deleted it with a sigh. Ishaan was frowning, staring at Asha like she was a beetle.

"How would you like to earn some cash tonight?" Seema said, rubbing her thumb and forefinger. She fetched a ten-dollar bill and pressed it in Ishaan's hands, saying this was his initial deposit for the first hour of his babysitting gig. All he had to do was keep Asha occupied.

Ishaan pocketed the note with a lopsided grin, and Seema arched an eyebrow at Jia with a "that's how you do it" look. When Ishaan clarified that his rate would increase to twenty after eleven p.m. since it would technically be considered after hours, Seema laughed. "Aren't you a smart kid."

Ishaan, suddenly solicitous, smiled at Asha while she offered to make him ice cream.

He snapped the lever on the side of the recliner, and as the footrest sprang up, Asha was pushed to the side.

"Stop it," hissed Jia. "You'll hurt her."

"I won't," he snapped back, his shoulders pulled up defensively. "She's fine. Why do you assume the worst?"

Jia flinched.

While she rarely gave Ishaan a hard time about his occasional B grade, she hectored him to be polite to others, especially women. Instead of inquiring what he did at school, she asked if he had shared his lunch with his friends. Between a failed marriage and a middling data-entry job, this part of her flesh was the sum total of her achievements on planet Earth.

She was determined to compensate for the deficits of nature with nurture.

A troubling possibility came to mind. Ishaan was rebelling against her forced altruism, like when she had woken her groggy son at seven a.m. on a Saturday to volunteer at the local dog shelter.

The aggression had been directed toward his classmate, but the message was for Jia: *Back off.*

Of all the aspects of the custody evaluation, Ishaan's interview racked her nerves the most. Jia wondered how Ishaan would paint her, with flattering brushstrokes, talking about his scrappy mom, describing their modest environment in pride-tinged tones? Or would he show resentment for the way she'd downgraded his lifestyle? Either way, Jia did not come off looking particularly good.

Ishaan sulked and gestured at the news playing on the television. "Mom, seriously, they're showing the same roof blowing off over and over again. Can't we watch something else?"

"Let me get Asha's tablet," Seema said.

"No," Jia said. "He doesn't use electronics." She and Dev had jointly decided to raise him away from phone screens, reading him storybooks instead, and Jia intended to continue this tradition.

She encouraged his love of electronics only by letting him attend coding classes. If he was going to be using devices, she'd rather he be in front of a computer trying to figure out programming than be sucked into watching endless videos.

"Where is Shefali?" Jia asked.

Seema's ebullient friend lived down the street and had a son the same age as Ishaan. A part of her had been expecting Shefali to be camped out here, chatting about the ridiculous circumstances. Her son would be good company for Ishaan.

Suddenly, Ishaan jumped up. "There's someone outside!"

Crackling winds jostled the house. Tree limbs snapped.

Jia looked, but the windows remained as dark as ever. "Must be a tree," she said.

"No, I swear, Mom, I saw someone."

Seema tousled his hair. "Probably a shadow."

Raj was leaning against the wall next to the fireplace, nursing a beer bottle. His expression grew serious as he read something on his phone.

"Work emergency?" Vipul laughed. "He writes a blog," he answered himself, putting air quotes around the word "blog."

Raj's eyes shot to his brother. Irritation flitted over his face. A slip in his laid-back demeanor before he gave an amiable smile. "Thanks, Bhai."

His eyes flicked to Jia. "I write finance-guidance articles geared toward millennials. Things like ways to improve your financial health on a small income, how to save enough money for a comfortable retirement, et cetera."

A thin smile spread on Vipul's lips. "Those who can't do, teach, right?"

Raj smiled affably. "Touché."

Lisa stiffened visibly. She scowled at Vipul and turned to Jia.

"His last post, a list of side hustles to boost income, had a thousand likes. All he needs is one article to go viral, and he can turn the whole thing into a book deal, basically."

"Just like that," said Vipul, snapping his fingers. "Viral," he repeated, saying the word as if it were a deadly flu one didn't want to catch.

Raj took a swig of his beer and kept quiet.

Jia squirmed uncomfortably. She wished for a button to unsubscribe from this conversation. Friendship highways had several exit ramps, but sibling relationships had no open doors, even if siblings who loved playing together as children grew up into adults with nothing in common, and family tensions wreaked silent damage like an undetected tumor.

As much as she loved Seema, their relationship had never been the same after her divorce.

In the past, Jia had never begrudged the providences of Seema's life and simply accepted that their lives were like the rabbit and the tortoise.

But divorce had corrected that metaphor. Life mirrored Chutes and Ladders. A single roll of the dice destroyed everything.

She didn't regret her divorce for a second.

It was a chemical peel for the soul, all frivolity denuded.

But after her life had forked in an opposite direction, it sometimes pained her to watch her sister have a complete family, a child with both parents in her life.

Did Raj harbor such resentments? He must have noticed Jia's hands clasped tight in her lap since he chuckled. "Don't worry, Jia." He jerked his thumb in his brother's direction. "Bhai is just giving me material for my memoir—'How to Succeed When Your Family Does Not Believe in You.'"

Vipul's eyes widened. "It's not that I don't believe in you." He continued, edging forward, the pendant of his gold chain swung out by the motion. He tucked it back inside his T-shirt. "What I don't believe in is taking out a loan for a fine arts degree that you know you can't pay off from the outset. Seema made the same mistake. I begged her to get some vocational training, but no, she wanted a master's in business administration. Well, she didn't even finish the degree and dropped out early, so I guess you're better than her, but now, if you'd listened to me and changed your major . . ."

With the air of a dancer performing a familiar routine in a rehearsed-to-death sequence, Raj put up both hands. "Yeah, I'm sorry I didn't do my bit in perpetuating the Indian-guy-in-tech stereotype. I'm sure some bloke from Bangalore is on his way as we speak to correct my giant mistake." He took a swig of his beer.

Vipul breathed heavily. "Do you know how much I've had to struggle? My civil engineering diploma meant nothing when I came here. I had to start from scratch, working night shifts at a motel while finishing my master's degree."

Seema nipped to the kitchen and returned with, by Jia's count, the third cup of tea for Vipul. She was more of a stickler for Vipul's persnickety feeding schedule than Asha's.

"Seema, you remember the night when the motel was burgled?" Vipul asked.

Without missing a beat, Seema said, "Lisa has been married to Raj less than a year, and even *she* has heard that story a hundred times."

The corners of Raj's mouth twitched.

Despite herself, Jia gave Vipul a sad smile. Immigrating to the United States after a certain age came with a unique set of challenges.

Like the Hindu caste system with the Brahmins at the top, the

Vaishnavas in the middle, and the Dalits at the bottom, Indian immigrants in the United States, too, belonged to tiers. At the very top
were naturalized citizens, many of whom, after finally finding themselves in possession of a US passport, had an epiphany: Something
had to be done about the immigrants taking jobs away from Amer-
icans! And they voted accordingly.

Below them were green card holders, slightly less smug, but having grown up in native countries with billion-plus populations, some
of them felt that the only sensible thing was to close any open doors
behind them. And this led to a delicate dance of griping for the need
for tougher immigration laws that also didn't block their own pathway to citizenship.

Work and student visa holders scraped the bottom of the immigration barrel, cycling through visas like a laundry machine, lives
governed by alphanumeric strings like "H-1B," "F-1," et cetera, visits
back home held hostage to visa-stamping appointments.

Seema and Vipul had arrived on the shores of the United States
as green card holders. But Vipul, in his mid-thirties, had to start
over and attend night school while toiling as a motel clerk, because
his civil engineering qualifications didn't translate in the United
States. Raj, on the other hand, went to college to pursue a bachelor's
degree and became an American by osmosis. Seema, having grown
up on a steady diet of Hollywood movies and McDonald's, had an
easier time than Vipul, absorbing the culture like a sponge. But
Vipul's worldview was as thick as a layer of oil: Any new experiences
floated to the top and formed a separate layer.

Vipul drew in a breath to respond.

Raj cut him off. "See, if *you'd* listened to *me*, we could have had
this very pleasant conversation at a bar on Sixth Street." Raj's smile
faded as he gestured toward the liquid bullets slamming the bay

window. "The roads near this area are dangerously flooded. We would've been stranded if it weren't for Lisa's SUV. We should have camped out at an Airbnb in Austin like I'd said."

"I don't care what they say, I'm not going anywhere," said Vipul, arms crossed over his belly.

Seema's gaze bounced from Vipul to the floor. Jia's breathing accelerated. *What is up with her?*

But Vipul was staring at the television screen, awestruck.

Hurricane Harvey had made landfall near Port Aransas in Texas, and its "catastrophic" classification was starting to make sense, because there was no other way to describe the damage. Fierce winds hurled a cargo trailer into a courthouse. Storm surges inundated houses in seconds, two-ton cars swept off to the side. Port Aransas and Rockport were suffering irreparable structural damage, entire businesses razed to the ground. The deadly combination of rain and wind reduced towns to rubble in the blink of an eye. Fatalities were climbing quickly, from people dying in accidental house fires to drivers trapped in flooded cars, but it was too early to capture the true toll of the havoc.

An extreme wind warning was issued in Corpus Christi with sustained winds blowing at the rate of 115 miles per hour, and tornado watches were issued for several areas of Louisiana and Southeast Texas.

Raj's phone started pinging incessantly, and after whipping out his device, he stared at the screen with a puzzled expression.

When he looked up, his face was pallid.

"Vipul," he said, his voice unnaturally high-pitched, "this is really bad. We can't stay here. The governor has declared a state of emergency for thirty-plus counties. This zip code is on the list of mandatory evacuation zones."

Lisa slid out of her seat and grabbed her purse. "We can leave right now."

Ishaan said, "Mom, what about us?" He chewed on a fingernail. "Our car's messed up."

"We're not gonna leave you here, buddy," Raj said. "Lisa's SUV is a seven-seater. If we squeeze in, we can fit everyone."

Jia was stymied. It didn't make any sense. "How can the government be so irresponsible? Wait till things get bad, then issue mandatory evacuation orders."

Raj frowned. "That's not the way they operate. They prefer to give folks time to prepare. This area has been listed under voluntary evacuation for a long time already, hasn't it? You both knew this all along."

Vipul gave an indifferent shrug, but Seema's cheeks turned red, and she avoided everyone's eyes, examining her nails.

Raj's mouth opened in a small O, and he raked his fingers through his hair. "You should've told us."

Jia gasped. The eerie streets. No cars. It all made sense now. People weren't hunkered down.

They had escaped.

Jia sagged forward. In retrospect, it seemed obvious that Seema's house, less than twenty miles from Jia's apartment, was under the same threat, but she had taken her sister at her word.

Seema's house had been a sanctuary for her for so long, it had assumed mythical powers, its towering structure and hilly driveway an insurmountable fortress.

"Mom, are we safe?" Ishaan asked, nudging his glasses up with an index finger. Asha, sensing his dwindling attention, tapped a magnetic scoop on his kneecap like an orthopedist.

Jia nodded and clutched the couch pillow to hide her quivering hands. She had surpassed her already low expectations of screwing things up.

That dangerous drive, they could have easily drowned, but for what? What kind of a person evacuated into a different evacuation zone? Jia wiped her sweaty palms on her jeans.

One thing was clear.

In a hurry to escape danger, she'd walked right into it.

Jia closed her fist, her nails digging into her skin, as she recalled Seema's evasiveness about the absence of her neighbors. She had invited Jia here, fully aware of the perils of her neighborhood, and Jia had followed her blindly.

Raj said, "Are you planning on ignoring the orders and staying?"

Vipul said, "Of course I'm staying." He threw his shoulders back. "If you ask me, all these people who left, you know what they are doing right now? Worrying about the state of their houses."

Raj raised one hand and scrolled through his phone with the other. "Listen. The mayor just released a statement. I'm reading it right now. He says based on the forecasts, the conditions are dangerous—"

"The mayor," Vipul said, his voice dripping with contempt, "is overreacting. I've lived through many storms. We will be fine." He rubbed his palms together. "I'm hungry. Seema, get dinner ready."

While Seema walked to the kitchen, Raj rubbed his forehead and exhaled. "But you do realize even if this house doesn't flood because of the driveway, the streets would be completely flooded. Meaning we could be marooned here for days."

"So?" Vipul swatted his hand. "Your sister-in-law has bought so many cans of cooked beans that we can eat rajma curry for months. At least if I'm here, I'll be able to guard my house. Make sure nothing happens to the luxurious furniture Seema has cluttered it with. What's wrong with that?" He grinned at Raj and said, "Think of this as an opportunity. You can use this experience to write your memoir: 'My Night Surviving a Hurricane.' Now that's a book that'll sell. Not your finance mumbo jumbo."

"It's not safe to stay here," Raj said.

"I'm not going anywhere," Vipul said firmly.

"But . . ." Raj said, coming closer to the edge of the seat.

"Didn't you say you were almost stuck in water on the way over here? How do you think the roads are now? It hasn't stopped raining even for a second."

Raj was quiet.

Vipul pointed in two directions like a flight attendant. "See the steep driveway, there's no way water will rise that high. On the backside, there's a storm retention lake, they are built to absorb water. We're covered from both ends."

Steep driveway. Lake. Jia repeated this in her head, hoping for once Vipul was right, but who knew for sure?

Jia's fingers shook with anger.

When she confronted her sister, she expected Seema to evade her or fake contrition, but she wasn't expecting an eye roll. "Duh, our house is fifteen miles from your place. What did you think was going to happen?"

"Why didn't you tell me all your neighbors had decided to flee?" Jia asked.

"I told you they were staying in hotels," Seema said, eyes flicking to Jia momentarily before she looked away.

"Yes. But you didn't tell me they had *evacuated,*" Jia said through clenched teeth. "And why did you make a big deal about my apartment flooding when this house was under an identical threat?"

"I didn't want you to be alone. You're used to snowstorms, not hurricanes. I couldn't let you face your first one by yourself," Seema said simply. "Isn't this better, to be with family?"

Jia sighed. Of course, in Seema's world, being alone was the worst. She would rather die surrounded by her family than face a crisis by herself.

"Why are you worrying so much? This area is as safe as any. I trust Vipul. And you should trust your brother-in-law."

How could Jia explain this decision to Hanna? Why would she leave her apartment and come to a location even closer to the bayous? She'd thought going to a shelter would reflect badly, show that she was incapable of taking care of her son. But this, this was way worse.

"Sorry, getting a call." Seema brought up a finger to silence Jia and disappeared with her cell to her room upstairs.

Jia crossed her arms, imagining Seema blithely chatting with a friend while custody of Ishaan hung in the balance.

Her phone trilled with a new message. A text from an unknown number.

When she read the words, she couldn't believe her eyes.

Hi Jianna.

There was only one person in the world who called her that. First he'd contacted Seema; now he was reaching out to her.

Dev was back in her life.

He'd been relatively civil till now, only talking through their lawyers like she'd asked. What had changed now?

Another message. Dev had sent an image this time. A photo.

At first glance, it looked like a nondescript building, but then Jia noticed the large "8" ribboned in a canary yellow sign.

Why did he send her a picture of a Super 8 motel?

But this wasn't any random motel.

Jia zoomed into the lettering on the board staked into the grass.

LOWEST RATES IN STAFFORD!

Jia quickly searched for motels located in Stafford, and when she found one, plugging in the address, she forgot to breathe.

Dev was less than fifteen miles away from this house.

FIVE

Her waist digging into the granite, Jia leaned on the kitchen counter as Seema opened the door of the enormous silver fridge and pulled out a carton of organic milk.

The digital screen embedded in the brand-new sleek fridge displayed a slideshow of Seema's family pictures.

Vipul, hair flecked with gray, an arm wrapped tight around Seema, fair-skinned and young, her Bachelor of Arts degree good enough to impress distant relatives with her snippets of English, but not enough to earn more than her husband. Essentially, a Powerball ticket in the arranged-marriage lottery. The first time Mom had shared Vipul's photograph, both Jia and Seema had mistaken him for some uncle. The passage of time had only made things worse because while Vipul's receding hairline exhibited the toll of maintaining their lifestyle, Seema had the age-defying disposition of a yesteryear supermodel.

Jia pulled up Dev's social media check-ins. His Facebook profile had no recent updates. The last post on his feed was from two days ago, hanging out with his office buddies in a bowling alley.

The timing of his arrival to Houston didn't make sense. He couldn't be looking at apartments in this weather.

Then what exactly was Dev doing here?

And why did he want no one but Jia to know?

Was this part of a plan to take Ishaan away from her?

Despite his initial bluster, maybe he'd realized how difficult it was for him to get custody. What if the custody evaluation was a ruse? But Dev was smart; he knew escaping with Ishaan to Chicago was not an option.

With a chill, she remembered the nostalgia Dev had for the village he grew up in, vague notions of moving back home eventually to take care of his elderly parents.

Was that his goal? Convince Ishaan to get on a flight to India to stay with his grandparents in a place away from US custody laws?

Jia's breathing turned sluggish.

Automatically, Jia went to Molly's profile. She brought up her Facebook page even though she knew there would be no new updates. Her dad had decided to keep her account active, a virtual cemetery for her friends to visit, with greetings and apologies that would never reach her ears.

A college friend had posted last month: "Happy Birthday, wherever you are Molly . . . Miss you . . . Wish you were here . . ."

A string of birthday wishes followed this, with Molly's dad thanking them individually. Then someone replied, "What about the elderly woman she killed? Teenagers need to learn drunk driving can have devastating consequences."

"Go away," one of her friends responded. "This is a space for Molly's friends. We don't need your sanctimonious BS."

"Young kids are too reckless, you're free to play with your own life, but not others'."

Jia put the phone down, her breaths coming in fast. Molly was not reckless, Jia wanted to scream at the poster. The Molly she knew turned her homework in early; she was gentle, calm, and meticulous to a fault. Yes, the toxicology report showed a blood alcohol concentration way above the legal limit, but no one knew the real reason behind her inebriation.

Molly had been like a daughter to her, and Jia had thought one day she would proudly attend her college graduation ceremony. But Molly never got to graduate because Jia was the worst kind of mother, destroying her life.

Seema closed a cabinet door, wrenching Jia back to the present.

On the television screen, a desk host said, "In addition to dealing with catastrophic flooding, residents of Houston must contend with a new worry: burglars."

His fellow host, a brunette, chimed in, "That's right, Mark. Tonight, we are covering a liquor store burglary."

She cut to a grainy video of three men, faces hidden under masks, stalking out of a gas station store with crates of alcohol, sidestepping the tree crashed through the glass door.

Mark continued in a somber tone. "Many areas are reported to have lost power, and with the lights out and authorities occupied with rescue operations, people have to be ever more vigilant."

Raj's eyes flicked to the bay windows.

Asha dragged her ice cream cart to the kitchen and pressed a vanilla cone in Jia's palms. "*Por favor.* No sad. Happy."

Jia forced herself to smile even as goose bumps broke out on her skin thinking about the tall windows. Seema's beloved layers of glass, excellent for bathing the room in sunlight and for taking bright selfies, were poor barriers for protecting the house from the torrential storm. An uprooted tree hurtling at the house would be enough to expose them to the bare elements of nature.

Vipul sucked his cheeks in. "That's double-pane glass. It's not that easy to break these windows." He gave a snort of dismissive laughter. "You're living in one of the premier zip codes of Houston. Nothing can happen here. They are just trying to scare people."

"I don't think the storm cares about zip codes," Raj said, a touch of wariness in his voice.

While the newscasters continued their discussion, a chyron appeared below: "Correction: The footage previously displayed was incorrectly attributed to the hurricane. The video was captured from a separate unrelated incident in Baltimore. The news channel regrets these errors."

Vipul pointed triumphantly at the screen. "See? I told you this is all propaganda—"

Out of nowhere, an explosive bang pierced the air.

SIX

Vipul jumped. His teacup slipped from his hands and landed on the floor with a loud clatter, tea spreading over the split shards.

"Gun?" Raj mouthed. Lisa's eyes, widening in alarm, darted in different directions while Asha, busy lifting the flaps of her picture book, sensed the adults' distress and started mewling. Ishaan leapt from his seat, knocking his shin on the corner of the coffee table. "*Oouchhh!*" Jia rubbed his leg and swiveled her head trying to place the source of the sound.

Another two blasts. Jia licked her lips, salty with sweat. Spaced roughly a minute apart, the bursts reverberated through the house, a cross between *phat* and *pop*, loud enough to be heard over the howling wind, and distinct from the cracking sounds of tree limbs snapping and the thunder that had been rumbling all evening.

Jia trembled, and by the time there was a fourth burst, it was clear that the bangs were occurring in the front of the house. Vipul barreled down the hallway. "Wait . . . hold on," Seema called out, but Vipul paid no heed and, grabbing a coat, stepped outside. Raj and Lisa rushed after him, Lisa clutching Raj's elbow with both hands. After turning off the stove with a hasty click, Seema slipped her phone into her back pocket and hurried down the hall.

Sweat pooled in her clothes, and with shaking hands, Jia lifted Asha and pulled Ishaan closer to her, but he wriggled out of her grip, an excited gleam in his eyes. "Mom, those are gunshots! I'm sure it's the man I saw."

When he started scampering down the hall, Jia waddled after him with Asha perched on her hip. She grabbed his arm. "Where do you think you're going?" Asha's whimpers were steadily picking up tempo, and Jia increased her rocking motion, knowing a full-on tantrum was close by.

"But, Mom—" Ishaan exclaimed, indignant.

"No arguments," Jia cut him off. Asha's wails pulsated in her eardrums, making it hard for her to think. She simultaneously rocked and shushed her till her cries subsided into soft sniffles. "Why don't you help me take care of Asha?"

Ishaan opened his mouth, but his words were cut short by Jia's ringing phone. She put it on speaker with tremulous fingers. "Jia," Seema said in an uncharacteristically small voice, "you need to come see this."

/ '/ '/ '/ '/

LEAVING A DISGRUNTLED ISHAAN BACK INSIDE WITH ASHA, JIA VENTURED out and snapped the main entryway door shut, a sense of foreboding rising within her. It took her a minute to get her bearings. As soon as she stepped onto the pebbled driveway, a sharp burst of wind almost knocked her sideways, slapping cold rain on her cheeks.

It was late evening by now. The rainfall had mutated into rain-throw, powerful winds hurling water pell-mell. Streetlights looked like sky-high shower heads with their white bulbs illuminating slanting sheets of rain. The swaying of tree branches had progressed to violent shudders, and the magnolia tree to her left shook aggressively, as though possessed by a demon, a spirit in the throes of exorcism.

Jia stepped over the bushes lining the front walkway to cut a path to the driveway.

Everyone was arrayed around her car, and even after squinting, she could make out only their blurry silhouettes due to the fog-machine effect of the windy rain.

Raj, Lisa, and Seema were all huddled on one side, struggling with their umbrellas twisting in the wind, while on the other side stood Vipul, his rain jacket hood pulled up. A flashlight, limp in Raj's hands, cast a hazy moon below. Their heads were bowed, gazes directed downward with the somber expressions of funeral attendees watching a casket being lowered.

Jia jerked forward, apprehension oozing out of her pores. There was something unmistakably off about the outline of her vehicle. Her nerves jangled as she narrowed her eyes, willing them to see clearly.

When he spotted her, Raj said, "I'm so, so sorry," and trained his flashlight at the bottom of the car.

Jia's insides contracted.

The Toyota's height was lowered by a couple of inches, tires deflated, saggy bottoms resting on the ground like an old man's jowls. The car resembled a camel sitting on its haunches.

Jia vaguely registered someone pressing an umbrella in her hand before she circled the car, her breath held.

One lap confirmed her worst fears.

All the tires had been subjected to the same fate.

Not a single one had been spared.

Hot shame flooded her face while Jia looked at her beat-up Toyota and struggled to remember the last time the tires had been replaced; car-maintenance chores always languished at the bottom of her never-ending to-do list.

The others were yelling, straining to converse over the roaring rain, but their words flew right over Jia's head while she continued staring at the car.

That uneasy feeling rose again.

One tire could be explained away, but what was the chance of all of them bursting at the same time?

Then an extended flash of lightning lit up the sky and brought everything into sharp relief.

Her stomach plummeted.

She finally understood why Raj was "so, so sorry" for her.

On the side, extending from the backseat door handle to the front of the car, a streak of jagged white gleamed on the gray metal. Squatting down, she noticed the inch-wide gash on both the front and back tires.

This was no accident.

Someone had methodically slashed each of the car's tires, lacerating the rubber with a knife blade, before scratching the side with a key.

Jia's feet wobbled, and she rested her forehead on the rain-washed car to steady herself, the surface ice-cold and wet on her skin.

Looking up, she saw Raj rub his chin while peering at Vipul's phone screen. Vipul said, "So you see, there's nothing on the side camera's feed, so if he escaped that way, he would've come up."

Raj straightened his umbrella, inverted by the wind, and sucked in a breath. "That's assuming he is gone."

A chill rose along Jia's spine. She stood up. Even in the hazy darkness, Jia could make out Lisa's quivering form, bringing her elbows close together like she was trying to make herself invisible.

Jia scoped the row of empty (*abandoned*, she reminded herself angrily) houses lining the street. How easy it would be for the perpetrator to hide in one of the many front yards, the dark storm a perfect cover.

Someone could be watching them right at this instant, crouched behind a hedge bush, knife in hand.

Seema's teeth chattered. "Let's go inside." Lisa, windy rain running down her face, nodded vigorously.

Vipul stuffed his right hand inside his coat as if securing something within. "I'm not going to be intimidated off my own property . . ."

Once the initial shock subsided, Jia's mind grappled with the practical implications of losing her car.

She needed her car for her appointment with Hanna next week. How was she supposed to go to her office in downtown Houston without a car? Even if she could take the MetroRail, she would still need a ride to the train station. On seeing Jia hooked to her mobile every day, eyes trained on the little car icon in the Uber app, the custody evaluator would give her a disappointed look before making a note in the report: *Based on the evidence I collected, the mother has a documented history of missing appointments or being late to appointments because she does not have access to reliable transportation.*

Jia clenched her fists. She wanted to strangle the person who had done this.

Her gaze lurched past her car to the SUV parked behind the Toyota. Lisa's car, backed up on the tail end of the steep driveway, looked pristine, sturdy tires untouched.

When she closed her palms, Jia had to suppress a childish urge to pound her fists on the ground. *Why me? Why not Lisa?*

Jia grinded her teeth.

Who would do this to her? Why?

Someone didn't want her to leave, even when the storm ended.

But if imprisoning her was the point, slashing the tires would accomplish that. Why go through all the trouble to damage the car as well?

Jia felt sick, light-headed. Trapping was never the goal; it was intimidation.

But who wanted to instill this kind of fear?

The answer came to her in a blinding flash.

Dev.

He'd checked into a motel nearby. What if he had snuck out hours ago when the rain wasn't so bad? Who would notice a rental parked on one of the many empty driveways?

But slashing tires was too crude for her charming ex.

In ten years of marriage, he'd never resorted to physical violence.

Emotional manipulation was more his wheelhouse. Why slap Jia when a cutting remark, delivered nonchalantly, could lacerate her just the same? When she gained weight after Ishaan's birth, he never complained about her extra pounds. But one day, Jia noticed a brand-new treadmill in the living room. Dev excitedly discussed the purchase, claiming it was on sale, and yet a week later, the receipt in his shirt pocket revealed the equipment had been bought at full price sans any discounts, the treadmill the only item on the crumpled paper ruling out an impulse buy among other purchases.

Currents of lightning ripped through the air, electrocuting the sky.

Jia wiped her sweaty palms. A surge of anger rose within her. Dev had to know how bad the hurricane could get. How could he do this to her and Ishaan?

The Dev she knew would never willingly put Ishaan's life in danger.

A gentle touch on her right shoulder. A quick comforting squeeze. Seema was next to her, and she whispered, "We'll figure something out."

In the house across the street, a window turned fluorescent yellow. Jia remembered the still figure watching her.

Raj gestured at the house as rainwater pounded the walls. "Here's an idea. Why don't we ask your neighbors if they saw something or someone?"

Vipul blew a breath out. "Not neighbors. Neighbor. Singular. Some fellow named Rafael moved in not long ago. He's recently divorced. He likes to keep to himself, doesn't mingle with the others on the street. But"—Vipul raised a palm—"don't even think about getting me to talk to him. I can't stand that guy."

"Well, he might know what's going on," Raj said. "What if his security camera captured who did this? What's your beef with him anyway?"

"He's a party animal. He has these loud parties at his house. All the time," Vipul said.

"Parties Vipul never gets invited to," Seema mumbled in Jia's ear.

Vipul said, "And his friends park their cars on the street, crowding it."

"Cars that are way more expensive than the ones we have," Seema muttered, her voice at a decibel level louder than the rain but still low enough that others couldn't hear her.

"You should see the state of his lawn the next day. All the beer bottles strewn about."

"Also known as having fun," Seema said.

Jia said, "But I need evidence, surveillance footage of some kind to prove someone did this on purpose. It's the only way my insurance will cover the cost of damages."

"Don't worry about insurance," Vipul said. Rain slithered off his jacket. "If you file paperwork reporting the crime, you should be fine." He finger-wagged her. "See, this is exactly why I told you to get rental coverage in your insurance. Your policy is terrible, and I'm sure they'll fight you at every step, but at any rate, they should foot the cost of repairs."

Seema stiffened and side-eyed Jia, but she remained silent. Surely the question would come in her mind, if not now, then later, when she had more time to think about it.

How did Vipul know the particulars of Jia's car insurance policy?

Her teeth chattering, Seema said, "Can we please continue this discussion inside now? I didn't want to alarm you all before, but my neighborhood group has been blowing up with incidents of burglaries. I swear, when we moved here years ago, we didn't have these issues, but lately such incidents have become common in our area." She gestured vaguely at the storm. "Something about tonight, it's bringing out the worst in people."

Raj nodded, scanning the dark skies. A loud clap of thunder sounded. Semicircular rain gutters installed on the house roofs vomited runoffs. "I agree. If one wants to get away with a terrible act, no better time than now."

Vipul shot a serious look at the others. "Could even be a hate crime. Someone targeting Asians."

The moment the words "hate crime" slipped from Vipul's mouth, Lisa shifted uncomfortably, hugging herself tighter, pinching her lips.

Seema exhaled loudly. "Lisa, chillax. No one here is accusing you, Lisa, personally, of this crime, you know."

Jia couldn't make out Lisa's expression properly in the blurry rain, but she suspected Lisa was blushing hard.

"We should report this to the cops ASAP," Lisa said.

Vipul snorted. "Yes, the cops are going to drop everything and look into this. A crime against a family in a brown community."

But Vipul was wrong. That was precisely what the cops would do. A call from an area with an average home price of a million would be answered promptly, any issues investigated thoroughly.

Money, in large enough quantities, razed inequalities to the ground. A posh house, fancy cars, markers of material success earned the respect of authorities, even if it was begrudging. However, Vipul had had an unpleasant experience getting pulled over, en route to his former modest one-bedroom apartment in a secondhand Honda, and nursed a grudge like someone stung by an unrequited first love.

"Maybe some teenagers did this," Raj said doubtfully.

Staring at the water gushing along the streets, Jia had a hard time picturing teenagers wading through knee-deep waters just to pull off a prank.

Bolts of lightning preceded an extended clap of thunder. Two houses down the street, a tree swayed dangerously in the front yard. The tree's scant branches were bare, and its trunk leaned perilously toward the house.

They watched aghast as angry winds jostled the tree, trying to wrench out the roots from within the ground.

The savage winds picked up strength, whipping the flooding water. Jia felt the air's resistance on her face, and she reflexively gripped Seema's arm.

The aged tree trunk snapped with a loud creak.

Lisa gasped.

The wind, failing to uproot the tree, had decapitated it instead.

The tree stump lay bare on the ground, its trunk having crashed onto the roof of the house. The limbs and branches stabbed the windows into oblivion.

Jia swallowed.

Vipul muttered, "Mr. Mehra is not going to be happy when he comes back."

Water filled the streets, the turgid waves dragging flotsam like the spoils of victory. An upturned trash can bobbed on the surface.

White-capped waves lapped greedily along the front lawns of all the houses on the street, licking farther with each ripple.

Jia sucked in her breath. How long before rainwater seeped into the houses?

"Still sure we're safe here?" Raj asked.

To Jia's utter surprise, Vipul tipped his head back and chortled. "I told you, my house is on an incline, so it is impossible to flood." He clapped his hands together. "This is fantastic. When every house lining this street except this house floods, the price of my home will skyrocket." He turned, vaguely gesturing to the front yard. "Yes, some of Seema's landscaping work will not survive. We can assess the damage once the rain stops in a couple of hours."

Raj exhaled and looked skyward with the look of someone rapidly running out of patience. "But, what happens, Bhai," he said, voice dripping with worry, "if it doesn't stop raining?"

Vipul dismissed his brother's concerns. "Your sissy generation worries too much." He looked down the driveway, where frothy waves rose and fell in an undulating pattern.

A fierce chill gripped Jia as a realization sank in.

The steep driveway was literally the hill Vipul was ready to die on, taking them along with him. She saw the arrogant curve of his shoulders pulled back, the jut of his defiant chin, and for the first time recognized his confidence for what it really was.

Delusion.

As they trooped back toward the front door, Jia overheard Raj talking to Lisa in a low volume, words meant for her ears alone: "I hope I'm wrong and he is right, otherwise we have roughly three hours before the house floods."

Jia's stomach turned rock hard as a panicky voice in her mind repeated Raj's words. *Three hours. Three hours before the house floods.*

She was still reeling in shock when there was a brush against her fingers. She startled and only then noticed Vipul sidling next to her, his pace slowed so they were the only ones left behind.

"I can see you're scared. But don't worry about your car," he said, misinterpreting her worried expression. He continued, "I'll take the car to repairs. I can even drop you at work every day." He smiled. "Wouldn't that be nice, we can carpool to work."

A wave of dread swelled inside her, and forcing herself to meet his eyes, she saw on his face a mixture of pleasure and cockiness, but also, to her utter horror, a sense of nostalgia.

Jia deflated, feeling the air leaving her body as if from a weeks-old balloon.

Of course he was happy taking a trip down the old memory lane.

After all, that was how the whole ordeal with Vipul had started. With one pesky deflated tire.

SEVEN

BEFORE

THREE MONTHS AGO

On a Monday afternoon, Jia leaned against the bonnet of her car parked under a canopy of trees in a residential area of Stafford. It was an average sunny day in Houston, with a temperature of 100 degrees Fahrenheit and a "feels like" index at least ten times that.

Jia raised her arms to air out her sweaty pits before jabbing a text to Seema.

> Where are you? Call me back please.
> I've got a flat tire. The towing company
> will take at least an hour to get here. I've
> shared my location on WhatsApp.

When a reply didn't arrive after ten minutes, Jia fanned herself with a crumpled magazine dug up from the pile of old mail on the passenger seat, and called her sister again. Seema promised to call back as soon as she could in an almost singsong voice.

Jia tapped her foot on the sweltering pavement. Beads of sweat pooled at the nape of her neck, rolling down her back, plastering sticky hair to her skin. Couldn't the heat do something useful and expand the air in the tire so she could be on her way?

She was starting to regret her decision to move to Houston.

Six months ago, after trading the biting windchills of Chicago for the sauna-like humidity of Houston, she had tried her best to keep an open mind about the city's quirks, even stashing dollar bills in her glove compartment for the squeegee guy, a disheveled man who cornered drivers at signals and went to town washing their windshields. But she was rapidly running out of patience.

No, she chided herself. This was all her fault.

The low-air-pressure icon had presented itself on the dashboard a week ago, but Jia had interpreted it as guidance, not something requiring immediate action. Why else would the sign be yellow and not the red alert of engine trouble?

Today, on her way to pick up Ishaan after work, driving felt off, as though the car was resisting acceleration, and Jia realized too late that the front tire was deflated.

A glance at her watch made her take rapid breaths. She was going to be late to pick up Ishaan. Pacing the length of the car, she called the towing company again. Called Seema again. She took a sip of bottled water and almost spat it out, the hot liquid burning her throat.

Jia gripped her cell. She'd informed the school, but her fingers ached to send Ishaan a text. A quick, reassuring *I am on my way, running a bit late.*

But she didn't let him have his own phone, even though he begged for one, even though all his friends were in possession of one.

She told herself it was for his own good; she was keeping him away from the addictions of social media, protecting his developing brain from the toxic radiations of the internet. But the truth was, his phone would be yet another thing for her to monitor. She didn't have the energy to worry about who he was chatting with and when, to screen his calls and install all the parental controls on the device, controls that didn't work most of the time anyway.

She didn't deprive him of screen time completely because games like *Fortnite* were a way for him to stay in touch with his buddies in Chicago, and sometimes Jia and Ishaan sat together on the couch and watched video game reviews on her phone. It was a solution that had worked for both of them.

Until today.

Blowing out a hot breath, Jia rolled up her sleeves and opened the trunk. Time for plan B. She popped the cover and found a floatation-device-looking spare tire and a useless ice scraper. One palm on the base of the trunk, she pulled up an instructional video on YouTube, but within the first two minutes, the guy said too many unfamiliar words like "jack" and "lug wrench," and Jia had to replay the video from the beginning, but of course the screen was stuck on buffering because of her phone's limited data plan, and before Jia knew it, her eyes were stinging with tears.

In that moment, although she was loath to admit it, she missed Dev with every fiber of her being.

None of this would be happening if they were still married. She would not be working a second shift as a receptionist for the dental company to make rent. The tires would be fat and happy with air, the engine's oil changed, the car buffed and washed.

During the peak of winter in Chicago, he was up while Jia and Ishaan slept in, ice scraper in hand, hacking away at the chunks of ice on the windshield, whorls of cool mist emerging from his lips.

But it was not the absence of these conveniences that caused her to break down in tears on the side of the road. No, what she truly missed was the presence of someone as invested in Ishaan's life as her, someone who cared equally about her son.

Dev would have dropped everything to pick him up. Her throat pinched at the thought of Ishaan, slouching by the school walls, pulling his backpack higher. His sigh releasing an emotion far worse than anger: profound disappointment in the one person entrusted to take care of him.

Jia took deep breaths. Wallowing in self-pity was a luxury out of her reach.

Just then, a swanky car pulled up right behind her and Jia's pulse quickened. *Am I going to end up on the evening news?*

But then her gaze registered the familiar congregation of an Om signage and Ganesh idol on the dashboard, the lettering on the license plate—"ASH-2014"—and she moaned in relief.

Stepping out of the car, Vipul strode to her side.

Jia blinked, pleased yet confused. "How did you . . ."

"Seema sent me; she's taken Asha to watch one of those Minion movies with Shefali and her kid," he said. He assessed the tires and cut off Jia's long-winded explanation by handing her his car keys. "You go pick up Ishaan. I'll take care of everything."

Jia thanked him, although inwardly she was really thanking Seema, who, like a divine entity, pulled strings to come to her aid no matter what.

In the school pickup lane, Ishaan slid into the leather seat and gave her a thumbs-up.

Jia beamed, assuming he was appreciating her timely appearance before he asked, "Whoa, Mom, did we get a new car?"

"I wish," Jia said as she pushed the car forward with a jerk, her feet still acclimating to the smooth controls. While she pulled out of the parking lot, bringing him up to speed on the day's incident, another SUV went past her and she caught sight of a driver in over-sized sunglasses, cascading hair framing her face.

Did she know her? Something about the familiarity of this woman perturbed Jia, but she could not put a finger on it.

A couple of hours later, when Vipul dropped off her car, Jia and Ishaan were schlepping trash bags to the community disposal area.

Embarrassment colored Jia's cheeks as she quickly put the bag on the side of the bin. They made an unpleasant sight, mother and son sweating profusely, the stench of rotten bananas emanating from the bag, an old screwdriver poking out from a ripped hole in the center.

Even the garbage from Seema's house smelled like lavender due to her special scented trash bags. Everything in her house was re-cycled and separated neatly.

But Vipul smiled warmly and gave an approving nod to Ishaan. "You are a good boy to help your mother. She works hard." He mumbled, after a moment's thought, "Certainly, harder than your aunt Seema."

Jia did not know whether it was exhaustion or guilt—after all, how many kids of Ishaan's age had to help with so many chores at the end of a long school day?—but for the second time that day, she found herself welling up.

Swiping her wet eyes with the back of her hand—what was wrong with her today?—Jia thanked Vipul profusely, but he waved his hand. "Do you ever thank your sister? She is your family and so am I. Now I also noticed your car registration sticker is expired. Make sure you take care of that." He declined her offer to come up for tea, gave her his work cell phone number if she ever needed to reach him in an emergency, and suggested adding him to the list of names authorized to pick up Ishaan.

After Jia tossed him his car keys, he said, "Oh, the kids loved that movie by the way. You might want to take Ishaan. And don't forget the inspection. You don't want someone sticking you with a hundred-dollars fine."

Jia watched as he reversed his car, her scalp prickling in unease as she mulled over his offhand remark. She remembered what had disturbed her earlier. Jia could have sworn the woman she had spotted at Ishaan's school was Shefali.

But Shefali was supposed to be at the AMC with Seema.

Jia shrugged off her concerns. It had been a long day. Her tired eyes must have misidentified her.

Later that night, Ishaan safely tucked into bed, Jia pondered Vipul's words and felt a surprising surge of warmth. *She is your family and so am I.*

Maybe a family did not need to include a father. It was the right decision to start over in this city. She picked up her phone to send Vipul a text thanking him again but thought the better of it. It didn't seem prudent for his device to light up with a message from her at this hour of the night.

They were likely winding down for the day: Vipul reading the news on his tablet, occasionally saying things like "Asha, listen to your mom" without looking up from the screen; Seema cajoling their daughter to finish her milk; Asha begging to listen to one more song before bedtime.

Their life was so perfect it was hard to imagine a scenario in which Vipul would need her help. Even still, she promised herself that if such an opportunity arose, she would do her best to be there for him.

But some promises were best not kept.

Some debts best left unpaid.

Hindsight was like a know-it-all friend who only ever showed up when it was too late to do anything, to throw in an "I told you so."

Jia didn't know then that each favor returned would spawn a gossamer thread of a new obligation, spinning a web trapping them both, until it was too late.

NOW

They headed back inside the house, filing down the pebbled pathway, and as rain streamed inside the soles of Jia's sneakers, she concentrated on not tripping on the slippery ground.

Reaching the front, she pulled up short.

Ishaan stood under the awning of the main door, skinny arms folded tight, sky blue shirt mottled with indigo due to the oblique rain.

"Ishaan," Jia snapped, indignation bursting through her pores. Her frustration with Vipul and fears over Dev and her car snowballed into blinding fury at her son, and she fully intended to scream at him in front of everyone, but when she opened her mouth, the words died in her throat.

Something was terribly wrong.

Ishaan's eyes were bulging, staring at the ground. His body stock-still like a statue.

"Oh God," Lisa whispered.

Jia tracked Ishaan's gaze below. When she saw what he was looking at, her blood ran cold.

EIGHT

Her heart leapt as she caught movement in the dark.

A thin pipe. Tan-colored. But pipes did not move.

And this one was weaving a path, curves undulating on the stones.

Jia's stomach dropped. Her insides melted.

Slithering on the ground, making its way toward Ishaan, was a long snake.

Jia's lizard brain activated. She wanted to leap toward Ishaan. Lisa gripped her wrist, but it was Raj's stream of urgent whispers that kept her feet rooted to the spot. "This is a copperhead snake and it's not here to harm anyone. Probably looking for a dry place because its burrowed home is flooded. But if a snake is surprised, it will think it is under attack and strike. We cannot make any sudden movements."

Seema said, "Oh dear, Asha's alone." She frantically plugged in the code to the garage and scrambled back inside the house, Vipul hurrying behind her.

Raj raised his palms and addressed Ishaan in a gentle voice. "Buddy, look at me. Why don't you try taking slow steps back inside?"

Ishaan's breaths came fast with rasping sounds, but he stayed in place like he was immobile, and squeezed his eyes shut.

The snake picked up speed, undeterred by the sheets of rain slamming its scaly skin.

Jia wrested her hand from Lisa's grip. She couldn't just stand here and do nothing.

With a lunging leap to her left, she followed Seema through the garage, raced through the house, and flung the front door open, rushing to Ishaan's side, but the snake was already too close, nearly touching his shoe.

The reptile reared its head. Ishaan blinked, clutched her arm. "Mom, Mom . . . help . . ." He kept repeating in a small voice, words she knew would haunt her worst nightmares.

Boom.

Jia's scream spliced into Lisa's shriek, her ears ringing from the shot.

Jia blinked rapidly, holding Ishaan close. He'd flattened his hands on his ears, looking around wildly, trying to make sense of what happened.

Vipul was back, standing on the pathway with his legs planted wide, a gun in his hands.

Blood speckled the ground as the injured snake slithered away past the bushes, into the darkness.

Raj wiped his forehead. "Was that necessary? We had the situation under control."

"Didn't look like it," Vipul said.

Raj eyed the weapon with disgust.

Ishaan buried his face in Jia's chest. He smelled of perspiration and urine, and to save him the embarrassment, Jia moved them toward the rain so the stain on his jeans would look like rain splatter.

Lisa pressed a palm to her throat, looking like she wanted to vomit.

Ishaan allowed Jia all of five seconds before pulling away from her hug.

"Why didn't you listen to me?" Jia said. She wasn't mad at him, not really, because her relief suppressed every other emotion. "I asked you to not to leave Asha alone. What on earth was so important that you couldn't wait to come out?"

Ishaan hitched his shoulders "I did wait, all right? But you were taking forever . . ." He gave her a sheepish look. "And then I got bored."

She rubbed her temples. He couldn't go five minutes without an activity to hold his attention.

Of course he wanted to be where the adults were, in the middle of all the action. His adolescent mind was unable to consider the consequences of his actions, like someone walking up blindfolded to the edge of a cliff over a bottomless crevasse.

"Mom, did you see how close the snake was? Whoa, like it was literally on my sneakers." His eyes sparkled, a lopsided grin played on his lips.

Gone was the terror of mere seconds ago, replaced by an excitement.

Like a woman using Photoshop, Ishaan was making the story better in real time, sharpening the edges, enhancing the imagery using artificial filters.

The snake's size would increase with each iteration, large fangs ready to strike. Instead of a single gunshot, a rapid rat-a-tat would take out the predator.

No doubt the encounter with the snake was the highlight of his weekend. Something worthwhile from his suspension period to report to his classmates. When he was prompted to talk about his experience in the hurricane, the snake incident would be front and center, whether it was neighbors, friends, or . . . a social worker.

Jia swallowed.

He might embellish the story, but the danger was no less real.

Her imagination conjured the worst-case scenarios. The snake biting the exposed part of his leg, venom spreading through his body, an ambulance stranded on a flooded street, help just blocks away but out of their reach. Vipul missing his target, a bullet grazing Ishaan's hand, Ishaan falling and bleeding out on the ground.

A lump formed in her throat.

He is not being provided the best care by his mother.

Wasn't Dev right?

Less than two hours after coming here, she had brought him closer to death than in all the years with Dev.

Vipul put the gun back in his pocket.

They huddled under the awning, and an awkward silence descended till Raj cleared his throat. "A gun? Guess y'all have really embraced the spirit of Texas."

Vipul's jaw tightened. "Someone has been sneaking around our house. Unexplained cigarette butts even though none of our backyard workers smoke, to my knowledge. You know what that means, right?" When Raj shook his head, Vipul sighed. "What's the first thing an intruder does before breaking in? They scope the house. I know it, I just haven't been able to prove it. I need to do everything I can to guard my home, wouldn't you agree?"

Ishaan perked up. "Can you teach me how to use the gun?"

Vipul nodded enthusiastically. "I'd be happy to. I took Seema to the gun range last month, and trust me, if I can teach her, anyone can learn."

"No," Jia said instantly at the same time as Raj gave a wan smile.

He said, "Let's wait for the kid to grow up before we push guns on him."

Ishaan stared at Vipul's coat pocket with such a longing it made Jia's blood pressure spike. She could tell his hands itched to grab hold of the gun.

Boys will be boys. Wasn't that what everyone said? At twelve years old, Ishaan was knocking on the door of teenagerhood, and fascination with danger was common. She'd seen him enthusiastically blow things up on video games with his friends. Yet it was up to Jia to discern what was normal versus what were signs she should see coming a mile away if she didn't want to end up on a documentary as a befuddled and distraught mother, at a loss to explain how her sweet-natured son had blown up half his classmates.

Without a partner to share her worries or even tell her she was overreacting, Jia's concerns mushroomed.

When Ishaan was a toddler and Jia chased him on the playground like a hapless zoo employee tasked with capturing an escaped monkey, her scalp smarting from the places he'd pulled her hair, her mother chortled. "Don't worry," she had assured her. "Boys are tough to raise in the beginning. They require a lot of energy, but once they grow older, they are easy to manage. Little girls may look cute right now, but wait till they grow up and give their mothers hell with their attitude."

Jia wondered at times if a teenage girl with mood swings and boy troubles would be easier to manage than her cipher of a son.

When she happened to look at Ishaan again, Jia did a double take.

His lips were pursed, and a shadow clouded his face. This time he was not looking at the gun, but at Vipul's face.

On his face, an expression of pure loathing.

And after what he'd witnessed months ago, who could blame him?

///////

AFTER ISHAAN CHANGED INTO A FRESH PAIR OF CLOTHES, JIA ACQUI-esced to letting him use Asha's tablet for a while. Raj and Lisa headed upstairs.

Jia had other things on her mind. If Dev thought she was going to sit passively, he was badly mistaken. He'd sent her his hotel snap to intimidate her, without realizing she could use that information to her advantage.

She dialed the number of the motel to ask the front desk if they had a guest named Dev and, if she was lucky, find out when he had left the room, but Jia had to hang up when dueling loud voices erupted from the living room.

". . . gone without bothering to clean up the mess," Seema's mother-in-law said, pointing to the broken cup pieces.

Seema's nostrils flared. "Why am I the only one responsible for cleaning in this house?"

Asha, her face red from crying, tugged at the loose end of Grandma's pallu. She was dressed in a Hindu widow's uniform—a white saree patterned with tiny flowers. She had a hunchback posture, papyrus skin stretched over her collarbones, and her scant wispy hair, which looked like sewing threads, was tied in a severe bun.

Her eyes, gray as concrete, swept over Jia, but she continued her rant at Seema. "You're lucky I heard Asha crying and immediately came out." She knocked her cane sharply twice. "I may look old, but I know everything going on under my nose."

"I would too if I had all this free time on my hands," Seema shot back.

"What kind of a mother leaves her child alone, even for a minute?" Grandma said, her chapped lips curling.

"That is not fair," Seema said, her face flushed. "I was gone for less than a minute." An all-too-recognizable cocktail of shame, guilt, and defiance was etched on her face.

What kind of a mother . . . ?

Those five words could manifest evil in perfectly reasonable human actions.

What kind of a mother parked her child in front of a television to watch cartoons for hours on end? What kind of a mother grabbed ready-to-eat food from the supermarket, chock-full of preservatives, instead of making fresh wholesome meals every day? What kind of a mother let strangers take care of her child so she could go back to work?

What kind of a mother did these things? A normal, exhausted mother at her wit's end. But the question was rhetorical, of course, because any mother who put herself first, even for a nanosecond, was a very, very bad mother indeed.

The act of giving birth was such a miracle, it was easy to forget that the mother performing the divine act was still very much a human being with all the attendant flaws.

Grandma blew out a breath, and Jia tried not to gag at her halitosis.

Her body odor was a curious alchemy of herbal concoctions and the chemical odor of Vicks VapoRub lathered on her chest and forehead. If there ever were a pharmaceutical dispensary in a remote forest, it would smell like Grandma.

Seema picked up Asha, glaring at Grandma.

Grandma and Seema were too alike, too dominating, born with

a killer instinct, to ever be comfortable in the same breathing space, and Vipul's marriage wouldn't have survived were it not for the concerted efforts of a third woman: Jia's mom.

Mom had asked Seema to give her all to make the relationship work. "Adjust," she said—a six-letter word used to justify a multitude of atrocities. "Adjust"—the same word Mom used to squeeze into the fourth seat on a local train built to hold three people.

Mom was only following a template commonly used by Indian mothers. The British set up the first railway track, paving the way for modern transportation, but they turned a blind eye to the nation's social ills, and failed to modernize the fabric of the country they ruled for a hundred years. The southern and northern parts of the country each had their own flavors of this injustice. Whereas a North Indian woman came home after an eight-hour shift and proceeded to whip out rotis like a machine, the woman in South India woke up before everyone else to serve rice crepes for breakfast.

The word "adjust" made its way into an Indian woman's vocabulary in the first year of marriage and in no time assumed complete control of her life. And this toxic word trickled down generations, its survival powers rivaling those of a cockroach due to a trifecta of culprits: abusive mothers-in-law, enabling mothers, and supine husbands.

Jia and Seema's mother had raised them with love and affection, but once puberty hit, she transformed overnight into an authoritative figure, hectoring her daughters to make perfect circular wheat rotis and scrumptious curry, all to please a future husband. Both Seema and Jia were more horrified at the changes in their mother than at those in their own bodies. And things only turned for the worse after their education was completed. While Seema saw her diploma as a pathway to a position in a multinational company, Mom saw it as a bargaining chip to get her married to a decent man from a cultured family.

Jia never had any issues with Dev's mother, but after Seema's marriage, her mother brushed aside all her sister's complaints about her new mother-in-law using this simple word—"adjust."

When Seema wanted to fly to India for her cousin's wedding, she had to obtain permission from Grandma similar to a work-leave approval process because now she belonged to Vipul's family. Mom responded to her outrage with "The first year of marriage is the toughest. Just adjust a little." When Grandma canceled Seema's honeymoon so Vipul could pay for a distant sister-in-law's wedding jewelry, Mom said, "Adjust."

One week prior to her first wedding anniversary, Seema packed her bags and came to her mother's house. "I'm done," she said, tears streaming down her face. But her mother, in anticipation of this moment, had saved her most potent weapon. She pulled Seema into a hug, wiped her tears, and fixed her a cup of tea. "I've never shared with you girls the things I've gone through. You won't be able to believe the abuse I endured. You don't realize, but you are much better off. You should be grateful. You're forced to simply greet your mother-in-law every day, well, you don't have to touch her feet like I had to. I was forbidden to enter the kitchen every month when I had my period. I had to wait and eat by myself on the floor once everyone was done eating. You only must ask for permission to come visit me. I wasn't allowed to see my parents till after you were born." She recounted story after story until Seema's trauma paled in comparison to her mother's horrific experiences.

Seema's outrage simmered down, seeing her experiences in a new, favorable light compared to their mom's, and that's when Jia understood why women's progress in India moved slower than Delhi traffic. Indians were wired to look back, and this compulsion to revisit history made it easier to celebrate incremental steps instead of seeing the future and envisioning the long road ahead.

Grandma trained her gray pupils on Jia. "Did your sister tell you about my nephew who's looking for a wife?"

Seema set Asha down. "My baby wants to watch cartoons with Ishaan?" While Asha made her way toward Jia's room, Seema addressed Grandma, her lips curling in disgust: "Your nephew is a useless fellow who sits all day smoking tobacco in his dad's shop. He's not the world's most eligible bachelor."

Grandma snarled. "You shouldn't talk about my nephew that way when your own sister is a *divorcée* . . ." Her mouth twisted at the last word.

Shame heated Jia's cheeks. It was a truth universally acknowledged that an Indian divorcée made for the least desirable bride.

When Grandma hobbled out of the living room, Jia assumed she'd retired to her bedroom, but she soon returned with a paper in her gnarly hands.

Her chest palpitating, Jia took the paper from Grandma's tremoring hands.

"This is the thanks I get for trying to help," Grandma said. "Your mother included this in her yearly parcel of snacks from India."

The back of her throat burned as Jia looked at the single sheet of paper, flecked with yellow oil stains.

The bold title mortified Jia: "Jia Shah Matrimonial Bio Data." It was formatted like a résumé, with bullet points at the top listing Jia's caste (Vaishnava) and skin color (fair), and at the bottom, in a miniscule font like a legal disclaimer one was obligated to include but hoped was never read thoroughly, it stated her marital status (divorced).

Jia cringed, heat emanated from her ears, and just when she thought she couldn't feel worse, she noticed the photo on the top right corner. Dev had been inelegantly cropped out, a fraction of his gray sleeve visible by her left shoulder. The photograph was from five years ago, and Jia no longer looked anything like the beaming woman in the picture, who had eyes brimming with happiness, the dark circles that were now permanently settled under her eyes yet to make an appearance.

WhatsApp proficiency notwithstanding, Mom was a technology noob, and Jia imagined her squinting through her glasses at a screen in a local computer café, enlisting the help of the café owner to truncate her daughter's personality and hopes for the future into a one-page summary. The paper shook in her angry hands. If Jia had a teleportation device, she would travel to Mom's kitchen this instant, roll up this document, and smack her on the head with it.

Seema mumbled, "I'm so sorry, I had no idea."

But it was Jia who was truly sorry. She had had a love marriage to Dev, but this was what Seema must have had to go through for her arranged marriage, an alliance she was pushed into in order to clear the way for Jia. When Mom discovered Jia was dating Dev in college, she gave her an ultimatum to either stop seeing him or marry him. Jia was only twenty-three years old, but she couldn't imagine a life without Dev. So Seema's plans for higher education went by the wayside as Mom started looking for a groom for her elder daughter so that Jia could marry Dev.

Grandma looked at the two of them, and if she had any eyebrows left, they would have been furrowed in confusion. "Frankly, I don't understand why you both are so upset. My nephew has not been married even once. You're lucky he is interested in coming to America."

Grandma said "America" like "Amreeka," and all Jia could do was stare at her, stunned. Was she supposed to be so grateful for a chance to be remarried that anyone willing to overlook her divorce was in fact doing *her* a favor?

"Umm," Jia began, at a loss for words.

Seema came to her aid, vein twitching on her forehead. "My sister is an independent woman who is raising her son on her own. She doesn't need to be married to your useless nephew." She snapped her fingers. "You know what, she is living such a great life that she doesn't really need to marry at all. In fact, I tell her, I'm jealous of her, living with freedom instead of being stuck with old in-laws who just keep on chugging."

Grandma threw her a dirty look and backed away, muttering, "This generation has no manners, no wonder the world is going to hell."

"You know who would be good for your nephew?" Seema called out. "Your best friend's cross-eyed daughter. Why don't you try matching them up?"

Once they were back in the kitchen, Jia nudged Seema. "Did you mean what you said? About me being lucky, that you're actually jealous of my life after divorce?"

Seema shuddered, eyes widening in horror. "Oh God, no. I can't imagine how you do it. You've gone from posting pictures of family outings to having a nonexistent social life. I couldn't live like that."

Seema had a point. When she was married, Jia's life too revolved around potlucks and Diwali dinners with her close circle of friends. Yet unbeknownst to her, it turned out a marriage certificate was mandatory for admittance to her friends' club.

After their split-up, their mutual friends chose charming Dev over his reticent wife.

Without his pleasant company, lifelong friendships devolved into awkward run-ins and lost conversational threads. The Indian community in Chicago eagerly gobbled deep-dish pizzas, electric cars, and the latest iPhones, but drew the line at divorce. A community accustomed to celebrating spelling bee winners and *Fortune* 500 CEOs didn't know what to do with a divorcée.

Western wedding vows granted a respite in death, but Hindu wedding rituals took this a step further.

Dev and Jia had circled a sacred fire in front of a thousand wedding guests and promised to spend seven consecutive lifetimes together, hauling their incompatibilities and resentments from one birth to the next. Such a culture had no room for people who stayed together for less than two decades.

While friendships in Chicago dropped like flies, her relations back in India were no less strained.

How could she face her family in India, after leaving the country with such fanfare, them crowding the airport while she departed as a beaming bride with Dev, only to return years later with nothing to show for it?

With thousands of visa applications rejected every year, an immigrant embodied success, and so a divorce was an epic fall from grace and made one a pariah.

An unmarried Indian woman, a divorcée, and an infertile couple could all agree on one thing: The road less traveled was also the road most lonely.

Seema said out of the corner of her mouth, "Actually, it's her I'm jealous of sometimes," pointing to Grandma. "She answers to no one. Has no filters."

Jia smiled awkwardly and patted Seema's back. Had she painted such a depressing picture of life as a single mom that a widow with more years of life left behind than ahead came off better in comparison?

Vipul strode around to his mother's side with a walking stick, gold lacquer gleaming under the lights. He gently prized her old cane from her grip. "Ma, I didn't realize you were awake. See, I got this new stick for you. It's got a bronze handle and everything. Specially handmade in India," he said. This was the first time Jia had seen Vipul do something nice for someone with genuine care, apart from for Asha.

Grandma, however, had eyes for only one person. As Raj and Lisa arrived downstairs, Grandma's eyes brightened and she croaked, "Raj, come here."

The corners of Vipul's mouth turned down, and just for a second, Jia had sympathy for the man. Vipul fulfilled his duties as a son and husband, but both Seema and Grandma treated him the same, with distance and indifference.

Raj and Lisa hurried to her side, and as Lisa approached Grandma, Jia was curious. What was the dynamic like between these women, five decades between them?

When Lisa clasped her palms together, namaste style, the gesture of supplication seemed to warm Grandma's heart, and her gray eyes widened, her thin chapped lips stretching in a smile.

Lisa bent forward with the grace of a ballerina and touched Grandma's brittle gray toenails. Touching feet was considered the highest form of respect, and so it wasn't uncommon for younger folks to lightly graze elders' feet in exchange for blessings.

Grandma pressed her withered hands on Lisa's head and said, "Bless you. May God bless you with a healthy baby *boy*. I know it's going to happen for you soon, I can feel it in my bones."

Even through the curtain of hair partially hiding her face, Jia saw a faint flush creeping up Lisa's cheeks while Seema rolled her eyes. Lisa sprang up, quickly tugging on her tunic, pulling it down as if showing the slightest skin would offend Grandma, which Jia thought was really unnecessary because Grandma's own saree blouse revealed much of her shriveled waist.

When Raj had announced his engagement to Lisa, Seema had

shared the news with Jia, her voice giddy with excitement. "He's marrying a white girl. Serves my mother-in-law right. Let's see how she feels when her daughter-in-law can't understand a word of her taunts. Ha!"

But despite their language and cultural barriers, Lisa turned out to be Grandma's favorite.

"Do you hear that?" Lisa said suddenly. The skin between her eyebrows creased as she leaned forward to concentrate.

The wind howls and rain patters pierced their ears ad nauseam, like white noise playing on a loop.

Jia strained her ears, and this time she heard it too. Not a wind chime, but a distinct continuous ring, an insistent thumb pressing on the doorbell.

Jia reeled back. Could that . . . ? Could that be Dev?

She closed her eyes and imagined him showing up at Seema's doorstep unannounced.

The touch screen fridge switched to front-door view, and a rain-splattered video filled the screen.

It wasn't Dev.

In the center stood a Caucasian man clad in a brown leather jacket. His head was lowered, rain plastering his auburn hair to his scalp, and something about the stillness of his figure made the hair on Jia's arm rise. If it were not for the raindrops sloping down the screen, the monitor would've looked frozen.

His relative placidity made the slightest movement, like a tilt of his neck, laden with purpose.

He looked up, facing the camera directly. Jia's stomach lurched, and she knew reflexively who this man was.

It was the creepy neighbor who had been watching her.

NINE

Vipul's face darkened. "That's Rafael. No way am I stupid enough to let that guy in."

Raj's eyebrows squished together. "Rafael . . . your neighbor Rafael?" When Vipul nodded, Raj threw his hands up. "C'mon, Bhai, this isn't the time for petty grudges, what if he is in some kind of trouble?"

"He *is* trouble. And when you buy a house," Vipul said, jutting his chin, "you can decide who you let in."

"*Atithi Devo Bhava*," Grandma said, hooded eyes fluttering.

Seeing Lisa reaching for her phone, Raj said, "She means a guest is the equivalent of a god."

Grandma closed her eyes like she was in a trance. "Let him in."

Vipul, chastened, fell silent as Raj marched to the door.

Rafael limped inside, one palm flat against the corridor wall, his other hand stuffed inside his jacket pocket. He lagged even after Raj slowed his pace. Rafael's jeans from the knees down were tainted a muddy brown, and water dripped from his clothes, leaving behind wet imprints.

At the slightest weight on his left foot, Rafael's face contorted into a painful grimace, and he staggered onto the edge of a chaise in the living area with an audible sigh. "Hi, I'm Rafael. I live across the street." Turning to Vipul, Rafael pressed a fist on his jacket pocket. "Thanks for letting me in. For a minute there, I was afraid you wouldn't open the door given our . . ." He gave a nervous laugh. "Colorful history. But I had to take my chances tonight." He scanned the windows as if expecting someone to jump out of the shadows. His pupils were dilated, and he kept tapping his fingers on his knee.

The sight of his hand firmly wedged inside the bowels of his jacket made Jia jittery, but she could not figure out why until she realized what it reminded her of.

Vipul hiding his gun.

Jia suppressed a shiver.

But Rafael's present distressed state could not mar his attractiveness. An expensive-looking, well-fitted leather jacket contoured sharply defined muscles, hinting at a physique propped up by weekly gym workouts and protein shakes. Scant freckles marked his white skin, and with his strong chin and thick hair a bright shade of red, he was someone Seema would call the "perfect male specimen."

Jia waited for Seema's usual cues in attractive company to appear—a casual tossing of hair, slight licking of lips—but her sister watched him with a stricken look. "Just tell us what happened already!"

"You won't believe the kind of night I've had," Rafael said. His Adam's apple jutted out, stretching the skin, oscillating the length of his throat like an elevator. When he moved to take out the hand buried in his pocket, Jia's senses went on high alert, and she sat up straight.

Rafael extricated his right hand.

Lisa covered her mouth, horrified.

A bandage was wrapped tight around his palm, scarlet stains percolating through layers of fabric.

The color was a deep red and had congealed like one of the paints Ishaan used for his craft projects.

The hair on Jia's nape of neck stiffened.

The air suddenly felt sharp, electric. Lisa worried the sleeves of her tunic while Grandma narrowed her eyes and Vipul, apparently setting aside his dislike for Rafael, asked softly, "What happened?"

"Someone broke into my house," Rafael said.

Having captured the room's full attention, Rafael appeared to relax somewhat, stretching his long legs. "I was fast asleep and suddenly I woke up to a crashing sound. I tiptoed out and saw someone entering my kitchen through a broken window. I quickly grabbed a lamp and hit his head. He stumbled for a second before I saw what he was holding in his gloved hand." Rafael paused here for a beat before continuing. "A butcher's knife. He tried to stab me but missed, and when I punched him, he whacked my knee with a chair leg before escaping through the window."

The next instant, lightning flashed across the sky, making them all jump.

"Did you get a good look at the guy?" Raj asked.

"Nah, it was too dark and he was masked." Rafael shrugged. "And then, to top everything off, my living room started flooding. I saw your lights were on and I figured I'd better get outta there while I still could. Do you mind if I hang out here for a while?"

"Of course," Vipul said, his gaze softening as Rafael rubbed his knee. "Stay as long as you need. You don't want to be at home if the robber comes back."

Rafael raised his palms. "I'm not even complaining, ya know? I'm lucky he had a knife, not a gun."

Silence, heavy as a fog, enveloped the room. A knife. Not the ideal weapon for a burglary but perfect for something else.

Jia's muscles twitched as the burst tires swam in front of her eyes.

Raj cleared his throat. "To tell you the truth, we haven't had the best night either. Someone slashed all four tires of Jia's car."

Rafael jerked his head in Jia's direction. "Oh, that was your car? Such a shame. When I saw that, I knew anyone staying put in their house tonight was in big trouble."

"What do you mean?" Jia said, alarmed. "Did you see it happening?"

He paused for a moment. Then Rafael leaned in like he was letting them in on a secret. "Didn't just see it. I caught it on video too."

Jia gripped the sofa while Rafael fished in his pocket to remove his mobile, pulling up a grainy video on the screen, blurry from the raindrops falling on the window.

Everyone crowded around Rafael to take a better look. The video was captured at an angle and showed a hazy outline of a person, back to the camera, a hoodie pulled up. The man was crouched, and in one swift action, he pulled out a knife.

It's just a car. Just a car. Jia quailed as he plunged the blade into the rubber of one of the back tires. Still squatting, he gingerly moved to the side and slashed the other back tire.

While capturing a violent act, Rafael's hands were unnaturally steady; the camera didn't jerk; there was no gasp, no sudden intake of breath, no sounds apart from the thrumming of rain. Jia would've dropped the phone in shock in one second.

It ended as quickly as it had started, a ten-second clip, and Jia felt herself crumpling in dismay. The video was not clear enough to rule out Dev. Rafael put his phone back, registering their disappointment. "Sorry, that's all I could get before my phone lost charge."

Lisa's hands flew to her chest, and she whipped her face in Raj's direction. "Honey, what if that man comes for us?"

Raj twitched as if Lisa had snapped him out of a trance, and while Jia expected him to start stroking Lisa's back in reassurance, he had a worried look in his eyes, and when Rafael's gaze dropped as he rubbed his injured knee, Raj nudged Lisa and they lapsed into fervent whispers.

The wind picked up, gusts thrusting against the glass, like it was trying to shove the house out of its way.

Jia swallowed hard. She and Seema exchanged uneasy glances. Even Vipul, for once, looked rattled. "Wouldn't hurt to check the locks again," he muttered.

A sniffling sound from the hallway startled them.

Asha toddled into the room, trailed by Ishaan. He said, "I watched soooo many toy-unboxing videos for her, but now she's bored. I instantly brought her here." He gave a pointed look at Jia, clearly trying to atone for his guilt at leaving her alone earlier.

Rafael pinned his gaze on Asha, who was dangling a plastic dinosaur. Smiling, he gestured for her to come over.

Asha regarded him with curiosity.

When Rafael spread his arms and reached for Asha, Asha rubbed one sleepy eye and wrapped her hands around his long legs, blubbering, "*Cómo.*"

Rafael burst out laughing and lifted Asha.

She tapped at his injured hand. "You got boo-boo?"

Rafael said, "*Muy buena, me gusta!*"

Asha looked quizzical, then said, "Asha bored. Bye!" and leapt out of his arms, losing all interest.

Raj and Lisa chortled, breaking the tension, and Jia too felt her tight muscles unclenching.

Grandma, who had been quiet so far in a corner, piped up:

"Seema, where are your manners? This isn't how we treat guests. The man is completely drenched. Get some towels for this fellow. If you stay in these wet clothes, you'll get sick."

Seema's lashes fluttered, and her mouth twisted like she'd been presented with Mom's bitter gourd curry. "Sure," she said, lips extending in a thin smile.

Rafael took off his coat, removing his bandaged hand from the sleeve gingerly, and laid it on the armrest. Grandma's hands trembled as she took Rafael's coat and lumbered in slow steps toward the passage before turning around midway.

Gesturing to Lisa, she said, "Would you be a dear and put this in the coat closet?"

While Lisa set off to help Grandma, Rafael's eyes flicked across his surroundings like a fly, touching on the pristine couch, the breakfast table, and the ottoman. A soft whistle escaped his lips. "This house may be the only one on the street to not flood. I expect mine to go completely underwater tonight. You're lucky."

"It's not luck," Vipul said. "I chose this house precisely because of its elevation and closeness to the water retention pond. If I'd listened to Seema, we too would be forced to take shelter in some neighbor's house."

Rafael smiled, but his eyes remained cold.

Vipul thrust his chest out. "Well, it doesn't really make a difference in your case now, does it? You're renting. Technically it's not your house anyway."

If Vipul meant that as a slight, it didn't land because Rafael was unfazed, checking the time on his fancy-looking wristwatch with an air of insouciance, and judging by his expensive-looking jacket, when it came to money, he adhered to Seema's "if you've got it, flaunt it" school of thought.

Grandma asked Rafael if he would like a cup of tea, with a side glance implying Seema would be doing the actual work of making said tea, but he didn't take her up on the offer. "I've had ten cups of coffee already," Rafael said, bouncing his leg like a smoker aching for a cigarette. "If I take any more caffeine, I'll explode."

Grandma nodded and returned with a plate arrayed with biscuits, but Rafael recoiled as though he were being offered poison.

"I can't eat anything with peanuts. Allergies."

"Allergies," Vipul snorted. His voice dripped with disdain. "This is the problem with growing up in America. Your biological systems are too soft. Coddled."

"I'm not from *here*," Rafael said haughtily. "I grew up in Spain."

Raj asked, "What made you move here?" His voice was calm, but his thumbs twiddled nervously.

Rafael hesitated, stroked his chin. "Let's see, I moved to Houston when my marketing project required me to liaise with our American office. My manager practically begged me to make the move."

"Okay, so Europe then," Vipul said, swatting his hand. "What's that thing Seema says." He snapped his fingers. "Oh yeah. Potayto, potahto. My point still stands. Ever wonder why Indians' biological systems don't have such problems?" He patted his paunch. "Because our bellies are filled with dust, dirt, from when we are toddlers. When I was a kid, we spent hours in the afternoon sun playing on swing sets, getting our hands dirty . . . But Seema here didn't even let anyone touch Asha without sanitizing their hands first . . . I mean it's incredible—"

Seema arrived with a plush towel, which Rafael took with a hearty smile, seemingly glad for the opportunity to escape Vipul's monologue as he excused himself.

Suddenly, as Jia was on her way to the kitchen to get a glass of water, the lights flickered. A second later, the electricity died, the house plummeting into pitch blackness. Asha's cries and Seema's shushing echoed in the dark. Vipul swore. "Mom, where are you?" came Ishaan's voice. Raj, Vipul, and Lisa simultaneously turned on the flashlights on their phones, beams bouncing like glow sticks in a concert.

In the slice of space separating the living room from the kitchen, Jia groped her way toward Ishaan. A scented candle flickered on the entryway table, and her gaze happened to snag on Rafael's profile on his way to the study bathroom.

Jia felt dizzy. Her hand flew to her chest.

Rafael was walking—*no, striding*—down the hallway, towel swinging in his hands, all traces of the limp that had so bothered him evaporated.

She blinked, not believing her eyes.

Then the lights came back on just as quickly as they had turned off, accompanied by the crank of gears whirring as the air-conditioning and fridge systems resuscitated.

Instantly, there was a reshuffle in his walk. He was back to his faltering comportment.

The transformation had happened in a flash, but there was no unseeing it.

Dread branched out from the seed of panic in the pit of her stomach.

He'd made it up. He'd made it all up.

Trapped in a once-in-a-lifetime hurricane, Rafael had taken refuge under the pretext of a fake injury.

Vipul was right. Rafael was trouble.

Letting him in was a mistake. A small, panicked voice in Jia's head amended: *Not a mistake. A blunder.*

And then he looked over his shoulder. Staring straight at her.

TEN

Jia rapidly swiveled away, every molecule thrumming with adrenaline. When she dared to look at him again, Rafael was inside the bathroom, but Jia's lips were glued together with shock. Her eyes searched for her safe harbor, Seema, but she was patting Asha into a state of calm, with Ishaan looking on helplessly.

And then the sensation of fingers pressed on her skin like cold gel. "We need to talk," Lisa whispered before retreating upstairs. Jia followed her—only later, much later, realizing the importance of this choice, how differently the events of that night would have played out if, for instance, she had stayed behind and confided in Seema instead.

When Jia appeared in the doorway, Lisa pulled her inside.

"He's lying," Jia blurted, while almost at the same time, Lisa said, "We know."

"'We'?"

Lisa drew in a breath.

"Raj and I know Rafael is hiding something," she said, combing shaky fingers through her hair. "His story doesn't add up. And when I saw your panicked face, I knew we had to talk."

When Jia explained how Rafael was faking his injury, Lisa was dumbstruck. She lowered her voice. "Raj noticed right away things were off with him. He said he was fast asleep when someone broke in. But he can't have tea because he's already had ten cups of coffee?"

"That's not the only thing he fibbed about," Jia said, remembering. "When he found out it was my car that was slashed, he acted surprised. But I noticed him peeking through a window when we arrived."

Lisa nodded, lost in thought. The downpour showed no signs of slowing down, the thrum of rainfall a constant reminder of their claustrophobic predicament.

Something else occurred to Jia. "Isn't it convenient that the video stopped just when we were about to get a good look at the guy who slashed the tires?"

"That video?" Lisa shook her head. "Raj thinks he didn't even shoot the video himself."

"What?"

"Let me show you what I mean." Lisa led her to the small rectangular window behind her bed. Pressing her phone screen on the rain-dappled glass panes, she said, "Now, imagine you're recording a video. See that tree outside."

Jia squinted, but the rain was a cataract film on her eyes. "What? I can't see anything," she said, pinching her fingers to magnify the focus.

"Exactly," Lisa said, pocketing her phone. "You zoomed. Rafael happens across a stranger cutting tires in front of him and he doesn't even try to get a better look?"

She had a point. The smartphone age had digits front and center, thumbs constantly scrolling, fingers flipping and magnifying on demand, but in contrast, Rafael's eerily steady hands looked abnormal. "Are you trying to say he set up the camera somewhere?"

"Maybe," Lisa said in a low voice.

"But why would he do that?" Jia said, before it occurred to her there was only one possible explanation.

Jia's stomach dropped, and looking at Lisa's stark face, she knew they had come to the same grim conclusion.

Rafael had slashed the car tires himself.

Was he watching from the window while Jia panicked over her damaged car? Jia squared her shoulders. "I say we point Vipul's gun at Rafael till he confesses what he's doing here."

"Wait a second, we've gotta think this through," Lisa said. "Raj is worried about Grandma and the kids. What if he's hiding a knife and he takes someone hostage?"

With a rush of apprehension, Jia started toward the door. How could she do this? She shouldn't have left Ishaan downstairs with him around.

But Lisa stopped her. "Raj is keeping an eye on things for now."

"Can't we tell the others what's going on?" Jia asked.

Lisa shook her head. "Not before we have a plan. Grandma looks strong, but what if her heart can't take all the stress?"

Jia nodded. Grandma was also a loose cannon and could even try taking matters into her own hands.

Lisa said, "We need to figure out a way to get Grandma and the kids to safety before we confront him."

Jia paced the floor; she had too much energy buzzing inside her to be still. "There is one way. We wait till dinner." She paused, inhaled deeply as she recalled everyone's routines. "After eating, Grandma goes to her bedroom to take her medication. Vipul heads to the loo, but we need to warn him so he can get his gun. I can get Ishaan to take Asha to the media room here upstairs."

Lisa chewed on a cuticle. "That could work. The plan's not perfect, but we've got to work with what we've got right now."

As they headed back downstairs, Lisa whispered, "If the plan is to wait till after dinner, we have to be careful. Knowledge is power. Rafael not knowing we're onto him is our biggest advantage. But right now," Lisa warned, "your face is a dead giveaway."

/′/′/′/

BACK IN THE LIVING ROOM, RAFAEL WAS NOW ENSCONCED ON THE chaise. Grandma doddered right up to him, and when she lifted her walking stick in the air, for a heart-stopping second Jia thought she was going to bring it smashing down on his head, but instead, she gently prodded his leg. "For your foot. Vipul bought me a new one."

Lisa and Jia exchanged nervous looks. Grandma was being a good Samaritan, but she had unknowingly handed Rafael a weapon. This was going to be a long night. Rafael accepted the cane he didn't need with exaggerated thanks, knocking it sharply on the floor, and then he rubbed his hands together. "This house is very lovely. Can I get a tour?"

Jia's innards writhed in fear as she tried to catch Seema's eye.

Say no. Don't go, Jia pleaded silently.

Seema replied, her voice bubbly, "I'd love that."

Why did she waste time talking to Lisa instead of warning her sister?

Knowledge is power. But Jia felt pretty powerless, and when Rafael pushed himself up with the cane, all she could think of was his hand effortlessly tearing into the tire with a razor-sharp blade.

ELEVEN

old up," Jia blurted. "I'd like to join you both."

Rafael leaned on his loaner cane, brows squiggled in confusion. "I thought you all were related. Haven't you seen the house before?"

Jia simpered, glad Rafael couldn't listen to her frantic heartbeats. "Seema renovates so often and does it so well, there's something new and cool to see with every visit."

Seema beamed.

Raj said, "I'll come too. I just need to stretch my legs." He kept his eyes fixed on Rafael's face, and Jia could tell he was trying hard not to let his gaze drop to Rafael's "injured" leg. Although Rafael shrugged, there was a slight wrinkle on his forehead, which would've gone unnoticed if Jia weren't looking intently. Whatever Rafael's plan was, Jia and Raj watching over his every move was not part of it.

Lisa stayed behind with Grandma under the pretext of wanting to look at baby photos of Raj, Asha enlisted Ishaan to read her a storybook, and Vipul declared that Seema's home decor initiatives were a dual waste of time and money.

They walked in the fashion of a search party, Seema and Rafael in the front, and Raj and Jia bringing up the rear. Jia wondered if they should confront Rafael now, since they'd managed to get him away from Grandma and the kids. But no, they couldn't confront him without Vipul. Or, more importantly, Vipul's gun.

THE BRIGHTLY LIT HOUSE WAS AT ODDS WITH THE PITCH-DARK SKIES, like a casino, with its own atmosphere, untethered from the outside world.

For all its contemporary trappings, the overall vibe of the house was at best confusing. It groaned with one foot each in Western and Hindu cultures. Seema had opted for cookie-cutter selections common to Hindus from Gujarat, the birthplace of Gandhi: Above the Italian stone fireplace hung a gold-trimmed poster of Lord Krishna with a diamond-studded chin, shipped from Rajasthan. In the spandrel was a statue of a village woman carrying a pitcher of water. An immigrant's house was a time capsule for the era in which farewells were said to their homeland. Hence, a decade later, Seema's decor choices would be as out of place in an ordinary home in Mumbai as they were in a suburb of Texas.

They traipsed through the gourmet kitchen equipped with an enormous five-burner range along with a griddle, where Seema gave a rundown of the recent upgrades she'd made, including a new marble-backsplash and a custom pot filler above the stove.

Reminders of Asha's presence were all over the place, from the kitchen-stove knob covers to the transparent corner guards fixed on all the tables. Seema gestured to the breakfast bar. ". . . And this is where Asha loves to eat her cereal because she gets a clear view of the television."

Moving farther along the passageway, Seema said, ". . . And here we have vinyl flooring, which gives all the sophistication of wood without the pesky maintenance stuff . . ." An armchair psychologist might attribute Seema's frequent inclinations to rip apart her house to a secret need to shake up the foundation of her life, but Jia knew better.

Her sister just loved renovating.

Coming to the foyer, she pushed a set of French doors open. "And this is the study room."

As they walked through the carpeted room, which had a coffered ceiling, Seema wrinkled her nose. Vipul's den stood in contrast to the rest of the pristine house. Asha's neon-pink blanket hung on the back of an enormous leather chair; a wood desk lay in the middle, cluttered with sheets of paper and picture books piled up like crooked stairs; there was a glass mug filled with tea dregs, and in the center of this chaos sat a laptop, its charger snaking into the outlet on the opposite wall.

The room had three windows, a small one on the side wall and two French-door-sized mullioned windows facing the front lawn. The front windows had wooden louvers with a rod in the center.

"Plantation shutters," said Seema proudly.

Raj cringed, but Seema, blissfully ignorant of the painful history behind the phrase, especially in the South, misinterpreted his expression. "Oh yeah, trust me, these are very trendy. All my friends' houses have them. We had them installed last year. Much better light controls." To demonstrate, Seema tugged on a rod attached to the frame, flipping the slats horizontal.

Lightning flashed relentlessly, a strobe light illuminating different parts of the front lawn. Jia gulped. Just as Raj had predicted, the rainwater splashing on the grass was also accumulating on the street, each drop bringing the water level closer to the house.

Rafael made his way over to the built-in floor-to-ceiling bookcase, and Raj followed him with a wary look.

Raj dragged out a magazine from a middle shelf, and said slowly, "I can't believe he kept this."

He opened the magazine and rifled through it feverishly, stopping at a page in the middle. His eyes were soft. "My first article in a financial journal. Benefits of index funds investing. The magazine had a circulation of less than a hundred, but I'd shared it with Vipul because I didn't want him to think his money for my education had been a complete waste." Raj shook his head. "I never imagined he would keep the article after all these years."

"He did," Seema said. "He even showed all his friends proudly when they came over."

"I did," Vipul said, striding inside the room. He unplugged a phone charger and was on his way out, then stopped at the door. "But I also told them my brother will be writing for the *Wall Street Journal* in five years. Still waiting for that day."

Raj gave a dry laugh. "Now there's the brother I know and love."

Crunch. Crunch. Ishaan entered, licking the tips of orange-crusted fingers. He popped a cheesy puff from a packet and asked, spraying orange motes, "Mom, how long before we go home?"

Why did he have to come near Rafael? Jia's brain skittered, searching for an excuse to get him out of the room. "Weren't you supposed to look after Asha?"

"She's with Grandma and I'm allowed to have breaks, Mom," he drawled.

Jia's eyes were drawn to Rafael, who had now moved toward the desk and was tracing his fingers on the walnut edges, clucking appreciatively, like a prospective buyer in an antique store.

Jia frowned, her body feeling chilly. What about this room interested Rafael so much? Moving past Rafael, Ishaan sat on the
chair, observing his movements. Ishaan then dragged the wheels in
a circle, rotating the chair so fast that even looking at him made Jia
feel dizzy.

A click of a knob. Rafael had nipped to the bathroom, and Jia
wondered if she had enough time to bring Seema up to speed, but
Raj took up position near the closed door like a sentry and, as if
reading Jia's mind, shook his head ever so slightly.

Jia agreed; it was too risky. What if he could hear them through
the door?

Ishaan grabbed a pyramid paperweight and shook it, sending
the gold grains in it rolling in a tizzy. Jia snapped, "What did I tell
you about going through other people's stuff?" before she could stop
herself.

Ishaan turned red as he clocked everyone witnessing his mother
berating him and left the room with his head down. Jia's throat felt
tight. She hated this version of herself, this brittle, prone-to-snapping
mom. But a month ago, Nikki had gently pulled her aside and mentioned that one of the other kids she watched after school alongside
Ishaan, Andy, was upset over a lost Nerf gun. Later, when an embarrassed Jia found it in Ishaan's backpack, he was surprised. "I must've
put it in by mistake with my other stuff cuz you were rushing me."
When Jia made him give it back the same day, Nikki was gracious,
even patting Jia's arm. "These kids, they are always misplacing
things. But Andy will be so thrilled to have this back."

A couple days ago, they were buying groceries when Jia recognized a couple of Ishaan's classmates hanging out by the candy aisle.
She urged him to wave hello and they called him over, but after mere
minutes with them, Ishaan was back by her side, ears red, mumbling,
"Can we leave now, please?"

When an elderly store clerk chased after them on the street, Jia assumed she must've forgotten something, but he addressed Ishaan. "Son, empty your pockets now," he said, panting. When Ishaan sheepishly pulled out a packet of mints, of a citrus flavor he *hated*, Jia was apoplectic. What was wrong with her boy?

A clap of thunder dragged Jia back to the present. Raj's eyes were fixed on his phone screen with a frown, but Jia knew what he was really worried about. Rafael had been gone for more than a minute.

Seema picked up the dirty cup and, nudging the leather chair with her hip into the gap of the desk, muttered, "Seriously, you need to take a chill pill and give the kid a little break. You don't have to be a nag all the time."

Jia crossed her arms stiffly. She didn't need advice from someone whose parenting largely composed of posing with Asha in color-coordinated outfits on Instagram.

"You've become paranoid after what transpired at his school," Seema said.

Jia jerked and blinked rapidly. How did she know?

Two months ago, when the principal's office had called her mid-day about an "urgent situation," Jia had grabbed her purse and dashed to the school, running three traffic lights. She scrambled into the office, where Ishaan sat ashen-faced in a wooden-backed chair in a corner, his entire body shaking uncontrollably, face wet with tears. Jia pulled him into a hug. "Are you okay? What's going on?" she asked the principal.

The principal, a mild-mannered woman with thinning hair, propped her elbows on the desk. "The children were out in the cafeteria during recess. Apparently, Ishaan and his classmate Sam exchanged some words and then that escalated into a fight and, well—" She peered over her glasses. "This would have amounted to nothing but a scuffle among boys, but unfortunately, when he pushed Sam, he slipped on the wet floor where someone had spilled juice, and his head collided with the steel leg of an upturned chair, bringing about a concussion."

Jia's palm flew to her chest. "Oh no."

"Mom, I had no idea he would get hurt that bad," Ishaan said immediately. "I didn't do it on purpose. I didn't want him to bleed."

"No one said you did," the principal said kindly.

"Is the boy . . . Sam okay?" Jia asked.

"His parents have taken him to the hospital. We are hoping to hear some positive updates later today. But he isn't in imminent danger."

Jia's heart rate, which had jacked up since the phone call, crawled to a slower pace.

"We called you so you can take Ishaan home. Unfortunately, we do have to suspend him for a day. We would've issued a punishment for Sam as well, but he's in the hospital, so we'll evaluate his penalty once he is discharged . . ."

Jia stood up to leave, and Ishaan dragged his feet out of the office, his shoulders slouching. When Jia's hand was on the door, the principal raised her index finger. "Actually, can we have a word in private?"

While Ishaan waited outside, Jia seated herself on the chair opposite to the desk. The principal said, "Can you please talk to Ishaan? He's clearly shaken up by this incident. Another classmate claimed Sam was whispering something in Ishaan's ear before this happened."

"What?" Jia said. "What did he say?"

The principal shook her head, took off her glasses, and cleaned them with a handkerchief. She straightened a pen on her sparse desk. "The boy wouldn't say. You know how kids can be, he probably doesn't want to get involved in this. Ishaan also won't say anything. We don't know. I've asked Ishaan, but it's almost as if he's taken a vow of silence on this matter." She put her glasses back on. "Maybe you will have better luck with him."

Jia said, "I don't understand. He's never had problems like this before."

"He is one of our quiet kids," the principal said. "Although his teacher tells me he got into a shouting match with Sam once before."

"Shouting?"

"The teacher announced the date for our 'bring your father to school' event, and Sam apparently said in front of the entire class that Ishaan couldn't bring anyone that day."

Heat spread in Jia's chest. "When did this happen?" Ishaan had not mentioned anything to her.

The principal's brows furrowed. "Last month probably."

Jia pressed her fingers to her lips. There was one morning Ishaan refused to go to school, clutching his stomach, saying his tummy hurt and he wanted to rest. Jia cringed, remembering how she'd complained about not having any more personal days off at work and forced him to take medicine before shipping him off to school.

The principal continued, "He would benefit from having positive male role models in his life. That may reduce his abandonment anxiety. He's well-adjusted mostly," she clarified on seeing the horrified look on Jia's face. "But divorce can have lingering effects on children."

Her cheeks burning, Jia foisted her bag and stood up. "I don't want to keep Ishaan waiting for long. Thank you for your time."

After leaving, Jia reminded herself that things could be worse. At least Ishaan's teachers were looking out for him.

That was before the lawsuit.

Then everything changed.

Sam's parents didn't wait for their son's release from the hospital before pursuing legal action. They sued the school for insufficient safety standards and lack of supervision. Apparently, the school had neglected to put up enough signs warning about the wet floor. The steel rod of the chair his skull crashed into was ancient and rusty, increasing the chances of a secondary infection.

The parents weren't filthy rich, but the mom had a currency more valuable than dollars in the social media age—a blog, popular among school moms and boasting a hundred thousand followers. Intimidated by her social media clout and afraid of the negative publicity that might be generated from a single viral post, the school swiftly responded by increasing Ishaan's suspension length to a week. Sam's punishment was dropped altogether, and Ishaan's return to school suddenly became contingent on the results of his interview with the school counselor. The "scuffle" was now unprovoked aggression. His shyness was a sign of his "inability to mingle with his peers."

The next time she entered the school's office, gone was the polite but kind principal. Instead the principal wore a severe expression. "If he stays on this path, the next stop will be a juvenile facility. We will monitor his behavior once he comes back after his suspension." At first, Jia snorted at this proclamation. He was, after all, a twelve-year-old boy.

"Is this because of the lawsuit?" Jia asked.

The principal shifted in her seat. "We take discipline very seriously in this school." She leaned forward. "Do you know Sam could have been seriously hurt?"

The principal's about-face threw Jia off kilter. In a lawsuit-friendly country, Jia worried she was next. She jumped like a mugging victim whenever a stranger approached. Two words, "You're served," would kick off her legal nightmare.

And even after weeks, the nagging question kept Jia up at night: What had the boy said to Ishaan to provoke such a physical reaction from him? Ishaan flat out denied that Sam said anything to him and shut down whenever Jia broached the subject. She'd even tried reaching out to a few of his classmates. Most of them claimed they weren't present in the cafeteria at that time, but their shifty looks made it apparent they'd been warned by their parents not to get involved. Only one boy gave her a cryptic "They're burying the whole story" before walking away.

This left Jia with two unpalatable options: Her quiet son was a bully in the making, pushing his classmates for no reason, or he did not have anyone to share his fears with. Without Dev to share her anxiety, her worries bounced in her mind, growing each day, until she was convinced that she'd proved her ex right. She was incapable of raising Ishaan on her own. She didn't even confide in Seema because what if Seema believed the rumors? Would she still let Ishaan hang around Asha? He had so few friends that Jia's heart couldn't bear a reduction in the number of family members in his life.

So Jia suffered in silence, concerns for her son mushrooming inside her, eating her away.

Seema drilled Jia with a piercing gaze. "You can never hide anything from me, sis." Cradling the cup in her hand, she continued, "Shefali told me. Her husband works for the law firm representing the parents."

Of course Shefali ran to her with this gossip. Jia's eyes burned with fresh tears, and under the pretext of coughing, she angled her body such that she didn't have to face Seema. It pained her to see Ishaan's story bandied about.

Seema said, "You know, it's fairly common for kids of divorced parents to have behavioral issues."

"He was provoked," Jia said through clenched teeth. The conviction of her voice took her by surprise—she'd been unable to summon it in private with Ishaan.

"Oh, really?" Seema said, eyes widening like a greedy collector, salivating at the prospect of acquiring new tidbits of information to barter. "The other kid was teasing him? About what?"

"I don't know," Jia said. Her body deflated. She had asked Ishaan, in turns pleading and threatening, to no avail. Sam's parents might be privy to the answer, but they would not say anything that could jeopardize their ironclad case. The shame in Ishaan's eyes, his shoulders curving inward at the very mention of the subject, led Jia to wonder if Sam had taunted him about his absent father. Kids had a cruel penchant for honesty.

She wondered who her son was. His dad was a maestro of secrecy and manipulation.

But taking him away from Chicago and forcing him to adjust to a brand-new city had made his life more difficult. She didn't know what was worse, finding out that her kid was on the wrong track or wondering whether her decisions had pushed him onto that path.

A gurgling sound of a flush. Raj quickly moved away as Rafael opened the door. Though Seema suggested skipping the house's second story on account of his leg, he was adamant, climbing up the stairs one ungainly step at a time.

As they rounded at the top, Seema waxed poetic about the wrought iron design. Rafael pulled out his mobile and tapped away, like he was texting someone, sending a frisson of annoyance through Jia. If he wasn't interested, why make Seema go through the trouble?

In one of the corridors forking off from the common area was a media room, equipped with a giant projector screen. Farther ahead was Seema's exquisite main bedroom.

Out of the blue, rising through the ground itself, an earthshaking crash like shattering glass tore through the house.

Jia clutched Seema's arm.

Rafael looked up from his screen, his eyes wide with panic.

"What was that?" Raj asked, his complexion sickly.

They hurried downstairs. The study bathroom door was flung wide open. Vipul was crouched by the windows. Raj pulled the blinds all the way up and touched the glass panes, looking utterly flummoxed.

Vipul scratched his head. "I don't understand. It's the strangest thing. You all heard it too, right? It sounded like someone from outside smashed the window."

They headed to the kitchen to inspect the windows there, but there was another strange noise—a faint shot that sounded like someone had fired a gun.

Rafael, who had been texting again, dropped his phone in surprise.

They scrambled back to the mezzanine hallway overlooking the foyer. Vipul looked completely floored. "I've no idea where these sounds are coming from. But I'd better check outside," he said, stomping out the front door.

A muffled *thunk* followed by a bawling sob erupted from the bowels of the house. As the high-pitched wail rose to a crescendo, the blood drained from Seema's face.

Asha.

TWELVE

mages with varying degree of gruesomeness ricocheted in Jia's head, so when they found Asha in the playroom, legs splayed, face pink from crying but overall okay, Jia wiped her clammy forehead and her breathing returned to normal.

Jigsaw puzzle pieces and geometric blocks were scattered on the floor. Ishaan lingered a few inches nearby. Jia grabbed his shoulders, shaking him. "Did you push her? Don't you know you have to be careful around her?"

Seema scooped up Asha, who buried her face in her mother's neck, cries amplified in the spotlight of attention. Bouncing Asha on her hip, Seema asked, in a lilting voice, "What happened to my baby?"

Asha hiccuped. "I tripped," she said, a chubby accusing finger pointing to an overturned plastic dump truck in a corner.

Ishaan wrenched out of Jia's grip. "See? I had nothing to do with it," he said through clenched teeth.

Jia's cheeks burned as her hands fell limply to her sides. Unable to meet her son's eyes, Jia stared at a storybook on the floor. When she mouthed "Sorry" to Ishaan, he stuffed his hands in his pockets and stepped away from her with a stiffness in his gait.

"Can Mommy kiss Asha's boo-boo?" Seema cooed. She planted kisses on Asha's elbow and gently put her on the ground like a baby turtle released into the ocean. Asha promptly grabbed Ishaan's hand and guided him to a neon-pink tent overflowing with dolls and drums, akin to a toy hoarder's lair.

Jia didn't know how to fix her relationship with her son, but berating him in front of others for something he had not done was not the answer. Jia rubbed her knee to alleviate her cramped leg.

She and Seema agreed that the kids were safer in this room. Slowly they backed out, hands clasped tight, fear regressing them into young girls, and Jia realized that this, the waiting, was interminably worse, their imaginations filling the silence, breaths held in anticipation for the next round of mysterious sounds.

Like prey anticipating the hunter's next move.

THIRTEEN

Rain pelted the patio roof with a sharp rat-a-tat-tat.

Seema and Jia returned to find the men huddled in the entryway.

"Are you sure one of the attic windows isn't broken?" Raj asked.

"I told you I already checked," Vipul snapped. "And there are no windows in the attic, just a small skylight. I'm telling you the sounds are coming from *inside* the house."

"But it doesn't make any sense," Rafael said. "What if the man who attacked me is trying to break into this house?" His eyes darted across the room. His anxiety looked authentic, but Jia didn't know if this too was a part of his performance.

Asha and Ishaan came over, and Asha tugged on Vipul's pants. "Dadda, Asha scared."

"Mom," Ishaan asked. "What's going on?"

Vipul rubbed Asha's back. "Nothing to worry about. It's firecrackers," he said with a pointed glance at the others.

"What are we going to do about the firecrackers?" Raj said cautiously.

"The firecrackers seem to have stopped. All we can do is wait and watch."

"Let's finish dinner," Raj said.

"How can you be hungry with all this going on?" Seema asked incredulously.

"Yes, the kids will be hungry," Jia said, palms sweaty. She knew in her gut that Rafael was responsible for everything, and finishing dinner was the fastest way to get to the bottom of it.

In the kitchen, a cacophony of sounds played out—pressure cooker whistles, the *chop chop* of coriander leaves being diced, loud sizzling as the buttermilk protested against oil tempering. Jia stirred kadhi, a gravy-like dish made of gram flour and yogurt that would typically accompany khichdi. Standing beside her, Seema twisted open the lid of the pressure cooker and stirred the khichdi, a yellow porridge of boiled rice and lentils.

Jia was dying to warn Seema, but Grandma kept puttering around, adding a dash of salt to the kadhi, muttering under her breath, ". . . This is what happens when mothers don't teach their daughters how to cook . . ."

Lisa hurried into the kitchen. "Can I help with dinner?"

Seema looked up and gestured to Lisa's hair. "You know you should be using a keratin-based conditioner that helps with dry-scalp issues. I can also recommend some products to repair damaged roots."

Lisa tucked her curls behind her ears. "Thanks for the tip," she said, cheeks coloring.

Jia sighed. Seema, with her heart in the right-adjacent place, often doled out well-intentioned yet unsolicited advice. She reminded Jia of the local beauty parlor lady who—after threading a client's eyebrows—asked, "And are we getting rid of our upper-lip hair today?" How could one respond to that? *No, thanks. I like my mustache.*

As Seema cut an eggplant, Lisa tried again, bouncing on her toes, hands behind her back. "There must be something I can help with?" she asked with the eagerness of a first-day-on-the-job employee. She locked eyes with Jia. "We can get dinner ready faster if we work together."

"No," Seema said, waving a hand. She called out to Jia, "Can you lend me a hand with the salad?"

Lisa's chin trembled, and she backed away in uneven steps.

Jia pinched her lips.

Seema wouldn't be so petty if she knew the real reason behind Lisa hastening their dinner prep. But Grandma was back, adding a dollop of ghee to the purportedly healthy khichdi, continuing commentary under her breath: "And she wonders why Asha is so thin. Forcing everyone to go on a diet, no wonder my poor Vipul is losing weight . . ."

Jia pointedly glanced at Lisa and said in a steady and strong voice, "I could use some help. I was going to make buttermilk. You want to do that instead?"

Lisa beamed. "Sure. I've seen Raj make it at home."

Annoyed, Seema stared at Jia, but Jia ignored her and, opening the fridge, grabbed a container of yogurt.

Lisa added spoonfuls of yogurt and water to a potbellied container with the precision of a chemistry student and then whisked the mixture.

Jia instructed Lisa to add a dash of mint to the buttermilk, and after pouring it into glasses, Lisa put them on a tray to be served as a beverage and left.

A tinny voice from a phone playing a video floated into the

kitchen. The singer was singing, "Let It Go," the lyrics inspiring on first listening, but *I'll do anything to make this stop* on the thousandth repetition.

Vipul ambled into the kitchen and, grabbing a banana from the countertop, asked, "Can you make banana fritters?"

Seema frowned. "Since when did you start liking banana fritters?"

Vipul shrugged offhandedly, peeling a banana and taking a bite. "Recently. It's an acquired taste."

Seema sighed loudly and trudged back to the stove muttering, "In ten years I've never seen him eat banana fritters."

Vipul glanced askance at Jia; their eyes met, and although it was a blink-and-you-miss-it gesture, Jia saw it.

He winked.

Jia coughed.

He wouldn't dare.

Jia glared at Vipul. He stared back, silent, the corner of his mouth lifted in a half smile.

Jia put the ladle aside and covered the pot with a lid, her appetite significantly diminished.

She knew exactly where Vipul had picked up the taste for banana fritters.

In *her* kitchen.

BEFORE

ONE MONTH AGO

Beeeeeeep. The smoke detector was emitting an unceasing beep with the urgency of an ambulance siren. Ishaan was on his tiptoes on a stool in the bedroom as he poked a broomstick at the round contraption on the ceiling while Jia stood below, covering her ears. It had started off as an annoying low-battery chirp that sounded every five seconds, and Ishaan had insisted he could take care of it, but then he had pressed the wrong button and now the sound grated against her ears, boring deep in her skull as they yelled over it at each other: "I got it, Mom." "Get down, let me do it!"

It took a few seconds for Jia to register that someone was knocking on the door and, opening it, she stared uncomprehendingly at Vipul. Stepping inside, he managed to silence the detector, temporarily disabling it, and Jia sighed, savoring the quiet. It was only then that the question popped in her mind: *What is he doing here?* Suddenly, she felt self-conscious, of her old sweatshirt stained with OJ, sweaty hair tied inelegantly in a side ponytail.

Why did he always have to find her in a distressed state?

Vipul said, not quite meeting her eyes, "I was on my way back from work and happened to pass by this area, so I thought, I'll stop by." Then he wagged a finger. "I noticed you still haven't renewed your registration. I could take your car for inspection and see if it needs an oil change too."

Jia twisted the end of her crumpled sleeve. Her apartment was not conveniently located to the nearest highway, and it would take a detour of a good thirty minutes for Vipul to drop by here from his office downtown, and although this fact caused her unease, more pressing was the fact that her car *did* need an inspection and she couldn't even remember when she'd last had the oil changed, and going to an automobile shop would shave off an entire afternoon, time she could use to do laundry or help Ishaan with his homework.

So, instead of expressing her reservations, she let a different set of words tumble out of her mouth: "Would you also be able to grab a carton of milk on the way?"

Vipul nodded, his face glowing in delight.

And that's when Jia understood what Vipul was doing at her apartment, miles away from his home. He likely did all these things and much more for his own family, but rarely received anything resembling appreciation from Seema. He was here for validation, to feel a little bit useful.

He returned two hours later, bearing a box of doughnuts for Ishaan, who accepted them cheerily. Vipul refused to take any money for the car-maintenance costs, even though he'd had all four car tires replaced with new ones, and Jia insisted he let her make a cup of tea and some snacks for him because it was the least she could do.

She poured oil in a pot and whisked chickpea batter seasoned with turmeric, red chili powder, and salt. After adding julienned onions and round cut bananas and potatoes to the mixture, she fried them individually.

Vipul blew on one of the pakoras and dipped it into dark week-old coriander chutney before taking a bite. "Mmmm . . . How did you know pakoras are my favorite? And these banana ones taste the best." He swiped another fritter through ketchup and said, "I wish Seema could be resourceful like you. More cooking. Less shopping." He shook his head ruefully. "Of course she will hate it if I compare her to anyone else."

He looked at Jia and waited, as if he had opened a window into his marital life and was inviting Jia to peek in.

She did not care for it one bit. Jia crossed her arms. "Seema is the best cook I know. I've learned everything from her."

The rest of the evening proceeded pleasantly enough, with Vipul engaging Ishaan in a conversation about football before rolling his eyes at Jia. "I'm a fan of cricket, but I have to keep up with American sports so I have something to say to my coworkers."

By the time he was on his way out, Jia had even forgotten about his nonreason for dropping by when she overheard him calling Seema while going down the flight of stairs.

"Yeah, I was late at work, I'm heading home now," he said, delivering the lie nonchalantly.

Jia's stomach lurched in apprehension, and all she could do was wonder: Had she eavesdropped on their conversation, or did Vipul make sure she would overhear him? His lie coiled around them both like a snake.

FOURTEEN

She felt the tea roiling in her stomach when she realized what was going on.

Vipul was purposely bringing up his visit to Jia's home because he knew Seema didn't know about it.

Her strategy of keeping Seema around had misfired.

Instead of being deterred by his wife's presence, Vipul was getting off on Seema's proximity.

He didn't see himself as a harasser and Jia as a victim of his overtures—in his mind, she was a willing participant. It was all a game to him. According to him, they were illicit lovers hiding a clandestine affair.

Vipul had correctly wagered that if Jia hadn't told Seema for weeks, she wasn't likely to do so now. Jia rubbed her sweaty palms against her jeans. Had he mistaken her silence thus far as an admission of complicity?

A clap of thunder pierced the sky, louder than the ones they'd heard all night, like the finale of a fireworks display.

Jia mopped her forehead, then steeled herself.

She wasn't going to let him know he had gotten to her.

Lifting her chin, she stared defiantly at Vipul.

Still smiling, Vipul tossed the peel into the trash can, and his gaze lingered on Jia, just for one additional second.

Jia's mouth fell open. She clenched her hands into fists.

Vipul had crossed a line. His behavior was becoming more brazen by the second, and she had to do something about it.

When Seema departed with a stack of dishes, Vipul took a step closer.

Jia jumped and cut herself. She swore softly as blood trickled from her skin, and sucking the edge of her finger, she glared at Vipul. He said, "Are you hurt?"

"I'm fine," Jia said. A sour feeling settled in Jia's gut as Vipul picked up a cucumber slice, swallowed it whole, and licked his lips. He reached across the counter to retrieve the salt and pepper shakers and whispered, "Blue looks good on you." With a wink, he whispered, "Check your phone. I have a surprise for you."

What fresh hell awaited her? She'd left the phone on her bedroom nightstand because it was the only way she wouldn't keep thinking about Dev's messages, and now Jia wondered if Vipul had sent another one of his asinine love poems.

Staring at him, Jia gripped the knife so hard her knuckles turned white. How she would love to press the knife into his pudgy neck, watch his skin turn red, and whisper, "The color of fear looks good on you."

When she saw him leaving, she turned her back to him.

A light tap on her bottom. She froze and whipped around. Vipul blushed like they were teenagers.

Behind her, his eyes wide, Ishaan stared at them.

When had he come in? How much did he see?

His muscles were tense, and his lips seemed to wobble.

Vipul cleared his throat like a singer before a performance. He said brusquely, "I'm going to go finish some work before dinner."

Jia's heart felt like it was going to leap out of her throat. What was going through Ishaan's mind right now?

He seemed frozen, his face an expression of pure repulsion.

"Ishaan," Jia started. She was buying time, trying to come up with an age-appropriate explanation.

"Don't bother," Ishaan said, turning on his heel.

Before Jia had a chance to stop him, he was gone, leaving his seething anger in his wake.

FIFTEEN

Hurricane Harvey showed no signs of letting up, barreling across the Texas mainland, decimating entire subdivisions, heavy bands of rain swamping several suburbs of Houston. Tropical storm surge warnings crossed borders into neighboring Louisiana. The local news station they'd been tuned into all night itself was flooded, television hosts scrambling to broadcast live on air.

The bathroom attached to the study was spa-like, with its wide vanity mirrors, bright marble counters, and a fully equipped shower. Jia splashed cold water on her face. The night was making her sick. She stared at the disheveled, harried face looking back to her, and as she was about to leave, she heard voices coming from the study.

". . . If you expect me to write a check for forty thousand dollars . . ." Vipul said.

Lisa's soft voice protested. "I'm not asking for a handout . . . I'll pay you back every cent . . ."

"He listens to you, why don't you ask him to join my company. He'd make much more as a technical writer . . ." Vipul said.

"No," Lisa said firmly.

Jia knew she was listening to a private conversation, but curiosity held her close to the door, wishing the rain would stall so she could hear clearly.

"I'm not going to crush his dreams. And his dream is to be a finance author, not spend days writing technical manuals for apps he couldn't care less about."

"But it's not practical. Now if we confronted him together, I'm sure he'd come around."

"Please don't do that . . ." Lisa's voice sounded anguished. "You can't tell him I came to you. He'll kill me if he finds out . . ."

Jia heard footsteps and suddenly realized she'd neglected to lock the door facing the study, and if one of them opened it, they'd come face-to-face. Slowly, she crept out with hushed steps from the bathroom into the hallway, their words buzzing in her head.

Why did Lisa need to borrow money from Vipul? Was the amount for a down payment on a house? A new car? But all these expenses were joint ventures, logical steps forward for a young couple like Lisa and Raj, so why would Lisa need to hide this from Raj?

Lisa's fearful voice rang in Jia's head. *He'll kill me if he finds out . . .*

$$/ \prime /\prime /\prime /\prime /$$

JIA JOINED THE OTHERS IN THE FORMAL DINING ROOM. VIPUL SAT AT the head of the table, his fingers steepled together. Sprinkling a pinch of tangy chaat masala powder on the cucumber slices, Jia perched on the chair adjacent to Lisa, rubbed her smarting finger, and tracked Vipul's disposition.

Rafael sat on the opposite end of the table facing Vipul.

Opposite her, Asha emitted a loud squeal of delight. She was riding on Raj's bouncing right leg as a makeshift horse while Ishaan flanked him on his left, eyes wide, swiping something on the smartphone in Raj's hand.

Despite her reservations about Raj, Jia was grateful to him for keeping the kids away from Rafael.

They were trying to hold it together for the sake of the children, but it was a facsimile of a regular family dinner. Lisa flinched with every flash of lightning; Raj's gaze kept flitting to Rafael, while Vipul craned his neck staring at the glass panes as if they would come crashing down on him.

Ishaan said, "Hey, Mom, can Raj come to my birthday party?"

"Of course, that would be great." At least Ishaan was talking to her again.

He would benefit from positive male role models. The school principal's suggestion had cut through her core. By the mathematical laws of divorce, children received two birthdays, one with each parent—but she had run away from Chicago after essentially blackmailing Dev to never contact them again. She had subtracted a father but doubled the amount of love. But now she doubted herself. Maybe that wasn't enough. She wasn't enough.

"And maybe my soccer match too?" Ishaan said. "Dad used to take me. We'd go for ice cream afterwards. He invited my teammates too. Even on days we lost the match. Made me really popular with my friends."

Vipul motioned to the bowl of khichdi. "Rafael, are you sure you don't want to eat anything?"

"I'm sure," said Rafael. He lifted the glass of buttermilk and inspected its contents. "Does this have peanuts?"

"No," said Jia. "You're not allergic to cumin, are you?"

"Not that I'm aware of," Rafael said, smiling.

Ishaan peered at Raj's phone screen and said, excitedly, "Go to my friend Nick's Facebook. He makes these crazy videos."

Jia's skin burned with embarrassment that after all her self-righteousness about not using social media, he had found a way. Her teeth gritted, she asked, "Ishaan, can you come with me, please?" As Jia marched ahead, Ishaan followed her, and it took all her willpower to keep quiet till they reached her room. As soon as the door shut, she burst out, "Why are you on these apps? Didn't I tell you I don't want you addicted to these things?"

Irritation flashed in Ishaan's eyes. "I'm not addicted. My friend showed me when I was using his phone, okay?"

"Is that why I haven't given you a phone?" Jia said, through clenched teeth. "So you can go look at your friends' phones? Why, Ishaan, why do you never listen to me? Why do you have to use a phone without telling me?"

"Because I wanted to talk to Dad, all right?" Ishaan snapped.

For a few seconds, Jia was stunned like a tranquilized animal.

"Why did you want to talk to him?" Jia said softly. "And why didn't you tell me?"

Ishaan shrugged. "I didn't tell you because you start crying even at the mention of his name. And I guess I missed him, especially after my suspension. I just wanted to hear his voice . . ."

Jia's skin tingled. That's how Dev knew about the suspension, not from Seema or through sleuthing, but from Ishaan himself.

Ishaan continued, "But Dad told me to stop calling him. You happy? He'll find a way for us to hang out the right way."

Jia went slack-jawed. The betrayal stung, sharp as a knife.

This was where the custody evaluation had come from. At Ishaan's behest, Dev was trying to legally find a way for them to be in regular contact. All this time she had hated Dev when he was merely following his son's wishes while balancing Jia's request not to be contacted directly.

But then she remembered the texts he'd sent her.

Jia's mouth turned arid as she grappled with the two opposite versions of Dev emerging in front of her, as if he had developed a split personality. How else could a caring father trying to do right by his son be the same man who was threatening her from a burner phone?

There was no good reason for him to be in Houston. He had cousins in Louisiana, so it would make sense for him to travel there, but why come to Jia's town if not to take Ishaan away?

Jia felt dizzy. The only thing she knew for sure was that because of Dev, Ishaan had lied to her. Hidden the fact that he was in contact with his father.

"You're right," Jia said, not looking at Ishaan because she knew he would hate her for her next words. "It doesn't matter now anyway. I forbid you to talk to him again, and if you care for me even a little bit, you'll listen to me this time."

WHEN JIA RETURNED TO THE DINING TABLE, ASHA BELLYACHED WHEN extricated from Raj's lap and moved to a high chair. Vipul said, "I think there's been an update on the hurricane." Everyone crowded around him as he pulled up the Weather Channel on his tablet.

The channel cut to a woman standing in front of a giant graphics screen. She traced the trajectory of a neon circle across the map. "The current gale-force winds have dropped to seventy-three miles per hour. We have confirmation that the hurricane has been downgraded to a tropical storm."

Jia's lips parted as a giddy relief overcame her. Compared to a hurricane, a tropical storm sounded benign. Even though the rain-fall outside continued with ferocity, she retrieved her phone and checked her email.

No messages from her building's management, notifying residents they could come home. There was only one email, but Jia ignored it as soon as she saw the subject, "Networking for single parents."

An end to this had to be in sight, yet when she looked around the room, no one seemed to share her hopeful optimism.

Vipul and Raj exchanged grim looks.

"It's just a tropical storm now, that's a wonderful thing, right?" asked Seema.

"No," said Vipul, and then gave a theatrical sigh. "That's *not* a wonderful thing," he said. "With high wind speeds, at least it was moving forward, and with any luck, it would travel away from Houston and go to Louisiana. But now, with reduced wind speeds, there's nothing pushing it, it's basically churning in place, dumping gallons of water." He waved his index finger in a circle.

"The problem is," Raj said, "when the land is so flat in Houston, where does all that water go?"

Crestfallen, Jia looked to the newscaster, who warned, "An additional fifty inches of rain is anticipated to cause flooding in all parts of Houston. If the rainfall continues at this pace, the Brazos River will rise by over fifty feet by tomorrow afternoon. Engineers will use state-of-the-art pumps to reduce the water level of the levees. But if the forecasted rain amounts come to fruition, the levee water will exceed the capacity of the pumps."

Lisa gulped. "Basically everything depends on the pumps? And what happens if the pumps don't work fast enough?"

Raj tipped his head back. "If the levees flood, ultimately streets will flood, holding water for days or even weeks."

Seema's eyes widened.

Lisa repeated, "Weeks?"

Raj shrugged. "It really depends on what happens in the next few hours."

The newscaster ended on a grave note. "Folks, we are not out of the woods yet."

WHEN SEEMA HAD FINISHED SERVING EVERYONE, JIA POINTED TO THE empty space on the table in front of Lisa and said, "I think we're one short."

Seema's hands flew to her mouth. "Oops," she said, her shoulders lifted theatrically. The exaggeration in her gesture, familiar to Jia, discomfited her.

Whatever followed would not be good.

"I'll be right back with the very special dish I made just for you," Seema said, winking. She returned with a plate that she set delicately on the dinner table in front of Lisa. When Jia glimpsed the contents, she took a sharp intake of breath.

The air in the room changed. Everyone's stares bounced from Lisa to Seema. Even Asha, boisterous moments ago, lapsed into silence, trying to comprehend what had made the adults go quiet.

Lisa's chin trembled, and her moist eyes blinked rapidly. On her plate was a single slice of cheese pizza, looking like Seema had it tossed in a microwave to reheat. Around Lisa, the yellow blobs of khichdi thickened as they cooled on everyone else's plates.

Seema scrunched her nose. "I know Lisa doesn't like my cooking. What did you tell Raj about my curry last year?" Seema tapped a finger on her chin and pulled a face like she was recollecting a long-lost memory. "Like a spice ball had exploded in your stomach?"

Lisa mumbled, "I was just kidding." Her lips parted and her shoulders bunched up as she said "I can't believe you told her" to Raj, who in turn gaped at Seema, evidently not having expected this betrayal of trust.

But Raj should have known better. To Seema, "I'm telling you something in confidence" meant you could confidently share this information however you wanted.

Seema shrugged. "This is the best I could do." She side-eyed Grandma, and the decibel of her tone increased. "I'm sure you eat all sorts of cow meat and beef in your house. But here, we have vegetarian food only."

"Bhabhi," Raj said with a sigh. His voice was laced not with anger but with profound disappointment. "You know Lisa likes your food and eats vegetarian meals." Stretching his arms, he opened the lid of the pressure cooker in the center, and a soft groan escaped his lips.

Seema scratched her cheek. "Well, I suppose it'll be enough, assuming the kids don't want seconds—"

Vipul dropped his spoon with a clang. "Enough, Seema. I'm sure there's something in the fridge we can eat."

Jia shot a glance at Rafael. He sat with his chin cupped in his hands, with the mildly amused look of someone tuning into an episode of a recurring soap opera.

Jia clasped her hands. If only Seema knew what they were up against, she would hold off on her dramatic productions.

She patted Lisa's knee under the table. Only Seema could weaponize food. Her white lies didn't fool Jia. Every Indian household, at any given moment, had enough food for three additional families. The so-called lack of alternate food options was no accident; the entire thing reeked of Seema's manipulative tactics. Even though the perceived slight had occurred a year ago, Seema had stewed in resentment, like marinated paneer cubes for a barbecue. And while she couldn't wait a day before buying the newest phones, she had the patience to wait for the perfect time to orchestrate revenge.

Things hadn't always been this bad between Seema and Lisa.

They had enjoyed a brief honeymoon period in which Seema drove Lisa to Desi clothing stores on Hillcroft to buy sarees and lent her bangles to match her outfits.

Seema probably thought she had found an ally against her mother-in-law. A tag team that would take down the matriarchy.

And initially everything was going according to Seema's plan.

Seema had kept Jia posted on all updates. Grandma was initially vehemently opposed to Raj's interracial marriage. "I'll eat poison before I let you marry her," she had threatened.

But everything changed when Raj brought Lisa along to a Diwali celebration and all the Desi aunties got a look at his girlfriend.

From the moment Lisa stepped in the room, a repressed reverence for white skin activated within the crowd like a long-buried gene, and they gushed over how perfect she was.

Suddenly, Grandma found herself the object of envy for having a foreign bahu.

Grandma delighted in this newfound cachet and in all the attention, and suddenly Lisa was invited to every family event, even distant ones. Pujas that were performed for new houses, baby showers for pregnant wives.

Grandma's interest in her younger daughter-in-law set the new tone for Seema's relationship with Lisa. Poor Lisa kept apologizing even though it wasn't her fault. Seema despised Lisa now, and Lisa kept trying to win her sister-in-law's affection back, hoping for things to return to the way they were when they were friends.

Seema's unrestrained venom tonight disturbed Jia. With a captive family, Seema had a built-in audience for her performance.

Grandma, settled in a corner, had been quiet so far. She said, "Don't worry, Lisa. I'll make something for you." She threw a dirty look at Seema and gripped the edge of the table for support, green veins popping on her papyrus-like skin as she struggled to rise to her feet.

Raj said quickly, "Please sit, Ma." He swapped his plate for Lisa's and said, "There. Problem solved." Back to his buoyant self, he smiled as he took a bite out of the pizza. "Mmm," he said. "Thank you, Bhabhi, you've reminded me of my college years."

Seema gave him a cloying smile while Lisa shot a grateful look to her husband and sighed. Vipul shook his head in exasperation and wolfed down his food. When Jia nudged the plate of cucumbers toward Lisa, Seema glared at her.

Jia stared back in defiance and added another spoon of ghee to Lisa's plate. "Sometimes you need more butter to make the taste better."

Rafael swirled the glass of buttermilk like he was at a wine tasting before taking a small, cautious sip.

When Lisa smiled weakly, Jia said, "I can give you the name of the Indian store where you can get the chaat powder. You can add it to fruits too."

Seema glowered at Jia, annoyance coming off her like a heat wave.

The dinner proceeded in silence, apart from the occasional sound of tree limbs cracking as rainfall continued unabated.

Seema picked around her food, pausing every minute to say, "Asha, don't sit there and play with your food." When Asha pushed her spoon away, Seema snapped, "Stop it."

Asha predictably responded to this by bursting into howling cries. Seema enfolded her in her arms. "I'm sorry. Mommy's tired," she said. The corners of her mouth were turned down. When Jia made eye contact, Seema looked away, and underneath the anger, Jia glimpsed a hint of disappointment, maybe even pain.

As Seema's motive for inviting her unspooled slowly, sadness gnawed at Jia.

Seema had invited Jia not because Jia was alone, but because Seema herself was alone.

With Vipul's support nonexistent, she didn't have any allies.

So, Jia's presence in the house was not an impulsive act of kindness, but rather a premeditated move. Perhaps Seema thought having an outsider present would preclude her from feeling like an interloper in her own family. Guilt squeezed Jia's heart. "Family comes first" was Seema's mantra.

As dinner wound down, Grandma, as expected, retreated to her room.

Raj patted Asha's head. "You finished your food, good job, kiddo." He motioned to Seema. "Bhabhi, why don't you take Asha upstairs and let us take care of the dishes."

When Seema left with Asha, Jia sent Ishaan off to watch television in the media room. Raj whispered in Vipul's ear, his eyes bulged, and he threw a furtive glance at Rafael drinking the rest of his buttermilk.

When Vipul left the room in a haste, a thrill fizzed through Jia.

He was getting his gun.

It was time.

Jia couldn't wait a second longer.

She cleared her throat. "Do you want to tell us what you're really doing here, Rafael?"

SIXTEEN

Rafael responded with a sneeze.

His cheeks turned mottled, and he frantically tapped his pockets.

Grabbing his throat, he said, "My jac—"

Rafael's hand, suspended in midair for a second, came crashing down, knocking a glass off the table. It shattered, scattering shards below.

"Hey, man, you okay?" Raj asked, throwing his chair back.

But Rafael was not okay.

His eyes bulged and his face contorted in anguish. His chest heaved, and he clutched his throat with both hands as if he was struggling to breathe.

A shuddering gasp. Rafael turned wide-eyed, red busted arteries crisscrossing his pupils.

Vipul, likely hearing the commotion, doubled back to the room and rushed to Rafael's side. "I think he's choking!"

Rafael slid off his chair and fell onto the floor with a sickening thud.

His cheeks puffed up. His left eyelid ballooned, shutting off one eye.

Vipul sat on his haunches on the floor next to Rafael, and placing one hand on top of the other, he started pumping Rafael's chest.

"Stop," Lisa screamed. "He's not having a heart attack."

Rafael struggled to breathe. "Get jack—"

"Who's Jack?" Vipul asked, wild-eyed.

Raj clapped a hand on his forehead. "He means his jacket! His EpiPen! Look at his skin, he's clearly having some kind of an allergic reaction. I'm sure he has it somewhere. Check his pockets."

"Yes. I put his jacket in the coat closet!" Lisa yelled, dashing to the living room.

Rafael's skin turned blue and his eyes rolled upward.

Lisa reappeared, clutching her stomach, like she was out of breath. She shook her head, her eyes horrified. "Couldn't find it." She laid the jacket on the chair.

"We have to call 9-1-1," Jia said.

"I'm on it." Raj plucked out his phone from his pocket and pressed it to his ear before disconnecting. He swore under his breath. "No one's responding. Network's jammed."

Rafael curled his knees up to his chest as his entire body shuddered. Another heave.

His lips parted, and it looked like he was trying to say something, but a stream of vomit burbled out of his mouth.

Raj recoiled.

For a gut-wrenching two minutes, they watched helplessly as Rafael convulsed on the floor, arms thrashing.

Then, just as abruptly as it had started convulsing, his body stilled. He stopped moving, limbs limp, a hollow look in his eyes.

Even though she didn't have a medical degree, Jia knew this: Rafael was dead.

BEFORE

Seema's invitation for a girls' night out was manna from heaven. Jia's previous foray into socializing in Houston had gone down in flames. She and Ishaan had gone with a Tupperware container filled with biryani for a coworker's potluck dinner event at her house. When they arrived, they heard a commotion from the backyard, and when they went around the house, Jia realized that coming here had been a mistake. Someone had procured firecrackers and was setting them off. The smaller kids were content perched on their mothers' hips, watching flowerpots light up while some of the older children waved around sparklers. And when one of the dads offered Ishaan a rocket, Jia could see him tear up. Lighting firecrackers during Diwali had been a yearly tradition for Ishaan and Dev, and it was always a special father-son activity because Jia couldn't stand the noise.

The next day, Seema called her. "You left early? And got drive-through Taco Bell? Jeez. Listen, Jia, you're not a turtle. You can't stay in your shell forever. I'm having a girls' dinner this weekend. I'll introduce you to one of my friends. Divorced for nine years. Never been happier."

Jia, who had been pacing the floor, came to a halt. She nodded. "You're right. I probably need to talk to someone who has experienced this firsthand." Seema's friend would be a crystal ball with a vision of the future, a woman with inner peace and confidence, untainted by the shame of divorce. The following Saturday, Jia gingerly climbed the stairs of a bar called Present Company, in heels she hadn't worn in months, a long-forgotten lighthearted first-date feeling in her belly. The upper-deck patio was an Instagrammer's wet dream: verdant walls interspersed with lush flowers, potted palm trees, bright-colored chairs. She found Seema inside a cabana, huddled with two of her friends, a smartphone in the air, stomachs sucked in, three sets of lips in variants of pouts.

"You made it," trilled Seema, spotting her. She lifted the velvet rope to let Jia inside.

Jia pushed a few Moroccan-style cushions out of the way. The ultrasoft sofa depressed several inches when she sat down. After greeting Seema's friends, she scanned their manicured hands for an empty ring finger. "Where's the divorced friend you were talking about?"

Seema took a long-drawn-out sip from a straw dipped in a wide glass. "She couldn't make it."

"Oh." Jia clasped her hands in her lap. "What happened?"

"Her babysitter canceled at the last minute. Poor thing. She'd been looking forward to this for months."

Jia's heart felt like it was shrinking. Divorce was a cancer, always in remission, never cured.

"Well, you're here now," said Seema. "C'mon. Let's get you a drink."

While Seema snapped her fingers to get the waitress's attention, one of her friends, Shefali, fanned herself with her hand. Her luscious hair was tied in a half-up hairstyle, waves cascading down to her waist like a goddess.

When the waitress arrived, Jia reached for the happy hour menu, but Seema pulled it out of her reach. "Relax. I'll order the best sweet red wine for you."

Shefali exhaled loudly and said, "You won't believe the kind of awful week I've had." Her kohl-lined eyes widened as she poked at a cherry in her drink with a tiny umbrella stick.

Jia scooted forward to listen better.

Shefali continued, "Our nanny is going back to India next week. Her husband has cancer and they can't afford medical insurance here. Where am I supposed to find a replacement on such short notice? My kid doesn't even eat without her by his side. If that wasn't enough, I have to find time to go shopping for our trip to Mali."

The other women tut-tutted. "Sounds like you could use a vacation right now," said Seema, before inhaling the rest of her cocktail.

Shefali ate the whole cherry. "Trust me, I need it."

Jia suppressed a sigh. On the pretext of adjusting the strap on her sandals, she peeked at her watch. Even with Ms. Nikki's discounted hourly rates, this insightful conversation had cost Jia ten dollars.

"Girls," said Seema slyly. "We're boring Jia."

"Oops," said Shefali. "Jia, tell us about yourself."

When they found out Jia was a single mother, she turned into an empty canvas to project their relationship insecurities onto, their reactions transparent enough for Jia to deduce the exact state of their marital lives.

Shefali sidled up to her. Coveting Jia's glass of wine, she took a reluctant sip of her mocktail. "Tell us about your single life, Jia. You must have so much fun. Tinder hookups and nights out. No husband to worry about. No sleepless nights because of infant babies." Copious layers of concealer had failed to hide her under-eye circles.

Bored-out-of-her-mind stay-at-home mom. Jia shook her head. "Honestly, most days, the highlight of my day is getting six hours of sleep."

Shefali put her drink back on the table, spilling orange drops on the wood. She frowned. "You're not dating?"

"No."

"One-night stands with younger men at least?"

Another shake of the head from Jia. Sweat rolled down her back, and she longed to pull down the band of the shapewear digging into her stomach.

Shefali took a gulp of her drink, leaving red smudges on the rim, and wiped her mouth with the back of her hand. "Then what are you using all this freedom for? To sleep?"

Freedom? Jia grimaced as her dejection gave way to reproach. It wasn't enough that Jia's marriage was a failure; apparently, she was doing divorce incorrectly too.

The third woman at the table, Palak, had yet to say a single word to Jia. Her skinny frame was slouched, and when her eyes met Jia's, she pursed her lips and lowered her head. She threw furtive glances in Jia's direction as if divorce were conjunctivitis, transmittable by direct eye contact. *Happily married but insecure wife, cherophobia sufferer.* Such women kept Jia at arm's length, switching places at parties so Jia wouldn't sit next to their husbands, guarding their spouses like lionesses because her presence was a reminder of the fragility of their precarious marriages.

As Seema got progressively drunker, she discreetly pulled out her phone and texted away, blushing. She occasionally chortled like she was high on happiness. Jia looked away. While Shefali and Palak ate their diet-compliant salads, checking in on their husbands and discussing times they were returning home, Jia sighed and took a bite of her sandwich. She checked a text from Nikki.

All good here. Ishaan's playing outside with Jim.

When Jia excused herself to go to the bathroom, Palak followed her. Stepping inside, she clutched Jia's arm. After a quick glance at the door, she whispered, "Hi . . . I need your advice. I can't do this anymore. I want to leave my husband." She spoke in hushed tones. "My mother-in-law expects me to make rotis and curry for the entire family after coming home from work. My husband used my last paycheck to pay off his brother-in-law's debts. I'm a business executive, for God's sake, how can I be expected to put up with this?" Her posture collapsed as the words tumbled out of her like an exorcism.

Having laid the case for her separation with the vigor of a thorough trial lawyer, her eyes watered, and she lifted her head and waited for Jia to render her judgement.

"Should I leave him?" she asked.

Jia handed her a tissue and gently stroked her forearm. Palak's gaunt eyes were pools of the inner turmoil Jia herself had experienced not too long ago.

Jia said, "I can't decide whether it's time to end your marriage. Only you can decide that."

Palak whimpered and swiped her hand across her face, brushing away fresh tears, smudging mascara around the corner of her eyes. "Thanks for hearing me out. I guess I better get going," she said.

"Hold on," said Jia, clasping her hand. "I'll tell you when *I* knew it was time. It was the moment I didn't care whether anyone approved of my decision or not."

Palak's eyes met Jia's; then she nodded vigorously and dabbed at her face.

"Either way," continued Jia in a soothing voice, "it's not going to be easy."

The suede bag hiked on Palak's shoulder vibrated, startling her. She answered her phone. "Yes, I'll leave in a few minutes. I *know* I still have to make dinner. You made that pretty clear when I left," she snapped.

After hanging up, she showed Jia the wallpaper on her phone— a cherubic baby girl, swaddled in pink. "She's six months old." She smiled. "My baby is the best thing in my life." The sight of her daughter cracked her not-yet-hardened resolve, and she shook her head. "I don't know if I can break up my family." Her face turned pale. "What's she done to deserve this?"

Jia squeezed Palak's shoulder. "Take my number. If you ever need to talk." Watching the sniffling, frail figure in front of her, Jia felt a weight lifted off her shoulders.

She had come here looking for relief in a glimpse of the future, but had instead found comfort in a reminder of the past.

Difficult as it was to be a single mother, Jia's current hardships paled in comparison to this woman's ordeal, trapped in purgatory.

Too miserable to be married. Too petrified to leave.

Jia pulled a stack of brown paper towels from the dispenser. It was a strange yet comforting feeling to be helpful to someone.

The restroom door opened with a bang. Seema stumbled in. "My girlsss . . . you're here," she slurred. Lurching to the basin, Seema tried to turn the faucet on but kept missing the tap. Jia and Palak exchanged a glance before escorting her outside.

The waiter arrived with a black book. "Ladies, are we paying separately today?"

Seema lapsed into a fit of giggles and snorted as though this was the funniest thing she'd ever heard. Jia looked at Seema's friends in alarm. "Did she drive here?"

"We carpooled together," Palak said. "I could drop her, but . . ." Palak glanced uneasily at the time on her phone. "But I still need to make dinner, and my husband just texted me we're also out of milk . . ."

Jia's call to Vipul went unanswered and Seema burped, "Don't bother. He's on a work call and I don't expect him to check his phone for hours."

"Guess I'll just drop you home," Jia said, whipping out her phone to text Nikki she was going to be late, but even in her intoxicated state, Seema apparently sensed Jia's reluctance.

"Chill, I'll get an Uber," she said, tapping on her screen. "Ishaan must be waiting for you."

With her arm looped around Jia's, Seema staggered down the treacherous spiral staircase, and Jia guided her toward the Uber. Seema swayed on her feet for a second before collapsing on the passenger seat and fumbled with her seat belt, insisting "I'm not drunk! I can do it myself." The driver observed Seema's struggle with thinly veiled exasperation.

Seema reached for Jia's hand, breath smelling of alcohol, and when she opened her mouth, Jia recoiled, expecting a projectile of vomit. But instead, Seema said, "How are you going to get home? Let us drop you."

Jia smiled. "I came here in my own car, remember?"

Seema hiccuped. "Text me when you reach home. Did you have fun tonight?"

"Yes," Jia lied.

Seema turned slightly cross-eyed. "I don't know how you manage living alone. I wouldn't survive a day."

"Luckily, you won't have to." Jia tucked Seema's stray strands away from her face. Jia said, loud enough for the driver to hear, "I'll be waiting for your text once you reach home." Warmth radiated in her chest as Jia shut the door. At least one of them wouldn't have to come home to an empty bed.

As promised, Seema texted her.

rchd hme. Gonna throw up now.
Hope you made it k 2.

Seema always looked out for Jia because Jia didn't have someone staying up, anxiously listening for the sound of keys turning in the lock. Seema lived in an extravagant house, but the real luxury was knowing that she could afford to sleep in the next day and nurse her hangover because, thanks to Vipul and Grandma, she knew her child would be fed, clothed, safe.

I wouldn't survive a day.

As Jia lay on the bed, drifting off to sleep, an uneasy thought took hold of her mind.

If Vipul was busy with work, who was Seema texting all evening?

Later that night, her phone beeped with an incoming text from Vipul.

Hello Jia. Thank you for taking
care of Seema today.

Jia clicked on a thumbs-up emoji, then reread his message again. Complete sentences. Seema's chats were short, full of emojis and abbreviations like she was being charged for every word, but the formal tone of Vipul's message reminded her of a business email. She deleted the emoticon and texted back.

> Happy to help. Can you make sure she drinks
> tons of water before sleeping? She tends to
> get these massive migraines the next day.

Vipul replied instantly.

> She is lucky to have such a caring sister.

Jia chewed the inside of her cheek. Things were the other way around. She was lucky to have Seema in her life. After replying "Ditto," Jia slipped under the covers, ready to go back to sleep, but seconds later, her phone pinged again.

> Can I ask you something?

Jia frowned at the phone and shifted her weight. It was weird chatting with Vipul this way—their previous chat history was basically a transcription of her sister's thoughts and whereabouts: "Seema still needs an hour to do her makeup." "Seema is taking a shower." "Can you please just call your sister?"
Before waiting for her response, he texted again:

> Our anniversary is coming up next week. Seema
> has been dropping hints for months that she
> wants a gift, but she also wants me to surprise
> her somehow. Can you help me buy one?

Jia let her head fall back on the cushion in relief. *Of course.* She typed right away.

> She loves purses and perfumes.
> I would stick to brand labels.

Jia rubbed the nape of her neck. Asking him for his budget would be rude, but she had to tell him to get something expensive, because Seema was notoriously skilled at finding out the sticker prices of the most obscure gifts.

Dots appeared on her screen while Vipul typed.

I'm going to pick out a gift next week.
Can you come with me to the mall?

Jia tugged at a fraying thread of a pillow. She was still mulling a response when more dots appeared on the chat window followed by another message.

I could really use your help. Our marriage
has been on the rocks lately.

Jia sat up straight. Where was he? Was he texting in the dark, Seema lying intoxicated next to him at this very moment, or was he perched on the toilet seat, discreetly laying bare his spousal troubles while his wife snored on their marital bed?

But Jia lived under a mountain of their favors, and here was an opportunity to repay him.

She typed up a message.

Text me the time and place and I'll be there.

The following Saturday arrived like most summer mornings in Houston, with the sun blaring in full view before seven, painting the sky in sepia tones, temperatures hovering around 80 degrees Fahrenheit in the early hours. Jia woke up and threw off her sweaty covers. Feeling queasy, she stared at the ceiling fan, her thoughts looping in tandem with the blades. Although she had agreed to meet Vipul, the idea of a clandestine encounter with Seema's spouse, albeit for a noble cause, made her heart palpitate.

After getting dressed in a loose, frumpy T-shirt and faded jeans, she sat in her car. Her fingers burned when she touched the steering wheel. As she turned her key in the ignition, the check-engine light came on. Jia sighed. The car was manifesting her reluctance. Interpreting it as a sign from the universe, Jia quickly sent a text.

> Sorry can't make it! Car's not
> working for some reason.

She went back inside with a measure of relief and thought, *Well, that was that.* She had dodged a bullet. It didn't feel right to meet Vipul in Seema's absence even though there was nothing wrong with their intentions. Jia headed upstairs, figuring it would be a while before she'd see Vipul in person.

Until he showed up at her apartment.

A week had gone by with no contact from Vipul. Jia had just discovered that Ishaan needed glasses, and she was so busy stocking her refrigerator with enough carrots to feed a forest of rabbits that her tête-à-tête with Vipul was long forgotten.

Then one evening, he knocked on her front door again, but this time Jia had an excuse ready on her lips. "Oh, we were just heading out to buy groceries."

"This won't take long," Vipul said, sidling inside.

From his pocket he removed a red velvet box and popped it open, revealing a silver ring encrusted with diamonds.

"What do you think?" Vipul said, staring at her hopefully.

Jia was flabbergasted. "I . . . uh . . ."

"Okay, hold on," Vipul said, fishing out another box with a

plain gold-banded ring and holding them side by side. "Is this one better? Which one will Seema like?"

Shaky laughter escaped Jia's lips as she sagged against the wall. *Of course he was referring to the anniversary gift for Seema.* Now relaxed, she looked at the two rings properly and personally would have liked the simpler one, but Seema was a fan of bling jewelry so that's what Jia recommended.

Vipul nodded, satisfied. "I thought so, but the saleslady had me all confused, so I wanted to make sure, and ended up buying both with return receipts just in case."

Then, stuffing the rings back in his pockets, Vipul asked in an offhand manner, not looking at Jia, "Is your sister having an affair?"

Jia was dumbstruck. He had caught her completely off guard.

Seema's words came back to her. *I don't know how you manage living alone. I wouldn't survive a day.*

"There's no one else in Seema's life. What would even make you say such a thing?" Jia said, mustering a confidence she didn't wholly feel inside.

Vipul pinched the skin of his throat. "She spends all her time on her phone."

This didn't surprise Jia. Seema's Insta feed often left Jia wondering when she found the time to truly live the life chronicled meticulously online. "Isn't that how she's always been?"

Vipul looked sheepish. "It's not just that." He shifted his weight from one foot to another. "She seems kind of happy."

Now Jia felt sorry for him.

But he was right. She did seem happier lately. A subtle difference that only the ones close to her would notice. A sunny disposition not despite her life circumstances but because of it.

It could mean nothing. Or it could be the key to everything.

Jia said, "You should just talk to her instead of talking to me."

His posture slumped. "What's the point? I feel like I could move mountains for Seema, but it wouldn't be enough."

Jia hunted to dig up something positive Seema had said about Vipul, but the only instance that came to mind was Seema once concluding "Vipul is completely reliable" before adding dryly "like a good package delivery service."

"Guess I'd better get going," Vipul said, and he looked so pitiable with his paunch, holding two rings worth an average person's monthly salary but still unsure if he would make his wife happy, that Jia's hand moved of its own accord, automatically squeezing his shoulder. "Seema is lucky to have you as a husband. Any woman would be."

She gave him a sympathetic smile, but as he locked eyes with her, she knew in her gut something was wrong.

His expression went from despondent to hopeful to excited in the blink of an eye, and before Jia could do anything other than recognize this shift in his demeanor, he pressed his hand on hers, the feel of his rough and dry skin making her toes curl.

Please leave. But the words caught in her throat, and Vipul, mistaking her distress for restlessness, leaned in eagerly.

Was he doing what she thought he was doing? But Vipul was already close, much too close, near enough for her to see the grays in his mustache, his eyes closed, lips puckered, and Jia cringed as she wriggled her hand free . . .

A cough.

Ishaan stood behind them, mortified, mouth hanging open, disgust and shock competing to take control of his face.

Jia's stomach contracted. Vipul, flustered, stepped back, unnecessarily straightened his shirt. "Aaah, it's getting late. I'd better get going."

He left in a hurry, and Jia faced Ishaan, but he didn't meet her eyes and stomped to his room, slamming the door shut.

Jia was calibrating her explanation to Ishaan when she registered the meaning behind Vipul's hurried exit.

A sick sensation rose up her throat.

As far as Vipul was concerned, their kiss would have very much happened if not for Ishaan's inopportune arrival.

When Vipul called her later that night, Jia ignored the call.

After a fortnight, he messaged again at eleven in the night, just as Jia was drifting off to sleep.

You were right. She loved the gift.

A warmth spread over Jia, and her fingers trembled with excitement as she typed, "That's great to hear!"

If Seema and Vipul's relationship was on the right track again, then the past would stay in the past where it belonged. The incident at the house buried forever. An embarrassing memory that would fade in time.

But before she could hit send, his reply came.

Jia's mouth fell open.

BEFORE

TWENTY DAYS AGO

Seema still didn't have sex with me.
Not even a hand job.

Jia recoiled and dropped the phone as though it were dirty, tainted. The candidness, the vulgarity of his words, left a sour taste in her mouth. She brought her knees together and wrapped her arms tight around them. She felt used, lured under the pretext of helping salvage her sister's marriage. She had never asked to be privy to the intimate details of their marriage. She certainly wasn't going to pimp her sister to Vipul.

When her phone lit up again, her heartbeat increased.

With growing trepidation, she picked up her phone.

Dots appeared and disappeared as Vipul typed. Jia had nearly tossed the phone aside again when his message appeared.

I didn't want to make you uncomfortable.

I don't have anyone to share this
with. Your sister has stopped
sleeping with me for months.

Jia took a deep breath and reminded herself of what was at stake
for Seema. He was a pig, but he was Seema's pig. She fiddled with
the phone.

After a few frantic searches on the internet, she forwarded him
a link.

Best recommended marriage
counselors in Houston.

No reply from him.
Then another week went by before he sent her a new message.

Want to catch a movie this weekend?

Jia cringed and immediately deleted the text.

Seema is going to visit her friend in California,
so she will be out of town for a week.

Jia's hands balled into fists. How could he presume that Seema's
absence would influence her decision?

After Jia's nonreplies to eight of his messages, he forwarded her
an image. Jia squinted at the block of purple text.

My heart was lonely for lack of love.
I confided to a friend but was spurned anew.
Oh heart how do I heal you now?

Jia clamped a mental finger on her growing irritation, clicked on the message, and hit delete.

Another week went by without his missives. Then one evening, while Jia was dumping the contents of her laundry hamper into the washing machine, her phone pinged.

> Can you send me the contact information
> of your divorce attorney?

Jia's face blanched.

He was punishing her for ignoring him. She had to find a way to fix Seema's marriage. She typed quickly.

> Please don't make hasty decisions. Why don't
> you take some time and focus on yourself?

Jia stared at the dots on her phone, holding her breath.

> Yes, you may be right. We have thousands
> of dollars of gym equipment in our house
> which I've never used. I'm going to hire a
> personal trainer.

Jia took a deep breath. For once, she agreed with him. It was perhaps the best course of action for him. She sent him a thumbs-up emoticon.

Over the next few days, he sent her stats from his workouts.

> Bench pressed 123 weights. Did 15 pushups
> in a row. Trainer says it's great for my age.

His shape was still far from Seema's ideal physique for a man, but it was a step in the right direction.

Jia replied.

Looking good.

On a Monday afternoon, Jia was seated at the very back of the DMV, suspended in time. Again, Jia squinted at the screen at the front, a one-digit difference between the number on the screen and her position in the queue.

Her phone pinged with a new message.

Jia paused and glanced at her phone. A selfie, Vipul in a sleeveless black tank, forehead glistening with sweat. A dumbbell in his right hand.

The sight of her brother-in-law, with his middle-aged paunch and sagging jowls, tugged at her heart. There was nothing wrong with encouraging him to get healthy. The number on the screen changed. Her turn was up. Jia quickly sent him a couple of smiley emoticons before hurrying to the counter.

It wasn't till she reached home that she read his reply.

I feel the same way.

Jia frowned. His reply made no sense.

What had prompted this response? She scrolled up, her eyes bulging in horror.

In a hurry, she had sent him a kiss emoji, the flirty cohort of the smiley emoji. Her insides shrank in embarrassment as she stared at the yellowed face with puckered lips blowing kisses into the air.

She instantly texted him back.

Sorry. I didn't mean to send that. Fat fingers. :)

But apparently for Vipul, an emoticon was worth a thousand words. He sent her another verse.

I was at my darkest point.
You lit up a single light and brought
me back to life.

Jia clapped her palm to her forehead. With the almost kiss and now this, she had cemented in his mind her intentions. There was no going back. What had she gotten herself into?

SEVENTEEN

They were trapped in a horrific tableau. Them by dint of shock, him by death.

Vipul crouched beside Rafael's still form. Raj sat next to his brother, knees crossed in a V, his phone facedown on the carpet. Lisa kneaded the side of her stomach, her breaths ragged. Jia's fingers gripped the edge of the dining table, the wood cold on her skin like Rafael's body, the same thought bouncing around the corners of her brain.

Rafael is dead. He is dead. Rafael's gone.

The air, minutes earlier suffused with the mouthwatering aroma of sautéed butter and spices, now reeked with the stench of vomit.

Seema entered the room, eyes glued to a baby monitor in her hand. "I swear every day it takes longer to put her to sleep."

After she placed the monitor on the dining table, her gaze landed on Rafael. She let out a sharp scream.

She blinked, disoriented. "What happened?"

When no one responded immediately, she jerked her neck to

look at each one of them in turn and shouted, "Will someone tell me what the heck happened here?"

Raj raked his hair. "Honestly, none of us are sure exactly what happened here. All we know is that he's dead."

Seema clutched her chest, edged closer, but as the funk of death and vomit apparently hit her all at once, she clamped her hands on her mouth and dashed to the nearest bathroom.

Her retching sounds interrupted the silence, and with each heave, Jia felt a wave of nausea swelling within her.

Vipul shot a nervous glance at Rafael's body, his mouth pinched in worry. "What are we going to do now?" He was slouched, sitting on his haunches, his voice several notes below his usual pitch, all traces of his bravado had evaporated with Rafael's last breaths.

Raj shrugged. "It's obvious, isn't it? There is nothing we can do to bring him back, so all we can do is keep trying to contact the authorities. Someone must respond eventually. Hold on, let me try again."

He reached for his phone and tapped on the screen, but before he could press the device to his ear, Vipul smacked his hand, knocking the phone on the ground.

Raj jerked. "What did you do that for?"

Vipul shook his head like a dog getting water out of its ears, an almost manic look in his eyes. "You can't call the cops now. He's *dead*."

"Yes, I know that," Raj agreed. "But it was an accident."

Seema reappeared, dabbing her mouth, her eyes glistening with a sheen of fresh tears. Spotting her, Vipul got to his feet. "Seema, you get why we can't call the cops, don't you? He clearly had some sort of reaction in our home."

Lisa said, "But he didn't even have dinner. If we consider the buttermilk he consumed, I would say he drank more than he ate."

Vipul clenched his hands. "Doesn't matter. I'll be detained no matter what. They'll call it negligence or something."

Raj gave an impatient snort. "Detained? Do you hear yourself? You are being ridiculous. This is clearly an accident. I know back home in India, nobody's bodies were sensitive to something as commonplace as peanuts. But trust me, in this country, allergies are more common than you think. I had three classmates in my high school who had the same issue. Unfortunate as they are, such incidents do happen. Hold on, let me show you the statistics." He reached for his phone, and again Vipul bowed and swatted Raj's hand.

"Ouch." Raj rubbed the back of his hand, chafed. "Have you lost your mind?"

"Have *you* lost your mind?" Vipul said. "I've seen enough true crime documentaries to know that the first thing they do is check your internet search history."

Lisa addressed Vipul with the calm yet firm tone of a hostage negotiator trying to reason with an insane person. "Understandably, you are in shock. But surely you can see that we don't have any options. We have to tell the truth and let the cops take it from there. They'll know what to do next."

Vipul's eyes bulged. "You, a young white woman, and I, a brown man in his forties, will never have the same experience with authorities." He stared at Lisa with such open hostility, she flinched. He jabbed his own chest. "Look at me. Now look at this European fellow. Who will they care about?" He balled his hands into fists. "You shouldn't talk about things you have no understanding of."

Lisa bit her lip before lapsing into silence, like someone backing away from an explosive device.

Jia knew the source of Vipul's paranoia. Seema had told her about Vipul's first brush with cops. A month after immigrating to the states, Vipul was out for a practice drive within their neighborhood,

Seema in the passenger seat, a retro Bollywood song playing on the radio of their secondhand Honda, when a cop car who had been stealthily parked behind trees like a predator pulled up behind them to let Vipul know he was being issued a ticket because he had failed to come to a complete halt at a stop sign.

Vipul balked at the hundred-dollar fine, and ignoring Seema's feverish pinches on his thighs, he argued with the cop, "The streets are completely empty. I was within the speed limit." Finally, he fished from his wallet a twenty-dollar bill as if the police officer were a local hawaladar in Mumbai, less interested in enforcing traffic rules and more in filling his own coffers.

The next thing he knew, the officer had his weapon drawn out and Vipul was being ordered to step out of the car and keep his hands where they could be seen. He was frisked, and the officer repeatedly pushed the gun barrel into his forehead telling Vipul to go back where he came from, and Vipul would've very well returned to his home country in a body bag if it weren't for Seema batting her kohl-lined eyes at the officer and pleading, "Sorry, Officer. We are new to this country. My husband is an idiot. It will never happen again. Did I mention my husband is an idiot?"

Now Vipul paced the length of the dining room table. "Okay, forget the cops for a second. What about his family? What if they sue me? We could lose everything."

"He doesn't have anyone. We know he's divorced," Seema said, her voice laced with pity, which felt out of place compared to the salacious tones she usually employed when discussing anyone's background.

"Don't feel too sorry for him, Bhabhi," Raj said before throwing his hands up. "Right, I forgot you don't know the truth about Rafael." As he walked her through the red flags in Rafael's break-in

THE NIGHT OF THE STORM

story and Jia's doubts about his injury, Seema gulped, and her face turned pale.

"I can prove it," Raj concluded, then fetched a pair of scissors to cut through the bandage on Rafael's hand and unfolded the layers of fabric.

Seema gasped. Rafael's palm was intact; not even a tiny paper cut creased his skin.

"I knew it," Raj said triumphantly. "Who knows what his plan was for coming to our house. This man has been lying to our faces all night. Do you really think once we tell cops our side of the story, they won't believe us? We're all witnesses."

Vipul's pacing came to a halt. He rubbed his palms on his pants. Staring at the ground, he said softly, "What about those witnesses who'll swear they think I killed him."

Raj cocked his head sideways. "Vipul," he said slowly, his voice tense, "why would anyone think you killed this man?"

Vipul exchanged a look with Seema.

She nodded. "You have to tell them."

Vipul swallowed. "Some of the arguments I've had with him may have gotten a touch out of hand." He sighed. "When I asked him to keep it down, we got into a yelling match, and other neighbors on the street heard us, some came out, some watched from their windows." Raj cringed, and Jia saw him shoot a sympathetic look at Rafael's body.

Vipul bunched his shoulders. "You see, I had no option, I had to complain to the HOA. I was already on edge from all the rumors of break-ins in the area."

Raj rubbed his cheek. "Okay, so, you had a bunch of petty fights. Doesn't automatically make you a suspect in a *murder*."

Jia pursed her lips. If that were the case, there would not exist a long-running reality television show centered on petty neighborhood squabbles that escalated to murder.

Lisa dragged a chair over and flopped onto it. "Like I said before, we tell the truth. He died here, so we have to have an explanation for it."

Vipul brought his palms together. "He died here. But that doesn't mean his body has to be discovered here."

"What?" Raj said, frowning.

"The lake," Vipul said simply.

For a second, Raj was quiet. Then he gave a mirthless laugh. "I don't know much about accidental deaths, but I do know that knowingly disposing of a body is criminal."

Vipul ran a hand over his face. He looked exhausted. "I don't know what to do anymore."

"What if," Jia said, "we tell the truth, but a version of the truth." Jia looked around the room. "We say he came to our house but omit the fact that he stayed for dinner. We just say he came to check on us and died minutes later."

"That could work," Raj said.

"I'm not sure," Vipul said.

"It's our best shot," Raj said. "As long as we stick to the same story."

His gaze flitted to Seema as if he were checking whether she was on board, and she gave a small nod.

"In the meanwhile," she said, "what do we do about his—" She paused, her breath hitched. "His body?"

"We can't leave it here, that's for sure." A raspy voice came from behind them, startling everyone.

Grandma limped in their direction, her cane hitting the ground with each step. *Tap. Tap.*

"Ma." Vipul jumped up and stepped forward so that he shielded

Rafael's body. "Why don't you get some rest? Rafael here is not feeling well."

Grandma sucked her teeth. "You think this old woman can't handle seeing a dead body? I've seen more than my share of deaths in this lifetime, more, in fact, than all of you in this room combined will ever see. When your father was taking his last breaths, I was the only one by his bedside." She closed her eyes, paper-thin eyelids shuttered against gray pupils. "I felt his spirit move through me as he went into the afterlife."

Seema's eyes went heavenward, and she muttered, "I can't deal with this right now."

"Something happened to Rafael after dinner," said Raj.

Grandma snapped her eyes open before narrowing them. "Did the man say anything before dying?"

"He had some kind of a reaction, he didn't have a chance to talk at all," Lisa said. "He was fine till dinner."

Grandma smacked her gray lips. "I'm not surprised he's dead."

The others stared at her in surprise.

Grandma continued, "What I mean to say is, he did, after all, eat Seema's food. I myself have many times expected to drop dead after eating her curries."

Seema's eyes bulged and she opened her mouth, but Raj raised his palm toward her in a placating gesture.

"It's a pity," Grandma said. "If I had the chance, I would've given Rafael a few drops of holy Ganga water. A last chance to wash away his sins on earth. Oh, that man has sinned. I could tell the second he stepped into this house. Of course cremation is the best way for his soul to be free to occupy a new body after reincarnation."

"Why don't we invite the whole neighborhood and sing dirges for his soul too?" Seema snapped. "Nobody has asked for a Hindu Death Ritual 101. What we need right now are practical tips."

"You want practical tips?" Grandma snarled. "Well, for starters, you should cover his nose and ears with cotton balls. His body will swell up. Tie his big toes, else you will find him sprawled wide. If you keep him here in this warm temperature, his body will start rotting," she continued. "You don't want the children to walk in on that, do you?"

"The garage then?" Lisa ventured. "The temperature will be colder there, so . . ." She trailed off, and Jia felt sick thinking about the implication.

The low temperature would slow down the decomposition of Rafael's flesh.

As Raj and Vipul lined up on opposite sides of Rafael and bent to lift him, Seema asked, in a rare show of empathy, "Should we not . . . cover him at least?"

Jia agreed. He might not have had the best intentions, but the man deserved to be laid to rest with an ounce of dignity.

Vipul hooked his fingers in his pockets and tilted his head. "He is what, almost six feet? I think a few of our tall kitchen bags should do the job."

Seema squirmed visibly. "He's not some trash we throw away."

Grandma said, "Forget about him, he's gone now." She picked up the monitor and pressed it to her ear. "I hear Asha stirring. Go before she starts screaming for her mother." While Seema left in a hurry, Grandma mumbled, "In my time, we didn't let machines raise our children."

She fetched an old scarf, which Raj used to tie Rafael's legs, and Vipul pushed Rafael's top half into an open trash bag, the black plastic swallowing Rafael inch by inch. Vipul and Raj hoisted Rafael and carried him away from the dining room. While Lisa kept the garage door propped open, they laid his body beneath a shelf stocked with tools.

Returning to the dining room, Jia scrubbed the carpet clean, her nose wrinkling as the stench of Rafael's vomit mixed with buttermilk assaulted her senses.

Next she fetched a broom to sweep away the shattered glass pieces.

Her eyes snagged on the moist carpet, the smell of disinfectant permeating the air.

Her chest tightened.

Rafael had died after consuming something here, but what? She herself had assured him that buttermilk did not have any peanuts. So, what set off his reaction?

And more importantly, it was an accident, wasn't it?

EIGHTEEN

Jia stared at the bowl in her hand, trying to recall the last time a scoop of rum raisin ice cream had felt less appetizing.

They were gathered in the living room. Jia felt claustrophobic, but there was no respite from the rain. As Raj had predicted, Harvey's downgraded status did nothing to help the city. The storm was stalled, dumping endless rain, sparing not a single suburb. Several areas, like Victoria, didn't have running water, and power lines went down, leaving people trapped in darkness.

Asha, fully awake after an episode of night terrors, had remembered that Seema had mentioned ice cream at the end of dinner and now held her mother to her promise with the zeal of a lawyer in possession of an ironclad contract.

Seema tried cajoling her, "Honey, everyone's tired," but predictably, Asha reacted to an adult's attempt to reason with her by throwing herself on the floor, and by the time her cheeks turned cherry red, it was evident to everyone that it was less of a hassle to just eat the dessert and pretend everything was normal.

But things were anything but normal.

The room was splintered in half between the two children bliss-fully unaware of the dead body stowed in the garage and the adults with fresh memories of Rafael's corpse.

Jia was wearing one of Seema's nightgowns with a low neckline and a lopsided proportion of sheer to opaque material she was not comfortable with. They had all changed into their pajamas because of Grandma's insistence that the clothes they were wearing must be discarded, followed by a bath to cleanse the impurities from being in the proximity of a departed soul.

Scents of sandalwood and jasmine from the bodywashes Seema had stocked in the guest bathrooms perfumed the air.

As far as Jia was concerned, they could shower all night long, but there was no washing away the sordid event of the evening.

Raj's hair, wet and messy, stuck out in different directions. Lisa played with her spoon, a soft ting sounding every time it contacted the ceramic surface of the bowl.

Seema kept sniffling, the tip of her nose red. When she offered Grandma ice cream, Grandma folded her knobby arms around her flat chest. "Do you want me to get pneumonia and die?"

Seema sighed but did not say anything, like all the fight was gone from her.

Vipul gobbled up scoops of ice cream as if his life depended on it.

Grandma kept her eyes trained on Vipul, and seeing her pained gaze, Jia had a feeling that she cared more for her elder son than perhaps she let on.

Jia rubbed her temples. She could feel a headache coming on. Every time Jia blinked, she pictured Rafael's face. His blank, empty stare.

Asha sat cross-legged on the floor, at a retina-damaging distance from the television, enraptured by the cartoons on the screen. Ishaan ate each spoonful of ice cream at a glacial pace, so that most of it would turn into liquid, at which point he would proceed to slurp it up like a soup.

It was a quirk that annoyed her, and usually she would try to hector him out of the habit—"Eat your ice cream before it melts"—but there was nothing like death to remind one of the ephemeral nature of life itself, and she sensed that she was still in the immediate period after witnessing a death when the smaller things suddenly did not matter anymore, before the shock wore off and gears of normal life cranked back into place.

When Ishaan asked for a second serving, she acquiesced. After all, it was bad enough that with the flooded streets outside, he was likely going to spend days stuck in this house.

Rainfall continued unabated, torrential winds slamming the house.

Jia remembered with a jolt that she had not checked her phone in a while.

Dev.

Rafael's death was a high tide that had swallowed every pressing concern, but now Jia's worries about Dev pierced her heart.

What if he had texted her again?

After refilling Ishaan's bowl, she checked her texts and flopped on the sofa next to Seema in relief.

There were no more messages from the mystery number. The absence of messages buoyed her confidence. For all she knew, he had simply texted her to freak her out. It was classic Dev. Playing on her worst fears.

When the bar at the top of her phone screen lit up with a notification, "You have new messages in WhatsApp," Jia pulled up the app, expecting a barrage of messages from the group chat of Indians in Houston.

But it was Vipul's chat that was highlighted in bold.

1 new message.

Jia scowled and pulled up their chat conversation. There was a single incoming new image. Jia blinked at the unfocused blur of the not-yet-downloaded image and clicked on it.

While she gaped at the downloading spinning circle, she had a premonition of things going horribly wrong.

The image loaded. She brought it into focus.

Her face blanched. Skin turned clammy. Completely still, she stared numbly at the picture.

As if her brain-processing speed had slowed to a crawl, she could only take in fragments of the photo.

Strands of hair peeking like weeds around a belly button. Gray underwear. An erection stretching the cotton fabric, wanting to be seen.

It was Vipul.

He was shirtless in a bathroom. Squinting at the image, she spotted a small vase of tulips in a corner of the photo.

Jia grimaced. This was not taken in just any bathroom; this picture was snapped in the main bathroom of this very house.

For a moment, Jia stared at the photo in bafflement. Was this one of the messages that he had sent earlier, which she had somehow missed and the app had incorrectly flagged it as read until now?

But the time stamp on the message indicated that this was sent an hour ago. Before dinner. A memory of his words floated to the surface. *Check your phone. I have a surprise for you.*

Jia recoiled.

"Oooh," Seema said. "Is that what I think it is?"

Her heart pounding, Jia felt the phone slip from her hands. "It's nothing. Just a spam message," she said, crouching on the floor, her face burning hot.

Seema arched an eyebrow. "C'mon. I know a sext when I see one." She furrowed her brows, looking hurt. "You started seeing someone and didn't tell me. Why would you hide that from me? I would be so happy to see you date someone."

"You got me," Jia said, bunching her shoulders. "I was embarrassed to tell you, I guess. It's some guy on Tinder." She hoped Seema would interpret her red cheeks for blushing.

When Asha ambled over and announced, "Mommy, Asha is done!" Seema patted Jia's knee. "I'll be back, but later on, you need to share all the deets, okay?"

Jia exhaled. *That was close.* She permanently deleted the selfie so she would never have to look at it again, even though she knew that nothing sent over the internet was removed permanently. She had a bitter taste in her mouth picturing Vipul's pixelated pecker sitting on some data server in a far-off country.

Sensing her sister coming back over, Jia put the phone aside.

She glared at Vipul, who was sitting across from her, still working his bowl, using the spoon to scrape every bit of ice cream.

She felt her facial muscles tighten and had to keep her hands crossed so everyone wouldn't see her limbs shaking with rage. It took all her self-control to not jump across and punch Vipul in the face.

How self-satisfied he must have felt, smugly snapping a picture just for her, knowing full well how uncomfortable it would make her.

But he was wrong. She was not uncomfortable.

She was livid.

The night had chipped away at her patience.

It was all too much. Seema's lies. Vipul's harassment. Dev's aggression.

Everything could ultimately be traced to her weakness, her utter inability to stand up to her family members.

But now she did not care.

Then an idea occurred to her.

She was going to make Vipul uncomfortable for a change.

And she did not even need to confront Vipul directly. She could communicate using his preferred medium.

She whipped out her phone and, before she had time to second-guess herself, sent off a text to Vipul.

Tonight, I'll tell Seema everything.

NINETEEN

When Jia's phone chimed with an incoming message, her heart rate picked up. Was Vipul that shameless? Had he responded to her threat by sending another selfie? Did he have an arsenal of nudes at his disposal ready for her viewing displeasure?

Her stomach churning, she pulled up her phone screen with increasing trepidation.

A new message from the unknown number.

Tomorrow, I'm coming to get Ishaan.

Here it was. Her worst fears realized. The past had caught up with her. A heaviness settled over her insides.

There was no running away from the mess she had left behind in Chicago. A flush of adrenaline tingled through her body as she realized she had only one option left.

Hating every fiber of her being, she took a deep breath and typed back:

If you do that, I will tell everyone
the truth about Molly.

No response.

A cocktail of dread and sadness whirling in her stomach, she again brought up the profile she visited periodically in secret.

Molly Wilson.

Her profile photo was one taken on her sixteenth birthday, auburn hair cascading past her shoulders, an open and welcoming smile of youth, eyes beaming with promise.

Molly's social media feed, previously filled with photographs of her making goofy faces over pieces of cake, now only had pictures her dad posted from the past, a childhood in reverse.

Jia had met Molly when she and her father, Jonathan, moved into their neighborhood in Chicago. From the day she helped them unpack, Jia became a go-to person for Jonathan. As a single father, he leaned on Jia to help him navigate Molly's teenage years.

When Molly wanted to get her nails done, Jia helped him research which paints did not have harsh chemicals. She bought organic deodorants for her to use.

Jia was the one to run to the drugstore when Molly had her first period. She helped pick out her prom dress and frequently invited them both over whenever she bought samosas from the store.

Molly developed a taste for Jia's cooking, and she often spent hours in her house. Together they tried and failed at making sugary balls of gulab jamun from the ready-made mixture.

When Molly was down with a cold, Jonathan would pop over at Jia's house. "Molly is asking for some of your yummy lentil soup. It's the only thing she can keep down."

Molly and Jia often went shopping together and had bought matching bracelets.

"Can you take her to the mall?" Jonathan had asked Jia when Molly started high school. "She wants to get these ear piercings, and I want to make sure her friends do not convince her to get her belly button pierced."

"Got it. I'll tell her to stick to tattoos on her back," Jia had said. She winked behind his back at Molly, and she had returned a shy smile. He had turned, alarmed, before he saw Jia laughing and realized she was kidding.

They were like her family.

She had seen Molly grow up, and when she entered college, Jia was certain she would have a front-row seat at her graduation.

Grandma's cough interrupted Jia's train of thought, and she saw her tapping a cane in Lisa's direction. "It's time for both of you to grow your family. When you get a son, I will name him after my father, Vishnu."

Lisa's eyes flitted in Raj's direction, and color crept up her cheeks.

"Ma, are you sure you don't want even a little ice cream? A glass of milk perhaps?" asked Raj quickly.

"It's fine. I don't want ice cream or milk. I just want to see a grandson before I die," Grandma said brusquely. She looked sideways at Seema. "At least one of you can give me a grandson."

When Seema and Vipul could not produce a grandchild after a decade of trying, it was a failure Grandma attributed solely to Seema. Grandma forced Seema to skip meals as part of monthly fasts and to chant mantras, and kept a Brahmin priest on retainer to perform pujas offering prasad of fresh fruits and rose water to jumpstart Seema's fertility.

Seema grew tired of this quickly and begged Vipul to go see a doctor. Instead, Vipul enrolled Seema in a university to get a master's degree in business administration. It turned out, distance from

Grandma was all Seema's eggs needed to flourish, because within six months, she became pregnant with Asha.

Grandma's mouth curled in annoyance, and she glared at Seema with the indignation of a customer dealing with a fast-food worker who just could not get her order right. Jia pictured Grandma spreading apart a baby's tiny legs like burger buns and pointing within: *I need to speak to your manager. I ordered a grandson, not a granddaughter! I demand a full refund.*

Grandma called out for Asha. "Don't you want a brother?"

Asha replied promptly, "Ishaan my brother."

Grandma swatted her hand. "He is your cousin. I'm talking about a *real* sibling. Like your dad has a brother, Raj."

"Huh?" Asha said, swiveling back to face the television, apparently making a snap judgment that Grandma's opinions on the nuances of sibling relationships could not hold a candle to the adventures of the animated pig playing on the screen.

Seema bristled.

Jia had a sick feeling of déjà vu. Her own grandfather often subjected her to similar disappointed looks, his vibes a mystery to her as a child. Later, she learned that he, too, had wanted a son after the birth of Seema; urging Jia's dad to have a second child, like a gambler convinced good luck was around the corner. Jia owed her life to the Indian law that banned medical professionals from revealing the gender of a fetus during an ultrasound. A country whose citizens ardently worshipped a thousand goddesses and elected a female prime minister in the '80s had collectively decided that not being born would always be a more appealing option than being born female.

The obsession with sons was not limited to Grandma. Despite all the progress Indian women had made, a son was still considered a prized possession. This mentality had made sense sixty-odd years ago, when dowries were commonplace, and a family had to scrounge together assets for the groom, ranging from cold hard cash to land, in return for the favor of marrying their daughter.

While the West considered it odd for a fully grown man to still be living with his parents, this was a normal custom in India, and for a son to start a new family with his wife in a separate space was basically parental abandonment because it was a son's noble duty to take care of his aged parents.

In short, an Indian boy was basically a 401(k).

A boy was raised with the expectation that he would support his parents financially, and in turn the parents would use their own savings to bestow gifts on their daughter's husband and in-laws. It was a vicious circle that made the birth of a girl undesirable.

Even though the younger educated generation didn't plan to depend on their kids for retirement, the desire for a son was hardwired into the DNA. Having a baby girl was akin to coming in second place, and the parents who immigrated to United States brought along these misguided convictions with them. The discrimination wasn't obvious, but any congratulations after the birth of a daughter still had undercurrents of consolation.

"A girl! Congrats! You're blessed with goddess Laxmi, the representation of material wealth in your house."

But the unsaid implication was: *You're getting silver.*

The birth of a boy was the real gold.

Raj cleared his throat. He and Grandma exchanged a look before she gave a subtle nod. Grandma said, "The family home in Jamnagar. I've decided to sell it."

A subtle shift in the mood. Vipul raised an eyebrow whereas Lisa became unnaturally still. Seema kept her eye on her bowl of ice cream while Vipul wiped his mouth and said, "Ma. We've been over this. The real estate market is tanking right now." He looked at Raj.

"You're the finance guy, I shouldn't have to tell you this." He counted on his fingers. "First, we have to pay the squatters to evacuate. Second, we must bribe the local officials to get the papers in order. We'll have a loss on our hands. If we wait for a few more years, we might make a profit."

Shaking her head, Grandma said softly, "I may not be around for another year. I cannot waste more time."

Vipul said, "But what about Dad's wish to keep the house in our family—"

Grandma wagged a puckered finger at him. "Your father was an emotional fool. I will not make the same mistakes. Start the paperwork. You can split the money between you and Raj." She bobbed her head in Seema's direction and gestured around the large dining room. "Keep your hearts as large as your homes."

Vipul turned red. "I don't care about the money." He looked at his mother with a pained expression. "But I can't let you all make a hasty mistake. You're getting desperate."

"Bhai, enough," Raj said, glancing sideways at Lisa. Lisa slunk lower in her chair, blond tendrils covering her face.

"I'm sorry," Vipul said, with the defiant tone of someone who was definitely not sorry. "But I have to put my foot down. We are not selling the land. I didn't say anything when you shortened your name from 'Rajendra' to 'Raj.' It's bad enough you don't keep the name Dad gave you. I can't let you wipe out his legacy completely." He thrust his chest out. "You will get my signature over my dead body."

Lisa's jaw tightened as she gave Vipul a cold stare. She rubbed Raj's knee. "It's all right. We don't need that money anyway. When Raj's agent gets him a contract, he'll get an advance five times over the selling price of the land."

Vipul smacked his lips. "There you go. Problem solved. Nothing would make me happier than seeing him succeed. It's why I poured all my savings into his education." He turned to Raj. "But how long have you been waiting for someone to buy your book? A year. Now I could make one call and get you a technical writing job. You'll be able to write *and* get paid for it."

"That's not necessary." Raj paused, as if he was making a calculation. "I've already found a publisher for my book."

Lisa clapped her hands together. "Oh, honey, that's great news. Why didn't you tell me?"

Raj's expression was soft. He rubbed the base of his neck, not looking at anyone. "I wanted it to be a surprise, I guess."

"Congratulations!" Seema trilled, then shot a glare in Vipul's direction, who said grudgingly, "Of course that's great news."

When Seema began collecting the empty bowls, Lisa offered to help.

Jia eyed them warily, annoyed at Lisa for giving Seema yet another chance to insult her. But to her utter surprise, this time Seema and Lisa exchanged a look and Seema's expression softened, and she handed the stack to Lisa. Coming from Seema, this felt like a giant olive branch.

When Jia trod to the kitchen with dirty spoons, Lisa and Raj worked in tandem—Lisa passed the bowls to Raj, who scrubbed them before arranging them on the rack.

Lisa dropped a sticky spoon on the floor, and when she bent to pick it up, her tunic hiked up, revealing a sliver of her waist.

Jia gasped.

She stared unblinking, unable to make sense of what she was seeing.

Three adjacent circular purple bruises on Lisa's waist, right above the hem of her jeans.

Lisa stood back up, and when her eyes met Jia's, a stricken look crossed her face. She tugged at the end of her tunic. Her cheeks turned pink as her eyes darted to Raj. "I can be so darn clumsy sometimes."

Jia's heart hammered. She had only caught a brief glimpse, and the small marks would've gone unnoticed if the purple didn't stand out so well against Lisa's pale skin. She turned to put the ice cream in the freezer, opening the door and placing the container on the top shelf, and let her face linger in the cool air. Why did Lisa have those marks on her body?

The bruises were a dark shade, suggesting they were fresh marks, not scars from long-past abuse.

A peal of laughter. Jia whirled around. Raj was sprinkling water from the running tap on Lisa's face. Lisa put her hands up. "Stop," she said, giggling.

The bruises burned vividly in Jia's mind. She pondered over the mechanics. Jia rubbed the skin near her collarbone. What secrets did Lisa's full sleeves hide? She wanted to gather Lisa in her arms and tell her everything was going to be okay. Raj, by all appearances, was a devoted partner, attentive to Lisa's needs and even willing to stand up for her against his family.

But Raj's very devotion convinced her of his nefariousness. Jia backed up against the refrigerator door, dizziness spreading through her veins. From her personal experience, she knew that outward shine was often just a facade for something rotten. The couples who bickered in public made love at night. But the so-called "perfect" couples, the ones who had nothing but kind words for each other, the ones whose public displays of affection made other couples uncomfortable—they protected wicked secrets.

She wanted to signal Lisa, let her know she would be there for her, but for that she needed to get Lisa alone.

After washing their hands, Raj and Lisa sauntered away together, his hand on the curve of her back.

A current passed through Jia. A kaleidoscope rotated, shifting the glass fragments, and once the pieces clicked into place, a new, sinister view reflected. It was like rewatching a movie with a twist and suddenly seeing all the clues hidden in plain sight.

Lisa's steadfast devotion to Raj, seeking approval for every action, ingratiating herself to his family, were the actions not of a smitten wife but a fearful one. Raj's puppy dog affection for his wife, not genuine love but an act.

Lisa behaved as if she were the luckiest woman in the world. Was that just a performance for Raj? He always had his hands on her, whether it was an arm resting on her shoulder or pressing against the small of her waist, gestures she'd chalked up as his way of expressing love. But now she wondered if that too was a sign of his possessiveness.

She had thought the brothers were a study in contrasts—Vipul a symbol of old-fashioned patriarchy and Raj a sensible modern husband. Now she suspected that they were two sides of the same coin.

But was Lisa not doing anything about the situation?

The loan. Vipul's check.

Suddenly, it was clear why Lisa didn't want Raj to know about the money. When Jia had first made up her mind to leave Dev, she didn't make an appointment with a divorce attorney or look at apartment listings. Instead, she'd walked into a bank and created a separate checking account in which she squirreled away small amounts from her paycheck every month, unbeknownst to Dev.

Jia could think of only one reason why Lisa would borrow money without Raj's knowledge.

Lisa was building an escape fund.

TWENTY

Alone in the kitchen, Jia was filled with an urge to check her phone to see if Dev had replied.

No new messages. None from Dev and thankfully none from Vipul either.

She spotted an empty beer bottle left on the kitchen counter. One of Raj's bottles. This lapse in Seema's housecleaning habits was a clear sign of how shaken up her sister was after Rafael's death.

Her throat ached at the idea that the body now rotting in the garage had been a living, breathing person walking among them mere hours ago. Rafael had happily sipped the buttermilk, unaware that he was consuming his last beverage.

Shaking off the morose feelings, she lifted the bottle and tossed it in the trash, before remembering how meticulous Seema was about separating her recyclables.

Scrunching her nose, she popped the trash bin open and leaned forward to retrieve the beer bottle.

That was when her gaze registered it, buried under a banana peel.

A yellow-colored stick with an orange cap—at first glance, it looked like one of the glue pens Asha would use for her craft projects. But a word marked on the cap caught her eye: "needle."

She pulled it out and twisted the stick. On one side was a drawing of an injection being jammed in a thigh.

Drugs? For a second, Jia pictured Raj injecting himself with heroin.

On closer inspection, she noticed the lettering on top of the stick.

"EpiPen."

The hair on the back of her neck stood up.

As far as she knew, no one in this family needed allergy medications . . . which could only mean one thing.

This was Rafael's EpiPen.

The one Lisa claimed she could not find in his coat pockets.

A dizziness came over Jia as she cradled the EpiPen in her hand, her mind racing to catch up with the implications of her discovery.

Someone had deliberately gotten rid of the one thing that could have saved Rafael's life.

Could it . . . could it be true?

Her pulse throbbing, Jia squeezed her eyes shut.

Rafael would not trash his own lifesaving medication. Lisa had offered to take the coat from Grandma to the coat closet. The coat whose contents had been rifled through.

Her skin turned so sticky with sweat that the EpiPen almost slipped from her grasp.

There was no other explanation.

Rafael had been murdered.

Lisa's distraught face flashed in her mind. She said her search had turned up empty, and no one had any reason not to believe her.

But why would Lisa kill someone she had met for the first time that day?

Her heartbeat thrashed in her ears as Jia walked through different scenarios.

Jia shook her head. *No.* It didn't have to be Lisa. Anyone could have snuck into the coat closet.

The kitchen had been a hubbub of activity. There was plenty of opportunity for any of them to slip into the kitchen and slide it in the bin. A fresh terror burst through her as she thought of the buttermilk glass by Rafael's side, her own reassuring voice to him. *There are no peanuts in here.*

Seema had taken the glasses out to the table. Vipul sat across the table from Rafael. Lisa had prepared the drink. Jia was more than convinced that one sip of the liquid had cost Rafael his life.

Anyone of them could have discreetly slipped a spoonful of crushed-peanut powder into the drink. Seema's kitchen had a bottle of crushed-peanut powder ready to use.

But why would Seema kill Rafael?

And if not her, then it had to be someone who knew the ins and outs of the ingredients in the kitchen.

Almost everyone in the house had opportunity to kill Rafael.

But who had the motive?

The answer flashed in her mind like a giant neon sign.

There was only one person in the house who openly despised Rafael. He himself had admitted they had a history. A series of public spats.

Vipul.

The man who had just convinced them all to lie for him.

Her chest heaved with the startlingly clear realization: Vipul had killed someone right under their noses and made them all unwitting accomplices in his murder.

Shuffling steps behind her.

"Hey," came Raj's voice.

Jia startled, dropping the EpiPen in the trash. Her heartbeats were so loud she was sure Raj could hear them.

She snapped the lid shut.

Raj looked strained. His eyes had bags and he exhaled loudly. "Weird night, huh? I think I'm still in shock."

Jia nodded, clasping her trembling hands behind her back.

"How are you holding up?" Raj asked.

His brows were knitted in concern, and yet, as she stared into his kind brown irises, a slight chill rose within her. The blemishes on Lisa's pale skin were imprinted in her mind. For all she knew, his caring routine was all an act. She could not trust him.

In fact, she could not trust anyone in this house.

"I've been better," Jia said.

Raj nodded and departed with a cup of warm milk Seema had prepared for Grandma.

Once he left, Jia took deep breaths, staring at the closed bin. She reached inside the trash can and placed the EpiPen exactly the way she had found it, partially hidden, because if the killer suspected her of finding the EpiPen, she would be next.

She had to keep Ishaan and herself safe before they could go home. A tall order.

Stay safe in a house trapped with a murderer.

TWENTY-ONE

"Sleepover, sleepover," Asha said, her chants muffled by the sheets of rain plunking against the living room windows.

As Asha pounded her tiny fists on her mother's legs, Seema increasingly resembled a harried general in an unwinnable battle. She exhaled. "I'd planned for Ishaan to sleep in Asha's room because she winds up sleeping in our bedroom most nights anyway. But if she wants to sleep in her room tonight, can Ishaan keep her company?"

"Well . . ." Jia stroked her eyebrows. Both Seema's bedroom and Asha's bedroom were situated on the upper story, a strategic floor plan, because the curving flight of stairs, difficult for an arthritic senior citizen to ascend, put one half of the residence out of Grandma's reach.

She could not tell Seema the real reason she wanted Ishaan close by: *I know that someone in this house is a murderer.*

Under normal circumstances, Jia's instinct would have been to go straight to Seema with her discovery, but she could not risk confiding in her sister anymore. Seema would blabber to someone.

This wide chasm between them stabbed her heart, but tonight, she had to think from her head, not her heart.

Her plan was to keep vigil the entire night while he slept next to her. She could not let Ishaan out of her sight. Not tonight.

"Can I sleep on the couch in that room?"

Seema shook her head. "I'm not letting my sister crash on the couch when we have so many bedrooms." She gestured at the corridor upstairs. "Raj and Lisa will sleep in the room next to our suite. I'd switch rooms, but yours has a smaller single bed."

"It's just that I—" Jia struggled for the right words to explain the knot of dread in her stomach. The winds whistling like ghosts roaming free didn't help her frayed nerves.

Asha was following the back-and-forth, and likely intuiting Jia's hesitation, and moved in for the kill.

Wrapping her chubby arms around Jia's legs, she gazed up, a vision of innocence. "Peees . . ." Her cherubic face tilted upward at Jia.

When her lower lip quivered, the sight squeezed Jia's heart. She nodded and patted Asha's head. "Fine. You can have your sleepover." Even if Vipul was responsible for Rafael's death, she knew he would never ever hurt Ishaan. She turned to face Seema. "Can you do me a favor? Can you please check on the kids at night?"

"I was going to do it anyway," Seema said. She leaned forward and prompted, "But you have to tell me what's going on. What are you so worried about?"

Jia felt her shoulders slump. She longed to ameliorate her worries, share something with Seema. "It's Dev. He has been messaging me tonight. He wants to see Ishaan."

Seema's eyes widened. "You don't say," she whispered. "But in this weather, you don't think he'll actually come here to get him?"

Jia said, "Maybe he plans to wait it out. Maybe he's just trying to scare me. I honestly don't know what his plan is."

"Dev? A kidnapper?" Seema rubbed her temples. "I don't know what went down between the two of you, but I can't help you unless you tell me."

Jia nodded like she was about to take a deep breath underwater.

Then she told her everything.

JIA DISCOVERED HER HUSBAND, DEV, CHEATING BY HIS ACTIVITIES on the platform where people conducted most of their lives: social media. Technology created a fresh problem for each problem it solved. Easy to date, easy to ghost someone. Easy to cheat, even easier to get caught cheating.

Standing at the foot of their bed, Jia was folding Dev's shirt. She had just plucked his sweatpants from the laundry bag when a beep sounded from the night table.

In the en suite bathroom, the electric shaver buzzed as he trimmed his beard. Jia placed the pants on the bed and was wondering which curry to make for lunch when she heard more incoming message pings. Jia scowled. She hated people who hit send after every other word. *Just finish your thought first*, she wanted to tell them. The cell sat on the corner of the night table, and with every vibration, it jumped closer to the edge.

It was for that reason alone that she picked it up. But just as she did, a new message popped up.

Her stomach lurched.

Three heart emojis. Jia swallowed and blinked uncomprehendingly. Her subconscious detected the shift in her reality, and fighting this change, she let herself believe this was just an auntie. Just a well-meaning auntie.

But doubt crept in like an intruder, and she broke her own no-checking-phones rule, on account of which they both never locked their phones.

She pulled up the conversation and squinted at the profile picture, a nondescript bunch of flowers, contact number not saved. She felt a prickle of discomfiture. This was unusual because Dev organized everything. Every person in his phone had a label, even the man they had called just once to install fans had a clear designation: "Alex repair services."

Jia scrolled as fast as her nimble thumbs would allow, and her breath caught in her throat while all her delusions quickly fell through. This was no auntie. A faucet turned on. Dev stepped into the shower while Jia read message after message.

I love you.
I miss you.

Her heart leapt in her throat as she scanned through again, this time searching for his responses, but she came up empty.

A new image appeared, a silhouette of a tank top, blurry in Jia's moist eyes. Jia clicked on the picture to download it.

Pulse throbbing in her throat, she stared at the rotating downloading icon. The face was cropped off, a skinny body in a tank top, her hand caressing her throat. A pink bracelet dangled on her wrist.

Something about the familiarity of the bracelet set off a painful tingling in her chest, and she was trying to nail down the reason when Dev emerged, his six-foot body wrapped in a towel, wet hair dripping on his shoulders. He saw Jia holding the phone and immediately put his hands up as if she were holding a gun.

"Jia, listen—" he sputtered. "It's not what you think."

Jia waved the phone in his face. "'Love you'? What else can that mean?"

"Calm down," he said, reaching out to touch her arm.

Jia snatched her hand away. "Don't tell me to calm down."

"It's not my fault. It all started a year ago. She's the one obsessed with me."

Jia shook her head. "Stop. Just stop. Stop trying to gaslight me." She slumped onto the bed, all energy drained out of her. She wished she could be angry like she had been a few minutes ago, cling to an emotion to anchor herself, but all she felt when she looked at him now was a paralyzing numbness. "I need to see my mom," Jia said, vacantly staring into the distance.

"Jianna," said Dev. "We can't be rash here. You can't go around talking to people. We have to keep this between us. We could lose everything." He ran a hand through his hair. "I mean we wouldn't be able to face anyone on the street. We'd have to inform the authorities every time we move."

"What?" Jia said, blinking in confusion. The gears of her brain cranked slowly into place.

She grabbed the phone and looked at the downloaded image.

Jia let out a guttural, animal-like groan.

A few seconds ago, Jia hadn't thought it was humanly possible for things to get worse.

She had been wrong.

This was much, much worse.

The picture sitting on Dev's phone wasn't of a random woman he'd cheated on Jia with.

It was Molly, their neighbor's eighteen-year-old daughter.

A girl with hopes and dreams in her eyes, having just headed off to college, a bright future ahead of her.

Jonathan, the quiet widower who lived a few blocks down, often invited both Jia and Dev for barbecues, going out of his way to find vegetarian patties for them.

He loved Molly more than anything in the world. Jia recalled with a jolt how Molly's father had stared wistfully at Ishaan and remarked, "Hope you cherish every second with your kid. Before you know it, he'll grow up and go off to college."

With a disgusted horror, Jia remembered how she had asked Dev to help Molly with her college applications: "She likes numbers. She wants to be a CPA just like you."

Nursing a beer, Dev had offered to take a look at the courses in the college syllabus.

Now, with a sour taste in her mouth, Jia did some quick math of her own.

It all started a year ago. Molly had started her first semester at a local university last month.

Jia leapt on him, grabbed his shoulders, and shook him. "She's a kid! What's wrong with you?"

He didn't protest or move away from her, even when her nails dug into his body. "It's a misunderstanding."

"Then how do you explain this?" Jia shrieked. She thrust the phone in his face. "Look at her. Why did she text you that she missed you?"

"Go ahead. Check the complete chat history. I have never responded, have I?" he said quietly.

Jia let go of him and cupped her hands over her mouth. His comment, weighed against his previous fear of changing neighborhoods, shuddered through her.

This was not an innocent man.

This was a man careful not to leave any traces. Plausible deniability.

Jia convulsed and jumped away from him. Who was she married to?

She ran to the bathroom, bile creeping up in her throat, and retched into the basin.

Collapsing onto the floor, she held her forehead as she realized how bad things were.

Dev had cheated on her, but Jia couldn't even have righteous anger at the other woman. Instead, she had to contend with the guilt of putting this girl in danger.

Her head still resting on the rim, she remembered how she'd been the one to suggest to Molly's father that Dev could advise her on classes.

When Molly had trouble with math, she set them up on the patio, letting them spend hours alone, thinking she was such a good person for helping Molly.

She threw up again.

She'd been the one to invite Molly to her house, to a predator's home. Yes, she realized, that's what Dev was. A predator. "Stay away from me," she said, voice dangerously low.

Dev took a deep, steadying breath. "I screwed up, okay? We kind of had a small fling, but then she got all obsessive. Listen, you know how teenagers can be."

Jia's head was spinning. It was too much. He was throwing too many things at her. Her mind groped for a way that would give her husband a pass. A way to hold on to the life she had before it came apart.

"We have to talk to her dad," she said, head still resting on the cold tile of the toilet.

"No," Dev said quickly. "We can't risk that. Honey, trust me," he said, reaching for her hand.

His touch repulsed her.

"Think of Ishaan," he said. "He needs both his parents. Once word gets out, everyone will crucify me. No one will care about my side of the story. My reputation will be destroyed. Do you want him to think his dad is a pervert? For his sake, we have to find a way to move past this. We will be treated like outcasts. Think of Ishaan's future. What girl will marry him when her father finds out about this?"

"Ishaan is not in India," Jia said. "And he's only ten. There's a long time before his marriage."

"Word spreads in this community and the stains will stay forever. Do you want to risk that?"

If Jia could go back and change one thing in her life, it would be this moment.

A fork in the road. She would redo this moment and stand up straight and march to Molly's father's house and tell him the truth.

Instead, the words that came out of her mouth were: "We have to move."

"Yes," Dev said quickly, glad that he had found a way in. "Obviously, we need to move. We can go to that area you always wanted."

The next week, Dev—who never had a free weekend—kept showing her vacation itineraries. On Sunday, he woke up early and made an omelet for her and pancakes for Ishaan. In return, Jia withdrew further from him. She began sleeping on the couch. Every so often, she picked up the phone, teetering on the edge of calling Jonathan. A father had a right to know. But Dev had fogged her brain with horrific possibilities, preying on her worst fears.

If word got out, the Indian community would shun them forever.

Ishaan would grow up a pariah. The family background checks, customary in arranged marriages, would dredge up Dev's unsavory past, and then who would want their daughter to be a part of her family?

The longer she waited, the more she turned into an accomplice.

After a month of his efforts at wheedling forgiveness out of Jia bearing no fruit, Dev's guilt gave way to frustration, and he erupted like someone who'd spent too much money repairing a used car, only to find it still sputtering. "Fine. You can't even bring yourself to look at me anymore. Just divorce me," he'd said. "But you know, Jia, you can't do a damn thing by yourself. You think you can do a better job of raising Ishaan? You won't last a day without me."

Jia knew he was right. She had sporadically searched on the internet for apartments and divorce lawyers; she had read a few blogs. But a mere look at the closet with one hundred sarees that needed packing would break her resolve.

"I told her I've broken up with her," Dev promised every day. "I'm one hundred percent committed to making our marriage work.

"But it's very important that you don't talk to Jonathan," he warned her.

Molly was already in college, and when Jonathan met Jia on the street, he was a typical empty nester, proud of the steps his daughter was taking toward her independence and at the same time nostalgic for the time she lived with him. But Jia had trouble meeting his eyes, so she cut the conversation short and left.

She'd lost a friendship too.

Overwhelmed, she continued to go through the motions. Seeing Ishaan ride a bike with his friends he'd grown up with, Jia wondered how she could turn his world upside down. He was oblivious to the seismic shifts in the family, happily planning which movie he wanted to watch next with his dad. Every night, Jia and Dev ate dinner together, urging Ishaan to finish his dal and rice, like nothing had changed between them.

Jia didn't want to stay with Dev, but she couldn't bring herself to leave him either.

Dev suggested they work with a marriage counselor, but before they could go to their first appointment, she noticed Dev was spending more time on his phone. But this time, she didn't confront him.

She decided to take matters into her own hands.

Molly readily accepted her invitation for tea. Jia set two cups of chai on the table in their backyard and reminded herself that it wasn't this young woman's fault.

Jia had rehearsed the speech ad nauseam . . . *It's normal to have crushes at this age, it's a time when being around someone with their act together can be comforting, even alluring* . . .

But before she got to say anything, Molly said, "I'm so sorry . . . I know how hard divorce can be . . ."

Jia's head spun. Molly had come here armed with a speech of her own.

"Divorce?" Jia said.

Molly nodded, not meeting her eyes. "He told me you had filed the paperwork."

Jia rubbed her temples. Of course he was duping them both again. Stringing Molly along with promises of a divorce underway while lying to Jia that his affair with Molly was over.

When Jia told Molly she'd not filed for divorce and Dev was, in fact, trying to fix their marriage, Molly's face crumpled.

More than her own hurt, Jia was left heartbroken by watching this young girl try to cope with the betrayal. She would be scarred by this experience forever, never able to trust someone completely.

The next day, Jia met with a divorce attorney.

This was rock bottom, she told herself every morning. The only way was up.

She was wrong on this count too.

One early morning, taking a walk, she spotted a police cruiser making its way up the street. The car stopped outside Molly's house, and an officer walked the driveway.

Immediately, Jia was worried that the cops would come to their house next. Someone might have tipped them off.

When Molly's father opened the door, the cop took off his hat and said something. Shaking his head, Molly's father clutched his chest.

The grim news spread through the community like a virus. Molly had died in a car accident. Speeding on the highway, she'd veered into the left lane, crashing into an elderly woman driving a sedan. Later on, her autopsy would reveal higher than legally allowed amounts of alcohol in her bloodstream.

From different members of the neighborhood, Jia stitched together Molly's last moments. She was not feeling like herself, one of her friends said. There was something going on with her. There was the predictable gossip about the dangers of youth binge drinking, but Jia knew. Jia knew the truth, and the guilt was an albatross around her neck.

Why did she think Molly, just on the cusp of adulthood, would deal with Dev's betrayal easily? Jia had been so involved in her own pain, she didn't think to care for Molly. If only she had warned her dad, Molly might still be alive.

Dev paced the bedroom floor. "The cops would've questioned me if they had found anything. She always deleted our conversations. It's a good thing we only used an app that doesn't store messages on the cloud," he said. "She was always smart about that."

Jia exploded. "You're worried about saving your own self! Molly is dead. Think about her father."

"My priority is you and Ishaan." Dev's voice quavered. "She's gone. I can't bring her back.

"Don't talk to Jonathan. You'll screw up our lives," he said, cupping her face. "Whatever happens, we need to keep this secret."

A month later, Jia saw Molly's father in a supermarket. He was hunched over the tomatoes, looking frail, lifeless. Jia snuck out, unable to face him. If only she had called him sooner. Her need to keep her own family intact had torn apart another.

"Let's move," Dev said. "Pick any city you want. We can start over. Even move to India if we have to. My grandpa would love to take care of Ishaan."

"I've already filed for a divorce."

"Now you want to divorce? Then all this will have been for nothing."

Jia pursed her lips in disgust. He wanted to rebuild their marriage using the bones of a dead girl. But she would use Molly's death to free herself and Ishaan.

She blackmailed him into giving her sole custody of Ishaan. If he came near them, she'd go straight to Jonathan with the truth. The day she signed her papers, she booked a flight straight out of Chicago to Houston to be near Seema.

/ /, / /, / /, / /

SEEMA TOOK THIS ALL IN SILENTLY. "ARE YOU SURE YOU'RE NOT PUNishing him?"

Jia blinked. This was not the reaction she was expecting.

"Come on," Seema said. "Sure, Dev did a ton of really horrible things. But I've heard nothing about him being a bad father to Ishaan. Are you sure you're not doing this out of vindictiveness?"

"What?" Jia blubbered, her self-righteousness rising. "How can he be a good influence on Ishaan?"

Then she fell silent. It did feel like karmic revenge for him to not see his son. He'd taken a child from a father; what right did he have to his own?

Asha let go of Jia, grabbed Seema's arm, and hoisted her feet off the floor, trying to use her mother's limbs as a makeshift swing.

"Asha, stop it!" Seema's shoulder blade jerked down in a motion that looked painful, and after settling Asha on her hip, she continued, "Our bedroom is right next to them. I'll check on the kids in the night. I know you're scared. I'm here for you."

This made Jia feel marginally better.

Vipul ambled into the living room and scooped up Asha. "Asha doesn't want to sleep with Mommy and Daddy?" he asked, grinning.

"No," Seema said quickly. "I mean it's not every day she has friends over."

"Fine," said Vipul. "I have some work to finish in the study anyway. So don't wait up for me."

The sleeping arrangements settled, Seema took Asha upstairs for a second attempt at bedtime, and Jia scoured her phone for hurricane updates for a while before finding Ishaan.

Upstairs, an owl-shaped white noise machine emitted staticky buzzy vibrations. On a bed plastered with princesses, Asha slept in a fetal position, blanket bunched near her feet, an arm slung over a soft teddy bear. Jia sat next to Ishaan on the main queen-sized bed and squeezed his shoulder. "You're a good sport. Thanks for doing this for Asha. The night's going to go by in a flash and it'll be morning before you know it."

But would it really? He often called for her in the middle of the night when he had a bad dream. And although he pretended to be brave, he flinched with every clap of thunder.

Jia released him and pinched his cheek. "All right. I'll be downstairs if you need anything."

Ishaan said, "Where is Rafael Uncle?"

The question caught Jia off guard, landing on her like a tree crashing into a roof. Jia swallowed the lump in her throat. "He's gone."

"Gone?" Ishaan asked.

"I mean," Jia said, "he's gone back to his place to pick up some stuff for the night."

"If you're going to lie to me, at least come up with something believable," Ishaan said, lips twisted in disgust. "I've seen all of you whispering together."

"I'm telling you nothing is wrong."

"What happened to 'we're a team'?"

Jia felt a wave of guilt. She lobbed the phrase "we're a team" whenever she needed Ishaan to help her with something, but how could she tell him the truth? The corners of Ishaan's mouth were turned down. "I wanted to sleep in your room."

Jia cupped his chin. "Hey, are you afraid? Listen, I'll be downstairs. Plus, if you need anything, you can call Seema if you want."

Ishaan scoffed. "I'm not scared. It's you I'm worried about."

Jia blinked.

"I don't want you sleeping alone."

"Why?"

Breathing out and rubbing the tip of his nose, Ishaan said softly, "Is that why you left Dad? Because you love Vipul Uncle?"

Oh God. Jia's heart stopped. Of course that's what it looked like to him. Jia not a victim, but very much a willing participant.

He dropped his voice to a whisper. "I've seen you guys."

He knew. A coldness hit Jia's core like ice water had been thrown on her.

She grimaced. What else had she expected? He'd seen their almost "kiss," had probably heard her excuses on the phone when Vipul wanted to drop by. Kids were intuitive. Any remnants of doubt he might have had were wiped out tonight in the kitchen when he walked in when Vipul's hand was . . .

Jia felt sick.

She rolled up the sleeves of the satin gown and took his hands in hers. "Listen. I know it has been just the two of us this past year, and I'm sorry I don't have my stuff together all the time—okay, most of the time—but I left your dad for reasons totally unrelated to Vipul, and I can tell you confidently, there's no one in the world I love more than you."

She grabbed him and pulled him into a hug.

Choking up, she smoothed his hair. "How about this? You get some sleep. Then tomorrow we'll get out of here and go to Kemah Boardwalk. We'll enjoy all the rides there, even the ones I'm too scared to get on."

He nodded, offering a small smile. She wasn't sure how many rides would be left standing after the deluge or whether they'd even be able to leave in the morning, but lies issued in the service of hope were not bad.

Suddenly, she saw something protruding from his pocket. "Take that out right now!"

It was a small rectangular contraption.

"What is this?"

"A mini speaker."

"Where on earth did you get this?" Jia asked.

"It was lying under one of Vipul Uncle's books on the study table."

Jia lost her temper. "You will return this to Vipul Uncle right now, do you hear me?" she hissed.

"I can't," he said. "It's not even his."

She frowned. "What do you mean?"

"It's Rafael Uncle's," Ishaan said. "I saw him pulling this out of his pocket in the study. I think he forgot it. That's why I was asking you where he was, because I swear I was going to return it."

But Jia was not mad anymore; she was burning with curiosity. "What is this exactly?"

"It's a Bluetooth speaker," Ishaan said.

"Is that like a walkie-talkie?" Jia asked excitedly. She remembered Rafael being glued to his phone.

"No, Mom," Ishaan said, rolling his eyes. He was looking at her like she was an idiot. "You connect it to your phone."

Jia frowned. "What's the point of it then?"

"You can do lots of things. Play music mostly."

Music. Jia pondered this. If it could play a song, it could also play the sound of things breaking. She had seen Seema play white noise videos to help Asha sleep. Any sound could be accessible on a phone these days.

The shattering noises. He'd used his phone and this speaker to set them on edge. To make them worry about someone breaking into the house.

But why?

TWENTY-TWO

After wishing him good night, Jia returned to her room next to the living room, flopped on the bed, letting her head fall on the nearest pillow, and closed her eyes. She pressed a palm to her warm forehead and glanced at the side table. The digital clock showed it was half past ten. Next to a glass of water was a round bottle of white pills. "Take this and you'll be asleep in no time," Seema had insisted. Jia sat up. The sound of the windows rattling in the strong winds made her head pound. She took out a tablet and brought it to the tip of her tongue.

What was she doing? The tablet represented the easy way out, but she was done escaping her problems.

Sitting up straight, she placed the bottle back on the table and tied her hair in a ponytail. She would stay up the whole night, ears attuned to the first signs of disturbance.

She couldn't believe only hours ago, they'd all sat down for dinner together, oblivious to the future. Rafael's death had splintered her experience into before and after, and now, a time in which she could be around her family without worrying seemed unfathomable.

In a different time, Jia had worried about Ishaan's birthday party. But now, that concern faded away as it became crystal clear that her first duty as a parent was to keep Ishaan safe.

Yet as Jia sat upright, she sensed a different feeling lurking inside her, making itself known above the drumbeats of fear.

It was a sense of control.

Jia was the only one apart from the murderer who knew about the EpiPen.

With knowledge came a sense of power.

All night, she had been caught off guard, in reaction mode, whether she was faced with Seema concealing information about the evacuation orders or Vipul sending her inappropriate pics, but now, she saw a glimmer of hope.

A chance to get her bearings.

If she was to survive, she had to be two steps ahead of everyone else.

Jia rubbed her face as she collated her thoughts.

She knew all the members of the family intimately.

But she'd barely known Rafael. It was time to change that.

Ignoring the 40 percent battery on her phone, she began searching for Rafael's social media accounts. Using his first name and address, she identified his profile.

Luckily, he was one of those people with nary a regard for privacy. All his updates and location check-ins were set to public by default.

She scrolled through pictures of him. There was a photo of him standing outside a cathedral. She assumed that was taken in Spain, where he grew up.

Deep down a rabbit hole of his older posts, her breath caught in her throat when she came across a picture of his family.

They looked perfect. His wife had short bobbed hair and was beaming at the camera, their toddler boy perched on her hip.

He'd added a caption underneath the photo: "Family is every-thing."

Her chest hitched. She continued scrolling.

She stopped at another picture.

On the surface, it was just like any of his other pictures. Him in a generic open-air sports bar, surrounded by his buddies in baseball caps, mini screens hanging behind them.

But there was something different about this picture. Some-thing that unsettled Jia greatly.

His hoodie.

Specifically, the words printed on it.

She zoomed in till she could make out the lettering: "University of Texas at Austin." A quick cross-verification of his LinkedIn profile confirmed that he had indeed studied in Texas.

Something about this pricked at her insides, but she could not figure out why.

She knew she was missing something important.

Then it hit her. Her pulse jacked up.

Rafael had been clear that he'd come to the United States for work, but here was proof that he had studied at an American uni-versity. Why would Rafael lie about something so mundane?

She was still processing this when she spotted something else in the picture.

Rafael's right arm was placed on his friend's shoulder, while his left hand dangled near his pocket, and nestled within his fingers was a cigarette.

She sat upright with a jolt.

Vipul had been driven to paranoia by those pesky cigarette butts he kept finding in the yard.

But what if Rafael was Vipul's secret smoker? Was Vipul right?

Was Rafael scoping out the house so he could steal something and blame someone else?

Why was Rafael sneaking around Vipul's house?

A sharp knock.

Jia jumped.

She padded across the room and opened the door. A chilly wave swept across Jia's body.

TWENTY-THREE

Vipul stood outside with a fleece blanket in his thick hands.
Startled, she shuffled backward, allowing Vipul to step inside, his frame now blocking the exit. A heavy feeling settled in her gut. His gaze was fixed downward; he cleared his throat. He ran a hand through his thinning hair, still not looking at her. His posture was stooped, making his bulky body appear diminished.

Jia kept her gaze locked on the sliver of space in the half-open door. "What do you need?" She deliberately raised her voice, on the off chance someone was nearby. But the light filtering into the room from the hallway was unblemished by shadows.

They were alone.

She angled herself so that her phone screen wasn't visible, with Rafael's pictures on it.

If Vipul was the one who killed Rafael, she couldn't let him know she was onto him.

Vipul. A killer. The thought made her dizzy.

"Sorry," he said, so softly that Jia had to lean forward to hear him.

He looked up, his ears red. "I'm sorry," he repeated.

Jia's shoulders curved forward as she struggled to respond. "What?"

"For the . . ." Vipul scratched his neck. "For the picture."

She blinked, confused for a second, before understanding what he was talking about. Her discovery of the EpiPen had obliterated everything that came before, including the selfie.

He proffered the blanket, a cloud of dust motes hovering above its surface. "This room gets chilly at night," he said, holding out the quilt, a woolen peace offering.

Jia tentatively reached for the blanket. When she grasped it, its coarse fibers rubbing against her skin, it was unexpectedly heavy and slipped out of her clutch. Vipul and Jia reached for it simultaneously, their arms outstretched, and both caught the blanket at the same moment. His hand slipped over hers.

She would've chalked it up to an accidental touch, an innocuous mistake, but his thumb caressed her fingers in a way that made her skin crawl. As she wriggled her hand out of his grasp, he resisted, locking her hand in place under his.

His skin felt rough against the back of her hand, and in the next second, everything changed. It was like she was having an out-of-body experience.

Her vision turned hazy, she started seeing black spots, and Vipul was no longer Vipul.

In him, she saw the face of every man who had ever wronged her. The passenger who had casually groped her in the local train, the security guard who leered at her every time she walked past him, and finally she saw Dev.

All these men who had taken advantage of her weakness.

She hated that Ishaan couldn't enjoy the simple pleasures of childhood because he worried about her. What effect did it have on him to see his mother pushed around?

He was protective of her, but underneath his resolute determination, she sensed pity for a weak woman.

Guided by instinct more than by any rational thought, Jia yanked her hand free and slapped Vipul hard across the cheek.

"What the—" Vipul said. His eyes bulged as he stumbled backward and stared at Jia with a dazed look. The blanket dropped to the floor.

"I—" Jia trembled and covered her mouth with her hands.

Vipul blinked. For a minute he was speechless; then he recovered himself. "Who the hell do you think you are?" he bellowed, his nostrils flaring.

Jia crossed her arms protectively around herself. "I didn't mean to . . ."

"Having a slumber party, are we?" asked Raj, moseying into the room. His gaze crossed from Jia's teary face to his brother's huffy countenance, and his smile faded. "You okay?" he asked Jia directly.

"She's fine," Vipul said brusquely. He put an arm on Raj's shoulders. "I need your help. We need to make sure everything is locked up and ready to go for the night. You start checking the locks on the windows and I'll join you.

"We . . ." Vipul hesitated. "We also need to put sandbags in the garage."

Raj looked stricken. The body in the garage. Raj swallowed, looking unhappy at the prospect of seeing Rafael's body again.

Vipul started to leave and gestured for Raj to join him, but he didn't budge.

Vipul sighed impatiently. "We don't have a lot of time, and I have something important to work on tonight, let's get going."

"I'll be there in a few minutes," Raj said, his voice uncharacteristically serious.

Vipul shot a pissed-off glance at Jia, then muttered on his way out, "I told Seema her sister was trouble."

Once Vipul was out of earshot, Raj repeated, "Are you okay?" his features etched with concern.

Jia's gaze darted to Vipul's retreating back before she nodded slowly.

Raj ran a hand through his hair. "Guess I'll get going, then. If you need anything, you know where to find me."

Again, she teetered on the edge of telling Raj everything, but pinched her lips and nodded instead.

Whatever one said about Vipul, his ugly flaws were right there on the surface. Raj, however, was a cipher.

Alone again, Jia sat on the bed cross-legged, gripping a pillow tightly, her tears leaving indigo trails on her blue shirt. *Pull yourself together.* But the salty streams leaked unabated as a stabbing pain spread inside her chest.

"Got a sec?"

Jia sat upright. Lisa shuffled inside. Dressed in a baby-pink nightgown with long sleeves, her loose wavy hair swept past her shoulders, she looked like one of Asha's dolls. In her hand she had noise-canceling headphones. Lisa gestured at the windows. "I don't know how anyone is going to get any sleep with the noise of all that rain outside. I know you forgot your bag and I happened to have an extra pair if you needed to sleep."

Lisa took a seat on the edge of the bed and stared at the wall as if fascinated by the beige paint, and Jia was grateful for Lisa's thoughtfulness in giving her a few seconds to compose herself. She quickly wiped her face with the back of her hand.

She glanced askance at Lisa, and her own pain dulled for a second while she stared at Lisa's attire. Even her nightgown had long sleeves.

A crazy urge to yank up her sleeves and reveal whatever horror might be underneath swelled inside Jia.

Apparently sensing Jia's gaze, Lisa tugged at her sleeves and crossed her arms as if she was suddenly cold.

Jia's own concerns were eclipsed by her worry for Lisa.

"This guy is a gym teacher," Lisa said.

Jia realized Lisa had her phone out, and glancing again at the screen, she saw the popular white-flame icon. A flash of recognition passed through her and she burst out laughing. "Oh, I'm not interested in dating." She brought the screen closer. "How old is this guy, anyway? He looks like a kid."

Lisa frowned. "He's not that young. Seema mentioned you were having a hard time. I really think you should put yourself out there."

Jia rubbed her hands together. "I don't think I'll be able to bring myself to trust men again."

"You have to let go of your past," Lisa said. "I know it's not easy. There was a period after my ex-fiancé ended things—"

"Wait . . . you were engaged before?"

"Yeah, high school sweetheart. I thought I would be married in my twenties. But we wanted . . ." Lisa hesitated momentarily. "Different things, I guess. To be honest, I took my relationship for granted. I didn't think his needs were as important as mine." She glanced in Raj's direction. "I'm not making that mistake again."

Jia stared incredulously at Lisa. The Land of the Free granted many freedoms, among which was the freedom to divorce, and half the people in this country took the option. Jia smiled to herself. It didn't make sense to live here but stay tethered to the norms followed back home. The divorce rates in India might be lower, but if someone surveyed the marriages for unhappiness, 90 percent would fit the bill. Lisa's flippant manner when referring to her previous engagement was so refreshing.

"But," Lisa continued, "if that hadn't happened, I wouldn't have met Raj. Now I'm the luckiest woman in the world." She smiled to herself. "So, it all worked out in the end. Trust me, someone somewhere is waiting for you."

"I'll think about it." There was an invite that had been sitting in her inbox. Jia pulled out her phone and searched her mail. "Networking for single parents." While she had no urge to date again, at least she could make new friends. She needed people like Lisa in her life. She accepted the invite and put the phone in power-saving mode.

Lisa half stood up, then hesitated and came closer. "You're not the only family member he's let down tonight," she whispered.

"Hold on, wait," Jia said. "What are you talking about? What happened?"

A dark shadow crossed Lisa's face. The emotion, so alien on her face, gave Jia goose bumps.

Before Jia processed her words, there was a sound from outside.

"Knock knock," Raj said.

Lisa sat up. "Just wanted to give Jia my headphones." She sprang to her feet. "I should get going. I want to wish Grandma good night before she goes to sleep," she said, hurrying out of the room.

Their relationship baffled Jia. Why did Raj feel the need to be near Lisa? Was that love, or was he keeping an eye on her?

Jia set the headphones aside, wondering if Lisa had been looking for an excuse to talk to her. She wished Raj hadn't arrived at the wrong time.

Had Lisa been about to reveal her reason she'd asked Vipul for a loan? Why didn't she say so outright?

Jia lay curled in a ball on the bed. Sleep was impossible, elusive, just out of her reach, much like the comforting embrace of her apartment. She lay on her side, face pressed against a wet pillow while melancholy winds howled in the distance.

After half an hour Vipul returned. This time, there was no knock. He flung the door open and put a folded receipt on the bed. "You can pay me back in cash or Zelle."

Jia unfurled the creased paper. It was an itemized receipt from an auto shop. The new tires alone cost two hundred a pop. Vipul's mouth curled in distaste. "Oh, by the way, Jia, when the sun rises tomorrow, I want you and your son out of my house."

Without waiting for her response, he slammed the door shut.

A sharp burning sensation shot up through her like acid injected straight into her heart. She dug her nails into her fists. The Band-Aid on her finger came loose, and she squeezed the cut. A fresh spurt of blood came forth. Her body didn't deserve to heal. She didn't deserve to heal.

Her worst fears had come to fruition. She was well and truly alone.

Her eyes glistened, parallel tear tracks sliding down her cheeks.

Going back to her apartment—still in the evacuation zone— was not an option, and even the certainty that her sister wouldn't actually let Vipul toss them out on the street in this weather provided little comfort.

What would Jia do once the skies cleared? Ask Raj to give her a ride? If her apartment was ruined by floodwater, would he and Lisa let them crash at their place while she searched for public shelters?

Exhausted by worry, she drifted off to sleep with one final regret burrowed in the recesses of her mind.

She should have slapped Vipul harder.

/ ' ', ' ', / '

WINE-RED LIQUID SQUIRTED FROM THE WOUND IN VIPUL'S CHEST, spraying drops on her face. His blood tasted hot, metallic on her tongue.

Vipul lay flat on his back as Jia hovered near the foot of the bed, transfixed at the body writhing in pain on the bed.

While his breathing slowed, hers accelerated. Like she was getting her life back by taking his. A cough behind her.

She whirled around.

Hands pressed flat to the sides of her head, she dropped to the ground like she'd been kicked in the stomach.

Ishaan was backed up against the wall, trembling hands clasped around a knife. Glasses speckled with blood.

A visceral mix of adrenaline and fear carved on his face.

"Told you, Mom," he whispered. "I would do anything to protect you."

/ ' ', ' ', / '

JIA SNAPPED HER EYES OPEN, DRENCHED IN SWEAT. DISCOMBOBU-lated, she threw back the covers and sat upright, blinking in the dim glow of the night-light. The dream was so vivid, she fanned out her fingers to see if they were tainted with Vipul's blood.

Hands fumbling on the nightstand, she turned on the lamp. The room was empty. She squeezed her eyes shut and leaned back on the headboard in relief.

It was just a dream.

According to the clock on the bedside table, it was half past one in the morning. Her parched throat burned, as though invisible claws were scratching into it.

She checked her phone. One new message from Dev.

> Go ahead, tell Jonathan about Molly, I dare you.
> But don't think you have such a good character.
> I know about you and Vipul. You have no moral
> high ground here whatsoever. Either you let
> me see Ishaan or Seema finds out what her
> dear sister has been up to.

Jia felt woozy like she'd been sucker punched.

Dev must've filled in the gaps from Ishaan's mentions of Vipul's frequent visits to their apartment.

Did a hurt Ishaan run to his dad after he thought he saw Vipul kissing Jia?

Good character. Something about that phrasing disturbed Jia, but she couldn't put a finger on it.

This one-sided conversation with Dev had to come to an end.

It was time to talk to her ex-husband.

She rolled up her sleeves and dialed the motel where he was staying.

After three rings, a receptionist picked up. "Hi, Michelle speaking, how may I assist you?" she said, voice muzzled by the rain.

"Can you patch me through to one of your guests? Dev Banerjee. That's *D-E-V.* Please, it's a family emergency."

Michelle put her on hold, and Jia held her breath, phone pressed to her ear, windy rain sounding as if someone were blowing air into the mouthpiece.

With a click, someone was back on the line, but it was Michelle again and her response jolted Jia out of the bed.

She had to put a hand on her chest to steady herself. "Sorry, I'm sure I misheard you," Jia said.

"Like I said, ma'am. I checked the system multiple times. No one named Dev Banerjee has checked into this location in the past week."

Jia hung up, feeling disoriented. What kind of a sick game was Dev playing?

If he'd checked in under a fake name, she had no way of guessing it.

She forced herself to think clearly through a maelstrom of emotions and reread his threat, her internal temperature rising with every word.

The solution was obvious, a glaring neon sign. What she should've done the minute she entered the house: come clean to Seema.

At the break of dawn, whenever Seema was up, Jia would tell her everything and beg her sister for forgiveness. Then she and Ishaan would leave as soon as it was safe to do so, move to a different city. Start over.

Straightening her back, she tiptoed to the kitchen to quench her thirst.

After downing a glass of water in three large gulps, she had pushed the lever of the countertop water filter for a refill when a movement upstairs caught the corner of her eye.

She squinted in the semidarkness. Raj was silhouetted in the corridor, his back to her, head bowed like he was staring at something in his hands. He twisted the knob of his bedroom door and disappeared from her view.

She felt the strangest sense of disquietude.

Her mouth still dry, she staggered back down the passage in a daze. The thrum of rainfall crashed in her ears, and anxiety roiled inside her as she thought about the state of the flooded streets and her slit car tires.

It felt suffocating to be trapped in a gilded prison.

Thump.

Jia jerked, startled. The sound appeared to be coming from somewhere farther down the hallway, but the roaring winds made it impossible to pinpoint a precise location.

Suddenly, a stinging sensation in her throat intensified, as if a bug were stuck in her throat, and she doubled over with a hacking cough. A stitch formed in her chest. She considered heading back for more water but then noticed a band of light beaming from underneath the gap in the door to the study.

Jia froze.

Vipul was up.

She gulped and pressed a fist to her mouth.

An explosive shot pierced the night.

Jia's leg muscles tightened. She cast a quick glance around her to check if anyone was there.

Did another tire get slashed?

Curiosity propelled her feet forward, and she knocked on the study room door. A faint clicking sound, like a doorknob turning. "Vipul?" No response. Jia gently eased the door open.

A scream died in her throat.

TWENTY-FOUR

Vipul was slumped in the black swivel chair, backed up against the desk. His head lolled sideways, and his right palm was pressed on his heart like he had been interrupted mid-pledge. A gunshot wound above his right eyebrow oozed blood, rivulets meandering past his stomach, carpet underneath his feet sodden crimson. Mouth open in horror, Jia awaited a scream to escape her lips, but her limbs froze even as wild panic surged inside, like a patient accidentally waking up in the middle of surgery.

Her eyes burned and watered as she stared at him, standing stock-still, her breath suspended.

The blinds of the side window slammed against the wall. The clatter burst her shock bubble, and she squinted at the open pdf on the laptop. An electronic suicide note?

But looking closer, she realized it was a partially filled-out form. The cursor blinked on a text box for "First Name," an impatient foot tapping away, waiting for Vipul's input that would never come.

When a gust of wind blew the blinds again, slapping her face with a blast of cool, wet air, she noticed the bookcase stepping stool beneath the window.

Jia's gaze alighted on the shattered glass, a jagged gap in the rectangular pane from which rain poured inside, waterlogging the floor.

Jia looked back and forth from the broken window to Vipul's blood-streaked face, and as she pieced together the horror that had unfolded in this room, her throat closed.

Someone had broken into the house and killed Vipul.

Jia gasped for air.

Hyperventilating, Jia whipped around, hands raised reflexively like a shield.

But there was no one. The door to the attached bathroom was closed, the bookcase undisturbed.

Jia switched off the lights, plunging the room in darkness, praying the absence of light increased the odds of her survival. The bluish tinge from the laptop screen cast a ghostly pallor on Vipul's face, and she snapped the device shut.

She curled into a fetal position, rain battering the walls from all sides with the force of a freight train.

A switch flicked. The room was awash in light.

A primal scream sliced the air.

TWENTY-FIVE

S eema was slumped against the French door. Jia's heart thundered, and she grabbed her sister. Seema was going to get them both killed. Jia whispered, "Someone broke into the house. Shot Vipul." When Seema issued a pained whimper, Jia clamped a hand on Seema's mouth hard. "Do you not get it? Someone is *inside* the house. We'll get the kids, but you cannot make any noises, do you understand?"

Seema's bulging eyes were orbs of fear, but she nodded, and Jia released her. Together, they crept toward the stairs, Jia's arm burning under Seema's terrified clutch. Her feet cold and wet, Jia grabbed a potted plant from the entryway table, which was no match for a gun, but it was better than nothing.

They heard footsteps above. A shadow formed on the staircase. Jia could just make out the silhouette of a man. Jia tightened her grip on the plant.

But as the figure came closer, Jia's body betrayed her, the plant slipped from her hand, and she shrieked.

"Hey . . ." Raj said in a frightened voice. Lisa trailed him. "What's going on?"

Jia quickly brought them up to speed in hushed whispers, cursing the precious seconds wasted when she could be checking on Ishaan. Raj took a sharp intake of breath on hearing about Vipul, and instantly put a protective arm around Lisa. They decided to search the house in pairs, and after opening the door to the kids' bedroom and peeking through the crack, Jia and Seema saw Asha spread-eagled on her pink toddler bed by the wall and Ishaan gently snoring on the main bed, his hair matted with sweat sticking to his forehead. It took all of Jia's self-control not to sweep Ishaan up in her arms.

Jia let out a delayed exhale, quietly increased the fan speed and Seema squeezed her palm, nodding. Jia's stomach unclenched as she looked heavenward to thank the universe for averting her worst nightmare, what she had been afraid of ever since coming upon Vipul's dead body. Ishaan was safe. Relief filled every pore of her being.

They tiptoed inside the room and checked the closets, peered under beds, repeating the process for every room in the house, including Grandma's bedroom. Grandma was not roused from her deep slumber even when Jia accidently knocked off a half-empty glass of milk on her side table.

Ten minutes later, they regrouped near the entryway. Panting slightly, Lisa said, "Looks like the burglar escaped the house. We've checked and double-checked every nook and cranny."

"Except for in there," Raj said, pointing his index finger, and at first Jia thought he meant the study, then realized he was referring to the bathroom.

A chill seeped through Jia's bones. How could she have missed it? The bathroom was a perfect hiding place, with dual doors, one into the study, the other opening into the passage.

As Raj nudged the door open, no one seemed to breathe.

But it was empty.

Raj stumbled backward, stepping on Lisa's foot.

"Sorry," he said, catching his breath, then gingerly entering the study.

Lisa hovered at the entrance door, close to Seema and Jia, not eager, for once, to follow her husband.

While terror and shock had stifled her senses the first time around, this time Jia discerned new details in sharp focus—the books scattered on the floor, smeared in blood; a sickly acidic odor tinged with the smell of urine emanating from Vipul, his eyes closed like his killer could not bear to look at his lifeless, vacant pupils.

Jia swallowed back the bile rising in her throat.

In a short time, the carpet had become soaked as rainwater streamed in from the broken window, cascading down the two tiers of the wooden stepping stool in the manner of a tabletop fountain.

Jia expected Raj to approach Vipul, but instead Raj hiked up his pajama bottoms, and giving his brother's body a wide berth, he grabbed a cricket bat lying near Vipul's feet. He knocked the wooden bat repeatedly at the power outlet till the plugged-in laptop charger came loose. "If there's an electricity surge, it could knock out the power in the whole house." His shoes made a sickening slushy sound and left a trail of bloody footprints in their wake as he passed Vipul's phone, which had been lying on the desk, to Seema.

Hands on hips, he gazed around the room, searching for something to put away, seemingly delaying the inevitable moment when he would have to face his brother. Finally, he turned slowly toward the lifeless body on the chair. All the color drained from Raj's face, and his shoulders caved as he moved closer to Vipul. With a soft whimper, he gently clasped Vipul's hands and examined his palms, frowning slightly. Then, sighing heavily, he stepped back, surveyed the sullied carpet, and said ruefully, "Vipul would die if he saw his study in this condition." Raj shook his head and pressed his palms on his eyes. "Sorry, that was crude. I do not know where that came from."

Lisa made her way to Raj. She shivered in her frilly nightgown, and her dilated pupils and staticky blond hair made her look like a shocked doll. She pressed her phone into Raj's hands. "Honey, we must call the cops right away to report this break-in. With the flooded streets, the intruder can't have gone too far."

She continued, "The newscasters had been warning us all night about burglars." She threw a pointed accusatory glance at Seema. "We were fools to ignore their warnings and now we're paying the price."

Raj nodded, although Jia didn't see what practical purpose the call would serve other than creating an official record of the murder, because the same flooded streets blocking the thief would also stop the cops from reaching the house.

One hand jammed inside a sweat-stained armpit, Raj dialed the phone. "Hello, I'm calling to report an emergency . . . A thief broke into our house . . . What's stolen? Ah, I'm not sure, but my brother . . ." His voice broke. "My brother was shot dead."

Muffled voices on the other end. "Are we safe? I think so . . ." His eyes drifted to the open window. "He escaped through a window." With a meaningful glance at the women cowering in the room, he said, "I mean he or *she* . . ." and Jia wasn't sure which feminists were clamoring for equal consideration as murder suspects.

"Uh-huh. Yes, I understand," he said, before hanging up, and just as Jia suspected, he reported that authorities had asked them to sit tight till they could arrive to the house in a few hours.

"His chain . . ." Seema spoke from the corner, looking at the floor. Faint shadows rested beneath her eyes, and vertical folds creased the skin between her eyebrows.

"What about it?" Lisa asked.

"You told the cops nothing is stolen," Seema said, looking at Raj. "But that's not true. His chain is gone and so is his ring."

Seema was right. Vipul's shirt's first two buttons were unfastened, and both his chain with the initial *V* and his wedding ring were missing.

Raj rubbed his chin, staring at the desk.

Jia's gaze passed over the sleek electronics. "What kind of a thief leaves behind a smartphone and an expensive laptop?"

"Maybe he was interrupted," Lisa said. Her face was taut with concentration. "Think about it. He and Vipul got into a fight. The chain broke during their struggle, and the thief slipped it in his pocket before making a run for it. Vipul wouldn't go down so easy."

Unified nods went around the room as they all agreed; acquiescence wasn't a quality one would readily associate to Vipul.

A fight in the study? Lisa's theory was plausible, and yet a discomfiting feeling wouldn't leave Jia. It wasn't exactly like fitting a square peg into a circular hole, more like an elliptical peg—close in appearance, but still it would never fit. Why break a smaller window on the side of the house when the giant French windows facing the driveway offered easier access?

Vipul evidently didn't come out on top in this fight, but where was the evidence of a struggle? Jia looked at the books swept off the desk and the cricket bat Raj had tossed in a corner. Had that made the *thwack* sound she'd heard earlier?

Gesturing to the bat, Jia said, "Maybe that's what Vipul used to defend himself. I think I might've heard him hitting the burglar with it."

Seema's eyes bulged, and she gasped, clutching her chest. "Are you all heartless? Coming up with theories for his last moments on earth when all that matters is that he's gone . . ." she said, whimpering. "He used to love playing cricket with that bat. I would give anything to see him go to the park again." Her face was dolorous; she appeared to have aged a decade, years of rigorous yoga benefits wiped out in a matter of minutes. Her eyes welled up as her body listed sideways.

Seema pressed her palms flat on the wall and banged her forehead onto it with a thud. "My life is over . . ."

Boom. Seema balled her hands into fists and pounded them into the wall. "Why did this happen to me . . ."

Lisa grabbed her wrists. Seema winced, wrenched her hands away, and before anyone could do anything, once more her forehead collided with the wall. "What am I going to do with the rest of my life?" she wailed.

"Please," implored Raj as the others restrained her together. "You have to get a grip on yourself."

Seema writhed in Jia's arms like a caught fish, and pulling free, she threw herself on the floor, thrashing around in pain.

Vignettes from her sister's life flashed in front of Jia's eyes—Seema, hands covered in a labyrinth of henna designs, laughing with her friends on her wedding day, then smiling next to Vipul in the living room, surrounded by moving boxes, the wall behind them blank and empty, soon to be filled with photographic catalogs of their happy memories. Jia hated how this night would be lodged in Seema's subconscious forever, nothing would ever be the same.

When Raj wrapped his arms around Seema, she grabbed a fistful of his pajama shirt. "My baby's going to grow up without a father. Who's going to love her the way Vipul did?"

Jia choked down a sob as she realized what was happening—while her memories had flashed back to Seema's life with Vipul,

Seema's imagination was doing the opposite, catapulting into the future, to all the moments in Asha's life that Vipul would miss, from dance performances to graduation ceremonies to her wedding.

Seema hugged her knees to her chest as Raj held her, tears inaudibly streaming down both their faces, and Jia and Lisa helplessly bore witness to their raw, authentic, and entirely silent expression of grief.

Jia used the pause to haul Seema away from the wall into a standing position.

"I'm going to let go of your hands now," Jia said. "But you have to promise you won't hurt yourself."

Seema nodded, sniffing, pulling herself together. Raj tenderly brushed her forehead, and Seema winced when his fingers grazed a bruise that had turned purple quickly.

"Don't you want to punish whoever did this to Vipul?" Raj said. "We need to get the facts right and give everything we can to the cops. Without all the information, they'll never find Vipul's killer. Don't we want justice for Vipul?"

When Seema nodded morosely, Raj continued, "Okay. So the intruder kills Vipul accidently, panics, and escapes with his jewelry using the same window he came in from." He walked toward the window and stared at the stool, frowning. He asked Jia, "Did you touch anything in here?"

Jia shook her head, finding his query odd. Any prints on the stool had likely been washed away by the rainwater.

After staring at the floor quizzically for a few more seconds, Raj looked up. "I'm assuming he used the stool to leave the room before regrouping with his partner. Someone acting as a lookout."

"Partner?" Lisa said, her eyes wide, her neck flushed.

Raj shrugged. "Partner. Partners. I don't know. I'm guessing if he expected to leave with a bigger haul, he'd need help. A two-person job."

Lisa sucked in a breath. "A two-person job," she repeated, twisting her hair.

But Raj wasn't looking at her; he was down on his knees, patting the carpet under the window. "Huh . . ." he said softly.

The next moment, Lisa clutched her chest. "Honey, look," she said, a quivering finger pointing to the wall behind Vipul.

Jia's jaw dropped. Water had begun to seep in from under the windows facing the front lawn, and now the room was flooding, soaking their feet. The water encroached quietly but at a rapid pace, like a guerilla warfare sneak attack. Tiny cracks had built up on the plaster of the wall encasing the window, and now Jia could see boils bulging on the surface.

When Raj flipped open the set of interior shutter blinds, Seema squealed.

Jia blinked rapidly. Every resident of the neighborhood was going to come back to a home destroyed.

The high elevation of Seema's house had not saved them, merely postponed the inevitable. The hill-like driveway of Seema's house, the supposed bastion against flooding, was now swallowed by roiling water. Water lashed against the parked cars. Gale-force winds whipped the rainwater in a circular churn, like a garbage disposal.

Eight hours after the hurricane's landfall, and after five hours of unprecedented heavy rain, Seema's house had finally been breached.

After covering Vipul's body with Asha's blanket, they blocked the windows with sandbags. When Raj suggested moving Vipul's body to the garage next to Rafael's, Seema shook her head, horrified, breaking down under a fresh slough of grief.

For the second time that night, they called the authorities, this time requesting a rescue, and were told assistance would be on the way within two hours.

A gust of wind blew an object from Vipul's desk, but with everyone's attention diverted to the storm, only Jia noticed—it was a mini ziplock bag, and it fluttered in the air for a second before landing near her feet. It looked empty, but when light caught it, she clocked something inside, something that made the hair on her arms rise.

Nestled in the folds of plastic were a few orangish strands.

It looked like cat hair, but Seema didn't own a pet and Jia was sure these belonged to a human, specifically the neighbor who had showed up at their doorstep mere hours ago.

Her knees felt shaky.

Using her foot, Jia pushed it under the couch, out of view, her heart galloping in her chest.

Rafael was dead.

What was the dead man's hair doing in Vipul's study?

TWENTY-SIX

They regrouped in the living area. Every few seconds, Lisa raised her head in a nervous tic to squint at the main door, barricaded with sandbags. Raj had used the circuit breaker to cut off the electricity supply in the flooded study, cloaking the front of the house in darkness, and then he'd stepped out to check the perimeter of the house to assess which other rooms might be likely to flood next.

Two hours. Jia checked the time on the clock, willing herself not to count every second, trying not to think of the hair strands in the study, like a horrific trophy. She'd assumed Vipul was the one who killed Rafael.

But did he?

And if not, was the same person responsible for both Vipul and Rafael's deaths?

Jia's skin felt unpleasantly damp.

She and Ishaan had to get out of here.

The back door leading to the patio opened, and Raj stepped inside, pinching the skin of his throat, his eyebrows furrowed in concern. He shivered in his pajamas, soaked through, as he sat carefully on the couch next to Lisa.

"Don't stress about the damage to any of the rooms," Raj said to Seema. "Your insurance should take care of it."

Seema nodded slowly, absently touching the swelling on her forehead. Jia felt sorry for her sister. Raj saw the damaged house as a pressing problem that could grant him some measure of control. Here was a circumstance he could do something about. To Seema, however, the flooded study represented the crumbling of her entire world. For the foreseeable future, every issue, whether unfamiliar paperwork or maintenance emergencies, was a reminder that she'd never had to worry about any of this before—Vipul had taken care of everything.

Raj assured Seema he'd make calls to file a claim and would even work with FEMA if they needed to. When Seema thanked him, Jia felt a curious jolt of reassurance, witnessing this tender moment between them.

She and Seema were technically the same now, single mothers, and yet their lives couldn't be more different. As a widow, Seema would always have someone willing to offer help. Help she could take without worrying about judgment and other baggage that accompanied a divorce.

When he crossed his ankles, Raj stared at the bottom of his muddy shoe with a perturbed expression.

He puffed out a breath and, bending down, yanked out something sparkly embedded in the rubbery surface.

It was a shard of glass, and Raj stared at it, transfixed, like it was an otherworldly artifact.

After gently placing it on the coffee table, he said, "I found glass pieces just like this strewn across the ground outside under the study room window." He cocked an eyebrow. "Isn't that strange?"

Seema, sniffling, said, "No, because we know that's from the broken window."

Raj rubbed his hands on his knees. "If someone broke a window to enter the house, the shards of glass would be on the *inside*, on the carpet of the room. But all, and I mean all, of the glass is outside."

"What are you suggesting, honey?" Lisa said, cautiously.

Raj massaged his forehead. "Look, I'm not suggesting anything. I'm merely stating the facts." He counted on his fingers. "All the doors and windows are locked and double bolted. I know that because Vipul and I checked them together. The only access point to the house is the study window, which I just discovered was broken from inside the house. Then there's the fact that some jewelry is missing but equally expensive electronics in the room are untouched."

"Yes," Jia interjected, "but that's because the burglary was interrupted."

Lisa nodded and leaned forward, eyes shining with intensity. "Exactly. Either Vipul scared him off or he heard someone coming by."

Raj dragged a hand over his bloodshot eyes. "Yes, there was an interruption. But it wasn't a burglary that was interrupted."

His eyes flittered over each one of them in turn. "I'm pretty certain whoever was interrupted was trying to stage an intrusion."

Seconds of silence stretched into minutes.

Lisa was the one to speak first. She cleared her throat and said, almost beseechingly, "No, that can't be right, because if what you're saying is true . . ."

Her unfinished sentence dangled over them like a precariously balanced sword.

Jia's throat throbbed as if she'd swallowed a golf ball. She was afraid to blink, to close her eyes for even a second. If Raj was correct,

Vipul, like Rafael, had died at the hands of someone inside the house.

Fear clouded Lisa's eyes. Seema gulped. Jia's horror was reflected in the petrified faces around her. Except one of them was putting on an act.

They'd been afraid before, but this fear was different. It cut deep.

They were scared of each other. Because someone in this room was a cold-blooded killer.

TWENTY-SEVEN

Rainwater pounded the windows, rattling the glass panes. Raj's accusation had opened a chasm of distrust between them.

"I would like nothing more than to be proved wrong," he said after a minute. "Jia, tell me, did you see anyone at all in Vipul's room?"

Jia shook her head.

"What were you doing in the study, by the way?" Seema asked, arching her eyebrows.

Jia bit her lip as she remembered Dev's threat, her prescient dream of finding Vipul dead, her impulsive decision to tell Seema about Vipul's messages. But considering everything Raj had just said, she couldn't reveal any of this to them.

Jia recalled her parched throat and dry mouth when she'd woken up. "I went to get water," she said.

Seema folded her arms and leaned back, but to Jia's relief, she didn't press the point further.

Raj had moved almost imperceptibly closer to Lisa, their fingers grazing—a natural alliance.

Jia's eyes met Seema's just for a second, and Seema said, "At least the kids are upstairs. It's best they stay there till we know what's going on." Jia gave a small nod. Even the gates of hell were closed for mothers who didn't look out for each other.

Could one of them be Vipul's killer?

If someone in the house had murdered Vipul, the first person to rule out was Grandma. Grandma's room on the first floor granted easy access, but the woman obsessed with male progeny had no reason to kill her older son. Her frail figure was no match for Vipul's hulky body. Raj was clearly Grandma's favorite son, and her biting remarks showed how much she despised Seema, but despite all that, Jia couldn't picture Grandma committing filicide.

Although Seema had a vindictive streak, her weapons of choice were passive aggression and public humiliation. Vipul was far from an ideal husband, but if wives started killing their patriarchal husbands, a significant percentage of the world's population would be wiped out overnight. Seema was unhappy in her marriage for sure, but she'd made it clear she would never divorce Vipul.

Her social media feed was carefully curated to suggest an idyllic life—the three of them next to a costumed Mickey Mouse, Seema and Vipul sampling wine in Fredericksburg. A husband and child were the fulcrum of her social status, and she needed him to keep up her "isn't my life great" facade. But what about Vipul's doubts concerning Seema's infidelity?

Jia squirmed and shifted in her seat. Seema was her sister, after all. Even considering the idea of Seema committing such a heinous act made her feel guilty.

Lisa played with her tresses absently. Was this diminutive figure capable of murder? Vipul had refused to loan her money, but was she so desperate for $40,000 that she would pick up a gun?

That left Raj. Raj, the unassuming, affable younger brother.

His jaw was clenched, and she caught him staring at Seema as if performing a similar mental exercise as Jia. There were worrying facets of his life hidden in plain sight. The marks on Lisa's skin. His obsessive need to be around Lisa. Love or a form of control?

If their marriage was so picture perfect, why did Lisa beg Vipul not to mention the loan to his brother?

Jia recalled the quiver in Lisa's voice. *Raj will kill me if he finds out.*

Jia jerked upright as her spine went straight.

Was that a figure of speech? Or a literal threat?

But Raj himself had essentially dismantled the burglar theory, and why do that if he was the killer?

Covering her face with her hands, Jia corralled her thoughts. She imagined Raj in the study, having just disposed of his brother, hearing Jia cough, his plan to stage a robbery abandoned halfway. He'd know the cops would figure it out anyway, so what option did he have other than forcing them to be suspicious of each other till he figured out his next steps?

In the study, he'd played the part of a distraught brother convincingly, but now she saw his actions—unplugging electronics, moving the bat, stomping all over the room—in an entirely different light.

Sweat broke out on her forehead. He had successfully disturbed the crime scene while they all watched.

Jia fidgeted. She had to talk to someone, share her suspicions. But Lisa had a Stockholm syndrome–like subservience to Raj and could not be trusted. Seema was her best option.

Just as Jia was formulating a plan to communicate with Seema in secret, her sister was on her feet, piping up, "I'm going to make tea." She marched to the kitchen, mumbling under her breath, "Just the way Vipul likes it."

She walked confidently as though she'd wished Vipul back into existence.

The others exchanged worried looks. Seema had quite simply gone mad. Or had they?

Raj's eyebrows wrinkled, and he scrutinized Seema with a pained gaze. "Bhabhi," he said, making his way toward her and steering her away from the stove, "why don't you go lie down for some time, get some rest."

Seema's hands flew to her mouth and her eyes watered. "I'm never going to hear him ask for tea again, am I?" she whispered. Her face was contorted in anguish. Vipul, gone for less than an hour, had already transformed into a better person in the halo of death, his rough edges blunted, flaws remembered as lovable quirks.

Raj took a deep breath. "No. Vipul isn't coming back." He gave her shoulders a tight squeeze. "But you gotta stay strong. Asha needs you."

At the mention of her daughter's name, Seema's face crumpled and she burst into hitching sobs.

"Sorry, Bhabhi," Raj said, grimacing. He pressed his fist to his mouth. "I wasn't trying to make you feel worse." As Seema's crying became louder, Raj craned his neck in the direction of the corridor. "Shhh . . . You'll wake up Grandma." His voice cracked. "I'm not ready to tell her." His face was haunted, and he looked permanently broken, as if he knew that for him Vipul hadn't died just tonight but would die over and over again every time he looked into his grieving mother's eyes.

"You're worried about *her*?" Seema said, her voice rising. She stepped away from him, tears streaming down her face. "My baby lost her father tonight."

Raj ran a hand through his hair and looked helplessly at Lisa, who shrugged almost imperceptibly. He moved closer and pulled Seema into a one-sided hug. "You know what," he said. "Tea sounds like a grand idea. We could all use some caffeine right now. I'll help you, Bhabhi."

Their eyes met, and he stroked her forehead tenderly. Seema nestled in his shoulder and sniffled. He opened the fridge and set the milk carton on the granite counter while Seema wiped her eyes and proceeded to light the stove.

Raj pulled up a stool at the kitchen counter, keeping a wary eye on Seema's back.

Seema pressed her temples like she was having a migraine. Then she whirled around and leaned forward, her waist digging into the granite's edge. The corners of her mouth twisted.

"I hated that tacky gold chain. I told him so many times after we moved to America to take it off. The design looked so unsophisticated. But he didn't listen to me." She threw a dirty look in Raj's direction. "He refused to take it off because it was *your* mother's gift. Said I would never understand it." She mimed air quotes. "'Sentimental value.'"

Raj looked on helplessly while Seema narrowed her eyes as if Vipul would still be here if he'd only listened to Seema. But Seema's impulse to overanalyze was understandable, because now she was condemned to a life of second guesses, tending to seeds of doubt with her guilt. She would be caught in an endless loop of what-ifs, wondering if the difference between life and death lay in some single mundane decision.

A loud whoosh. The tea overflowed, the spilled milk sizzling as it came in contact with the flames. Seema rushed to turn the stove off while Lisa grabbed a paper napkin. There was a scramble of activity as Seema ducked into the pantry to fetch extra paper towels and Lisa and Raj helped her clean up.

In the hubbub, Raj's phone was unattended, lying innocuously on the countertop.

Jia had a few seconds. The pull of his blank screen was hypnotic—could she risk it?

She grabbed his phone and, after bringing it under the bar stool, pressed the power button on the side. The phone was locked; evenly spaced dots appeared on the screen prompting her to draw an unlock pattern. She'd never be able to get in. With a sigh, she was about to put it back when she saw a notification at the top, and clicking on the down arrow, she expanded the email snippet.

Subject: Re: Book Update.

We regret to inform you that while your proposal sounds great, we unfortunately cannot make you an offer to publish "Keys to Financial Success." Your blog has less than a hundred unique visitors each month, and those numbers would need to be significantly higher before we can move forward. Once you build a bigger platform, we would . . .

She was reading the words so fast, the text became a blur.

Raj had announced his book deal during dessert, lying without qualms to the people closest to him.

Lisa's bruises suggested he was a potential abuser.

Was Raj also a killer?

TWENTY-EIGHT

Seema wiped the counters with a rag while Raj sipped the half cup of tea they had salvaged.

Jia's heartbeats were arrhythmic. If her suspicions were correct and Raj had murdered Vipul, she had to alert Seema before it was too late.

After dumping the tea dregs from the strainer, Seema scrubbed the steel vessel, pausing every other second to wipe her eyes against her shoulders as her body spasmed with each incoming wave of sorrow. Jia cocked her ear toward the patio, trying to discern Seema's wails from the rain. She rubbed her eyes. The clock on the wall showed four a.m.

Although only three hours had elapsed since her discovery of Vipul's dead body, Jia felt as if she had been stuck in this nightmare for days. Her retinas burned with every blink, and she felt light-headed, like she would faint any second.

When Seema reached for one of the glass-encased cabinets and pulled out a medicine bottle, Jia quickly made her way over to her.

Seema popped an ibuprofen before washing it down with a glass of water.

The bruise on her forehead from banging against the wall was even darker now, morphing into an ugly shade of maroon.

"Listen," Jia said, after checking that Lisa and Raj were talking among themselves. "I have to tell you something."

Suddenly, like an ill-timed orchestra, shrill sounds emanated from all their phones one after the other. Raj swiped on his screen ruefully. "Emergency alert letting us know homes in this area are flooding. Like we don't know that already."

Seema was holding both her phone and Vipul's phone, and though she set hers aside quickly, she pointed at Vipul's screen with an excitement in her eyes. "We should've checked his phone. Maybe that'll tell us something."

Raj shuffled close to Seema, tilting his face. "That's a great idea. Check his recent calls."

As Lisa and Jia tiptoed around them to get a better look, Seema scrolled through the call logs. "The last one's a spam call," she muttered. "Let me go to his messages."

After a couple of seconds of scrolling, Seema gasped, then angled herself to face Jia directly, eyes ablaze with fury.

Jia's pulse jacked up, and she had the distinct feeling of being chained to a train track, ears ringing with the piercing horn of an incoming train but frozen in place, unable to do anything other than watch the blazing light grow bigger.

Seema tipped her head at the phone. "What the heck is this?" she demanded, her voice dangerously low.

"What happened?" Lisa asked.

Jia was shocked by the whimpering sound her mouth made, like a cornered puppy.

Seema thrust the phone in her face, Vipul's underwear inches from her eyes.

Jia recoiled, squeezed her eyes shut. "I can explain."

"What's going on?" Raj asked, looking confused, craning his neck to get a better look at the phone.

"What's going on," Seema said through gritted teeth, "is that while I was giving shelter to my sister, she was busy shagging my husband."

"Please," Jia begged. "That's not true. Vipul had been sending me these inappropriate messages. I didn't mean for this to happen. I hated how things had gone in this direction."

Seema scrolled through the messages. She held up the phone for Raj and Lisa to see. On the screen was Vipul in the gym; underneath it, Jia's message, "Looking good."

"Does that look like hate to you?"

"I was just trying to encourage him to get healthy . . . For you," Jia said, cringing as she realized how lame her defense sounded.

Seema's eyes flashed with anger. "For me? Aren't you one generous sister." Her thumb continued flicking through the conversation.

"Ah," Seema said, her eyes wide like she'd hit a jackpot. She brought up another snippet. This time, a snapshot of Vipul in a gym, dumbbell in hand. Underneath it, Jia's response: a single kiss emoji. "Explain this."

"I sent it by mistake," Jia said. "Read the next message, it says I'm sorry." She vividly remembered the panic consuming her on realizing that she'd sent the wrong emoji. How her insides had shrunk in embarrassment as she stared at the yellow face with puckered lips blowing kisses into the air.

Seema erupted in laughter; her voice tinged with hysteria. "That's what you are using to get out of this? A typo? Wow, you must really think I'm dumb."

Her digit resumed exhuming Jia's past.

"'Want to catch a movie this weekend?'" Seema fixed her with a cold stare. "Did you lovebirds go to a cinema hall?"

"It sounds worse than it is. He just showed up at my apartment, what could I do? Not let him in? Honestly, I had no idea at the time that we would end up here. Trust me, I was never ever interested in him that way."

"'My heart was lonely for lack of love . . .'" Seema read aloud. "Why don't these messages support a single thing you're saying?"

Jia grimaced. "Don't you see it? He's the one who misunderstood everything. I thought I was doing him a favor."

Another flick of her thumb. "'You light up the lamp of my dreams.'" Seema tilted her head. "Sounds like you both were close. You don't have a man to do things for you, so what, you go and steal your sister's husband?"

"No. Please." Jia rubbed her face, exhausted by the fusillade of Vipul's messages. "No, it wasn't like that."

"Stop with your lies," Seema said, her voice rising. "Look at this. Sunday, eight p.m. 'Seema is going to visit her friend in California, so she will be out of town for a week.'" Her mouth curled in disgust. "Ugh, did you guys do it in *my* bedroom?"

"No," Jia said, instantly. She glanced helplessly at Raj, but he looked away as though he was too embarrassed to even look at her.

Jia's eyes flicked to Lisa, who shot her a sympathetic look before addressing Seema: "Let's at least give her a proper chance to explain her side."

"This doesn't concern you," Seema snapped. "This is my family matter." She pulled up yet another text, this one a listing of websites selling high-end purses and designer watches, and this, more than anything else, seemed to hurt Seema. Her voice wobbled. "You made him *shop* for you?"

"These links were suggestions for *your* gift," Jia said, weary. "It all started when he wanted to buy something extravagant for your anniversary. He said he wanted to surprise you and asked me for my help. I sent him a link with the kinds of gifts I knew you would like, but he insisted I come check them out with him in person. But I didn't go with him, I swear, and I obviously couldn't tell you because it was supposed to be a surprise. And I honestly thought that would be the end of it, but somehow . . ."

She sputtered like a car engine out of fuel. Taking another breath, she plowed on. "After our first meeting, he had told me about issues in your marriage and I wanted to be a sympathetic sounding board, and yes, I found myself leaning on him when I was overwhelmed with my never-ending list of errands, but never did I imagine it would lead to this." Jia's shoulders caved. "I may not be perfect. But I would never betray you."

"My anniversary?" Seema said, keeping her eyes locked with Jia's, as if they were the only ones in the room. Jia swallowed. A beat of silence. Seema narrowed her eyes. "My anniversary was *three* whole months ago. Are you telling me this has been going on behind my back all this time and you didn't tell me? How could you do this to your own sister? You have the nerve to go on a coffee date with my husband behind my back. After everything I've done for you." Her face appeared pained, and she looked on the verge of tears.

Jia felt blood drain her face. "I was planning on telling you today, I swear. I just . . . just didn't want to cause problems in your marriage."

"And sleeping with my husband was supposed to help my marriage?" Seema exploded.

"I never slept with him!" Jia yelled back. "Listen, I know, I know. I should have told you about the messages sooner." She clasped her hands together and sighed. "But I didn't have an affair. I wish I could go back in time and do things differently. But it doesn't change what happened. I didn't sleep with him, and I never wanted to. That's the truth."

Seema sneered. "I don't trust a word that comes out of your mouth." Twice she opened her mouth to say something, then stopped. Her jaw was set. "It's my fault. I should have never taken you in. Guess what they say is true, you can never trust a divorcée around your spouse."

The words lacerated Jia like a knife. Her mouth became slack, and she reeled as her face burned white hot. A stab of pain shot through her. Seema, like everyone else, thought of her as lesser simply because she was a divorcée. Blood was thicker than water, but the difference in their marital statuses had shattered their sisterly bond.

"Wait a second," Seema said, the indignation on her face replaced by fear. "Is that why you were in the study with him?" She put a hand on her mouth. "Oh God, were you two hooking up?"

"No, no," Jia said. "I already told you I woke up to get water when I heard sounds."

But Seema wasn't listening. She whipped her head back and forth between the study and Jia. "Oh my God, did you do this to him? Did you kill my husband?"

Raj said, crossing his arms. "C'mon, Bhabhi. Now you're taking it too far."

Seema silenced him with a raised finger. "Aren't you the one who said one of us did it? Why can't it be her?"

Lisa clutched her hands tight. "We shouldn't make such wild accusations."

Raj shot a warning look to Lisa and shook his head ever so slightly as if to say, *Stay out of this.*

"Why are you taking her side?" Seema snarled. "You have met her what, two times before this? How do you know they didn't have a lovers' tiff that got out of hand?"

Lisa flinched, but Raj's eyes widened for a second and his lips parted slightly, like something in his mind had clicked in place, and Jia knew he was remembering the scene he'd walked into in Jia's bedroom—Vipul, red-faced and shocked, and Jia, flustered and angry. At the time, his immediate reaction had been concern for Jia, but now his imagination was filling in the missing bits of information, processing the same visual with new context, coming up with a very different interpretation of the scene he'd witnessed.

"I can't believe I have to say it," Jia said, looking her sister in the eyes. "I didn't kill anyone. And I certainly didn't sleep with Vipul." Accusations of sleeping with Vipul were far more hurtful to her than being suspected of his murder, perhaps because, though she was guilty of neither charge, she actually did wish she'd handled the former situation differently.

"We have to get through this night," Lisa groaned. "Let's let the cops decide who killed Vipul."

Jia's chest seized. *Cops.* The realization that she would be part of a murder investigation jolted through her, terrifying her more than Vipul's dead body.

If she couldn't convince her own sister, how would she fare when the cops asked her the same questions? Her insides clenched when she thought of all the text messages the cops would no doubt see on his phone.

A detective, overworked and underpaid, would sit her in a windowless room, offer stale coffee, and ask her to explain her relationship with Vipul. At first, the detective would deploy a soothing voice, but his patience would ultimately give way to frustration, and he would come straight to the point: *How long were you sleeping with your brother-in-law?*

Jia swallowed, and her glance tracked the others, Seema in the center, flanked by Raj and Lisa, and although she couldn't be certain, it felt like the physical distance between them and her had increased by an inch.

A closing of ranks against her.

Seema cleared her throat loudly and broke Jia's train of thought. She raised her eyebrows at Lisa and Raj like she was a seasoned prosecutor performing for a jury. "But here's what I don't understand. Why would you go to the kitchen to get water? I'd put a bottle on the nightstand right next to your bed. I did that for every guest room, in fact."

Jia's insides tightened. Seema was correct. She lowered her head and mumbled, "I'd forgotten about the bottle." Seema's head was cocked, face tight with skepticism, as if the quiver in Jia's voice, her hesitation, implied she was lying.

Seema pursed her lips and glared at Jia. She didn't say anything, but she didn't need to, because her silence spoke volumes. Raj and Lisa exchanged quiet glances.

In the interminably long minute that passed, a partnership formed, and a narrative stitched from their disparate fragments of information.

Jia pictured Raj talking to the detective. *Yes, things turned ugly between Jia and Vipul.*

Seema would wipe away a tear and chime in. *I had no idea my own sister could stoop so low. I'd never seen this side of her.*

Lisa had come to her defense earlier, but Raj had an impossible hold on her and it wouldn't be long before she fell in line with the rest of her family.

The detective would leave the pivotal query for last, a question posed to every person currently in the house: *Is there anyone you suspect of Vipul's murder?*

Given Seema's unconvinced expression, her rigid posture, Jia was certain that when the time came, Seema would point one trembling, manicured finger in her direction. *Without a doubt, Jia Shah killed my husband.*

TWENTY-NINE

Jia tried not to think of Vipul's waxen skin, his body bloating every second under his daughter's blanket. After all the problems he'd created for her when he was alive, making her life miserable, she had never imagined that his death would be the final nail in her coffin.

The leather clung to Jia's skin like Velcro as she peeled her sweaty elbow away from the sofa's armrest. Lisa cranked the curtains closed, covering the bay windows, and joined Seema and Raj. All three of them were situated on adjacent bar stools such that they faced Jia, their backs to the kitchen island.

The message behind their choice of seating arrangements was not lost on Jia. Their vantage point allowed them to keep a watch on her.

The arrangement was fine. She needed to keep an eye on them as much as they needed to keep her in their crosshairs.

Lights blazed from every direction in the room, from the kitchen skylights, the ceiling recessed lights—even the tiny lamp in a corner was turned on. A palliative measure, a false hope that enough light could keep danger at bay.

Jia imagined a lie detector strapped to her wrist. *Did you ever think about hurting Vipul?*

She would fail that test with flying colors.

She clasped and unclasped her hands. If only she had confided to someone about Vipul's harassment, if not Seema, then someone else.

When Lisa had entered her room earlier that night, she should have shown her all the texts.

Without a witness to her harassment, it looked like a case of she said, and he didn't get to say anything because she had killed him.

But, she realized with a terrifying jolt, someone did know about Vipul's behavior.

Ishaan.

Time seemed to come to a halt as her head spun.

He'd witnessed multiple incidents between Jia and Vipul, without the benefit of full context. His observations of their interactions were stripped of nuances, and as far as he was concerned, there was something going on between his mother and Vipul Uncle.

The dream flared again, but this time the details shifted like grains of sand contouring to fit a container.

Ishaan woke up and couldn't go back to sleep, so he came to Jia's room but ended up wandering into the study instead. An unlocked drawer granting him a chance to caress the gun he so coveted, making him feel like a man. Vipul entering without notice, making him jump. Ishaan pulling the trigger by accident. Blood-soaked Vipul. Cowering in a corner, Ishaan gripping the gun he never intended to fire.

What if Vipul had forgotten to put the gun safety back on, after firing at the snake?

Her body broke out in a cold sweat as fear set up camp in her heart.

Her decision to come here might have driven her son to murder.

Her head throbbed as if her scalp were being drilled, and she was tempted to pop one of Seema's painkillers herself. She'd considered Seema a natural ally, but after the discovery of the messages, her sister refused to even look at her. Jia ignored the wary glances coming her way because for the time being, the spotlight of suspicion trained on her was an advantage. It meant no one was thinking of Ishaan.

He was sound asleep upstairs, and Jia shuddered thinking that the bedcovers might conceal blood-splattered pajamas. He was a boy still developing his moral compass; he wasn't a stone-cold killer, but he'd inherited his father's ability to compartmentalize. Perhaps his sweaty forehead was not the mark of a heated room, but of a terrified boy hoping to sleep away his nightmare. Jia had to get to her son and find out the truth before the others did.

But how could she sneak away? She couldn't so much as cough without Seema glaring at her.

Abruptly, the power went out.

"Oww, my leg," Seema yelled in the dark.

The blood in Jia's veins drummed with a rush of anticipation. This was it. Her only chance.

A white beam of light flashed straight into Jia's face. She squeezed her eyes shut.

"Sorry," Lisa said.

"Don't waste your phone battery," Raj said. "Where's the flash-light?"

While their search led them into the kitchen, Jia went along with them, but midway, doing an about-face, she padded upstairs, one quiet step at a time. Halfway up, she slipped, hitting a knee on a staircase edge, and yelped in pain.

Jia grimaced and threw a panicked look over her shoulder. But they were arguing: ". . . what's the use of saving battery on a phone when there's no network . . ." ". . . you talk as if the world's ending . . ."

Under the cover of a burst of thunder, Jia picked up her pace, crept down the hallway, and finally stood outside Ishaan's room.

All the answers were on the other side of the door.

Her hand stilled, a fluttery feeling in her belly.

She froze. She couldn't do it. Accusing her son of murder, even an accidental one, would take their relationship to a point of no return, and she wasn't ready to cross that threshold. She rested her sweaty forehead on the smooth wood, wanting to linger in the liminal space where Ishaan was innocent.

Suddenly, an idea popped in her head.

There was one way.

A way to prove Ishaan's innocence.

Pin the guilt on someone else in the house.

The jewelry. Jia felt a tiny flame of hope ignite within her. Just like her, Ishaan had no reason to take Vipul's chain or ring.

Raj had fit all the puzzle pieces together with Sherlockian accuracy, but hadn't considered the location of the chain and the ring.

Blood rushed to her ears. Had Raj crumpled under the weight of financial pressures, burdened by his doting wife's faith in him to have a successful career? With Vipul out of the way, he'd be the sole heir to the family property. Was this his plan all along?

The chain and ring must be hidden somewhere in Raj's room,

and she was going to find them. Insides tingling with fear, Jia headed down the black corridor and snuck into his room. Standing in the doorway, she brought up the flashlight app on her phone and scanned the twin night tables. A water bottle just like the one in Jia's guest room, a leather wallet. But no sign of gold, though of course she was not exactly expecting Raj to carelessly toss his dead brother's items onto the nightstand.

She saw the bottled water and felt a tight knot form in her belly. Seema had insisted on the bottled water, made a big deal about Jia going to the kitchen. Had she spiked the water? What about the pills she'd insisted Jia take for her health? Were they even a legitimate medication?

Jia checked the door again before flinging open the top drawer of the dresser that faced the bed. Holding her phone in her left hand, she scrabbled for the feel of metal amid the satin nightwear. Her fingers initially grazed timber, but in the far end of the drawer, her skin rubbed up against soft velvet.

Bingo. Her pulse fast with excitement, Jia pulled out three plush jewelry boxes of different sizes. This must be it. Jia's heart leapt. She would find Vipul's chain here along with his ring. She knew it even before she opened the smallest box.

When she unclasped the snap closure to flip it open, though, her heart sank. Encased within a padded lining was a gold necklace with a green emerald in the center. It reminded her of Mom's jewelry. Jia quickly opened the remaining boxes, heat rising in her cheeks, disappointment coursing through her as each one of them revealed similar old-fashioned women's jewelry pieces. Her panic-stricken face reflected back at her in the mirror atop the dresser.

A particularly loud gust of wind jostled the house, startling her. She stuffed the boxes back in their place.

Jia had to pivot to another plan. The best thing to do would be to get herself and Ishaan away from the murderer, even if she still didn't know who he or she was. She had to secure a way out of here, if not in her own car, then in Raj's SUV.

With every fresh clap of thunder, Jia's apprehension spiked. The closer she got to uncovering the identity of the murderer, the more danger she and Ishaan would be in. What was she playing at, thinking she could be a detective? What she needed to do instead was find a way out.

She just needed to get the keys.

Stealing is wrong. She'd lectured her son not to take other people's possessions, but her moral righteousness buckled under the weight of reality. As it turned out, when it came to saving her and Ishaan, there was no right or wrong.

Raj would have left the keys on the mantelpiece downstairs or hooked them on the key rack by the entryway. She gave a heavy sigh and was about to leave the room when she remembered.

Lisa's SUV. That's how Raj had referred to the car. If Lisa was like most women, she would hook the car keys by the front door in our own home, but at her in-laws' residence? Everything important, including a set of her home keys, would be safe inside her purse.

Jia scoured the room first and then made a beeline for the closet, where, nestled within the bowels of a leather satchel, was a set of keys, among them a car key. The fluffy pom of the keychain felt soft against Jia's hand.

Clutching the key like a talisman, Jia came out of the closet and glanced out the window that overlooked the driveway. The waves of water churning on the driveway suggested the SUV's back tires must also be submerged.

To drive in current conditions was akin to a death sentence. Jia could picture the article in the *Houston Chronicle*: *Tragedy in Sugar Land. In the early hours of the morning, residents of Fort Bend County made a grisly discovery: two bodies trapped in a car, both mother and son drowned. County officials blamed the deaths on the mother's poor judgment.* Jia shuddered involuntarily and shook her head. She would wait till daylight broke in two hours. Hadn't Raj said it would stop raining soon? Whenever it did, she would be ready.

THIRTY

As Jia beelined to the door, her elbow brushed against the edge of the dresser, causing a photo frame to fall over with a soft thud. She winced and crouched to pick it up, ears attuned to the sound of any approaching footsteps. The dual-hinged frame lay facedown on the ground like an open book. Jia turned it over. The glass covering both pictures was intact. Exhaling a sigh of relief, she traced her fingers over its intricate design, the word "Family" etched over and over across the glossy wood frame. The pictures had a professional stock-photo feel, and Raj featured in both of them—in the first picture on the left, he wore a graduation robe, clutching a diploma, while the right picture framed him on a beach next to Seema and Lisa, their toes covered in sand, translucent water blending into the clear blue sky. Lisa gripped Seema's arm tight like they were best friends, while Seema beamed into the camera. It was easy to forget that the two sisters-in-law had once had a good relationship before Grandma's favoritism fractured their bond.

She snapped the frame shut so she wouldn't have to look at their happy faces. What was she thinking, suspecting Raj of murder?

These people were not killers; they were normal people in extraordinary circumstances. Jia cupped her face in her hands and rubbed vigorously. Sleep deprivation and anxiety were taking a toll on her, hindering her ability to think rationally.

Traces of Lisa's perfume lingered in the air, and as Jia breathed in the lavender scent, the set of keys in her pocket filled her with shame. She hadn't hesitated before deciding to abandon everyone else for her own safety.

Jia opened the frame again and stared at Seema's photo. Her head was inclined toward Lisa's shoulder. The idea of Seema becoming a widow at such a young age broke Jia's heart.

Would Seema, like her mom, bloom in the absence of a rigid husband's shadow? She was thirty-seven years old, young enough to remarry a man her own age. A Vipul 2.0.

Jia's legs buckled, and she covered her face with her hands. Mom's voice screamed in her head: *Jia, do you hear yourself? You're saying your brother-in-law dying is a good thing!*

She stared at Raj's graduation photo again and asked herself whether he was capable of murder.

The notion was ridiculous, impossible.

But a day ago, she would've thought thirty hours of nonstop rainfall was impossible. Just like finding her brother-in-law's dead body in her sister's house was impossible.

The last twenty-four hours had blown apart all presumptions of plausibility, placing every outcome in the realm of possibility.

"Hey!"

Jia jerked as the room flooded with light.

"You nearly gave me a heart attack," Lisa said, standing in the doorway, hand on her chest. "The power's back."

"I heard something," Jia said quickly. She squinted and blinked as her eyes adjusted to the sudden brightness.

Lisa took a step backward. "What? Where?"

"No," Jia said, her pulse racing. Lisa could not find out about the missing car keys. "I was mistaken . . . I think it was just the wind hitting the window." Jia cringed as soon as the words tumbled out. Her lame excuse crumpled against the mildest of scrutiny.

Realizing the picture frame was still in her hand, Jia set it on the table.

Lisa frowned. Her eyes flitted between Jia and the window behind the bed, gauging the distance, and she appeared to be testing whether the facts matched Jia's account. Jia, hunched near the dresser, shrouded in darkness seconds before, did not by any stretch of imagination look like someone investigating a sudden sound from the window.

Jia's cheeks flushed. "Looks like there's no one here. Guess we can go downstairs now."

"Guess we can," repeated Lisa. She frowned and tucked her hair behind her ears, looking skeptical.

The temptation to confide in Lisa was strong.

Lisa had been the solitary voice of support for Jia, and she'd even felt a sense of kinship earlier over their prior failed relationships. Yet staring into those blue eyes made her realize that while she knew Lisa on a surface level, Jia didn't have any real understanding of her motivations.

The contradictions in her unsettled Jia. If Lisa had such a healthy relationship with Raj, why would she try to borrow money behind his back? If she was so besotted with her husband, why did her bruises tell a different story?

The burning question was what she had meant by the comment *You're not the only family member he's let down tonight.*

When Lisa started to back away from the room, Jia saw her opportunity to question her privately slipping away.

Jia pursed her lips.

Briefly glancing over Lisa's shoulder to check the coast was clear, Jia lowered her voice. "When you said I'm not the only one he's let down," she asked, "what did you mean?"

Momentary silence. Lisa worked her lower lip for a minute. She shrugged. "Just that he's a creep. He behaved inappropriately with one of my friends at our wedding reception. Tapped her behind on her way to the bathroom."

Lisa maintained eye contact the whole time she was speaking, but the way her eyes slipped to the floor at the end made Jia feel that while she was getting some version of the truth, it was not the entire story.

Lisa looked over her shoulder. "We shouldn't stay here longer. The others will worry about us." She drew her arms around herself, and Jia wondered if she was subconsciously touching her bruise.

"Make sure you give a different address to the bank or go paperless," Jia said.

Lisa blinked in confusion. "Excuse me?"

"If you're opening a secret separate account," Jia said. "I made that mistake. The first statement went right to my ex-husband. That's why you were asking Vipul for money, right? I overheard you talking to him in the study."

Lisa looked at Jia uneasily. "I have no idea what you're talking about."

Jia leaned in and touched Lisa's elbow. "Listen. You don't have to hide from me, I can help you. It's one thing to end a relationship. Ending a marriage, however, is a different ball game. It's not easy."

Lisa's eyes went wide like they'd pop out of her sockets. "End my marriage?" she blubbered. "Why on earth would I do that?"

Jia said, "I just had a feeling . . ."

"Why? Do you think Raj isn't happy with me?" Lisa's voice brimmed with panic.

Jia shook her head. "No, not at all. I thought it might be the other way around."

Lisa blew her breath out. "Oh." She pushed Jia's hand away firmly. "You've got it wrong." She gave a decisive nod. "I would never ever leave my husband."

Jia pressed on. "But then what did you need the money for?"

Lisa evaded her eyes. "I didn't ask Vipul for money." She glanced at a spot on the wall behind Jia and pressed her lips together. "I was . . ." She cleared her throat and clasped her hands. "I was discussing stock investments with him. You clearly misunderstood me."

Jia sighed. She wasn't the only one coming up with ridiculous excuses tonight.

Without waiting for a response from Jia, Lisa turned on her heel and headed out to the hallway.

Jia lowered her chin and followed her, but Lisa walked quickly and lengthened the distance between them.

Her trip upstairs had been a total failure. Not only had she not found the missing chain and ring, but she'd also managed to truncate the very short list of people on her side.

When they reached downstairs, a fresh burst of thunder tore through the sky, and the subsequent rumble sounded like schisms had opened within the ground below, dislodging enormous boulders.

They all turned to see two figures standing at the head of the staircase.

THIRTY-ONE

Mommyyy . . ." Asha yelled. Ishaan bounded down the stairs. Seema clambered up the stairs and quickly lifted Asha, who, like any other kid her age, didn't handle being disturbed in the middle of the night very well. Her face was splotchy, bottom lip turned inside out, and soon enough, she started bawling.

While Seema rocked Asha on her hip, Jia gestured for Ishaan to sit next to her on the sofa. Seema shushed Asha back to sleep and gently laid her on the sofa, covering her with a blanket.

Ishaan's eyes were alert. "Whoa, Mom, did you see those lights? It went on forever . . . and then boom." He bumped his fists to show an explosion.

He sounded so innocent, just like any other twelve-year-old.

The creases and folds on the side of his face from sleep gave her a small measure of comfort. Ishaan's brows were knitted together. "You all have been up all night?" he asked, gaze sweeping the room, disappointed like he had missed out on all the action. His head snapped up to look at her directly. "Where's Vipul Uncle?"

Doubts niggled the back of her head. Why was he asking after

Vipul but not Grandma, who was also not around? "Vipul Uncle is checking . . ." She hunted for words, but Ishaan cut her off.

"Whatever, Mom," he said, shaking his head. "I can tell when you're lying to me."

She sighed, hating herself.

"I don't think the power will last very long," Raj said, keeping his voice low for Asha's benefit. "They'll turn off the electricity in the area on purpose so all the flooded homes don't catch fire." Raj tapped the flashlight. "We need extra batteries. I want to make sure we don't run out. I think Vipul had kept some in Jia's guest room." He gave Seema a guarded look, as if afraid she was going to break into sobs again on hearing her husband's name.

"I'll get them," Lisa said, walking to Jia's room.

Jia was struck by an idea. From the first mentions of the nascent hurricane, she had been helplessly letting the storm dictate her actions. Trapped by the elements of nature.

But now she would use the environment to her advantage.

The next time the power went out, she would grab Ishaan and escape, taking her chances stranded on a street. She would get them to the nearest gas station if she could.

Jia grabbed Ishaan's arm. She whispered, "When the lights go out next time, I need you to come with me."

But in the next second, Lisa's scream pierced the night.

THIRTY-TWO

Raj leapt off the sofa and scrambled after Lisa in raw panic. Before Jia could stop them, Ishaan took off after him. Seema stayed behind with Asha.

Lisa and Raj stood at the foot of the bed, staring at the bedsheet as if hypnotized.

At the entrance, Jia cupped her mouth and let out a stifled scream.

Like a glittery snake, hidden under the soft pillow, was Vipul's chain. Its surface stained red.

Lisa's voice cracked as she spoke. "I was searching for the batteries, and I noticed something shiny peeking out from beneath the pillows . . ."

Jia's lips trembled. Here it was, in her bedroom, the missing chain.

Her knees wobbled and felt like they would give away at any second. Jia leaned against the door for support and gaped at the blood-speckled chain, her heartbeat thrashing in her ears.

Raj's forehead creased in worry as his gaze ping-ponged between Jia and the chain.

Unease settled in the pit of Jia's belly.

"So . . ." Raj was the first one to speak. "Any idea how this came here, Jia?"

All heads snapped in Jia's direction. She felt a tectonic shift in the air. Lisa stepped a fraction away as if she was afraid of her.

"I swear," Jia said, "I have no idea where this came from." She raised her palms. "Don't you guys get it? This proves the killer moved inside the house."

"But we checked all the rooms," Lisa said, wrapping her arms tight around herself. "Including this room. Right, Raj?"

Raj ran a jerky hand through his hair. "I checked that the rooms were empty. I didn't think of checking under every pillow."

"What about that one?" Lisa said, pointing at the other pillow, resting innocently on the mattress. Fear unfurled in Jia's chest, shaking her body.

Anticipation hovered like a thick fog pressing down on them. Their gazes bounced off each other.

Raj sucked his breath and edged closer to the bed. He glanced back once as if to say *Ready?* And lifted the pillow in one swift motion.

A gun lay near the head of the bed, its trigger pointing toward one of the floral bedspread's rosebuds.

Lisa erupted in a hysterical shriek.

Jia doubled over, struggling to breathe. Lisa looked like she was about to throw up.

"Mom," Ishaan said. The way his brows were crinkled in fear made Jia's heart tremble. "Isn't that Vipul Uncle's gun? Where is he? And why is that in your room?"

Jia's stomach twisted. The gun.

Raj pulled an arm around Ishaan and nudged him away from Jia. "Hey, buddy, why don't you leave the room. Let the adults figure this out."

Once Lisa had led him away, Raj continued scrutinizing Jia.

Jia felt a gut punch, and her chest hitched so hard she felt afraid of collapsing.

"We can't touch anything here," Raj said. "It's part of the crime scene now."

Crime scene. A sense of dread filled Jia's insides at his words.

Raj said, "Let's keep this room closed for now."

They plodded back to the living area.

Seema sat at an awkward angle, one palm on Asha's chest, the other cupping her forehead, a flesh eye mask for her daughter. "What happened?" she whispered.

When Lisa brought her up to speed, murmuring in her ears, Seema's eyes glinted, and she mouthed to Jia, "I knew it."

Raj fetched a glass of water for Jia. "You seem pretty shaken up."

"Thanks," Jia said. She thanked him, surprised by the relief the cold water brought to her sore throat.

Minutes passed, and as she saw Lisa attempting to engage a still-rattled Ishaan in conversation, Jia felt light-headed with relief.

The chain. It proved beyond a shadow of doubt that Ishaan had nothing to do with this. Like a terrifying nightmare that lost its power the instant a person woke up, the notion of Ishaan killing someone already felt ridiculous, otherworldly.

How could she ever have suspected him of killing Vipul?

But just as hope buoyed her, the wary looks from Seema and Raj sank her back to despair.

For the others, the gun had shredded any remaining doubts about Jia.

Crime scene. Raj, who hadn't hesitated to stomp around Vipul's study, was careful about preserving the one bit of evidence that implicated Jia, and if his objective was to frame her, he'd succeeded because she had no allies.

She would never be able to piece together the shards of her broken relationship with Seema because Seema would always see her as a home-wrecker.

A deep roar of thunder erupted, as if an earthquake had ruptured the sky. Winds blew against the house, and this time Jia sensed a familiar emotion lurking in the howling sounds.

It was the sound of mourning.

How did the gun get under the pillow? After the damning texts and the gun, all her resources would be funneled to securing her own freedom.

In the morning, once the rainwater receded, cops and medical techs would swarm the area and passersby would gawk at the house marked with a yellow crime scene tape. The neighbors forced to discard their moldy furniture on their lawns would exchange secret grateful glances. *Sure, our carpet was destroyed, but at least we're not dealing with murder.*

When the formal inquiry began, who would stay with Ishaan if the detectives whisked her away for questioning? Jia's chest froze. Did police stations have play areas? She was still paying back Hanna's fees in installments. How could she afford another attorney? Where would she even find a criminal attorney? How would Ishaan's school principal react when she found out Jia was involved in a murder case?

Jia's head pounded as the questions ricocheted in her brain.

The reality of her situation came crashing down, knocking the wind out of her.

Ishaan's well-being was the fulcrum of her existence, but was it in Ishaan's best interests to stay with her? For the first time, she wasn't sure.

The answer came to her in a flash, something buried within her all along and yet it filled her with unbearable agony. Divorce was not her rock bottom. This right here was the nadir of her life.

She looked at her phone. Her chest felt hollow. Blinking through the teardrops falling on the screen, she drafted an email to Hanna.

Each syllable hurt to type.

When she was done, she hit send before she could change her mind.

We don't need to fight for custody. I would like
for Ishaan to stay with his dad in Chicago.

THIRTY-THREE

Sending the email was just the beginning; now she'd have to face the person whose life was about to be turned upside down again.

Pulling Ishaan to a narrow passageway near Grandma's room on the pretext of checking on her, she decided that for the first time that night, she was going to be straight with him.

"Someone has hurt Vipul Uncle. He's dead."

He gasped, pushed his glasses up, his lips a circle of shock.

"And Rafael's dead too," Jia said. "I'm sorry for not being straight with you earlier."

"Who did it? Are we safe?" Ishaan asked. He grabbed her. "Mom, the gun in your room! Do you think the killer was coming after you?"

"I don't know," Jia said. She couldn't bring herself to meet his eyes. He'd reciprocated her doubts about him with unwavering faith in her.

"Can we not just leave?" Ishaan said, and Jia was struck by the resilience of a kid's mind, readily accepting these disturbing facts, focusing on the present.

"Soon we will," Jia said. "But until then, you have to stick with me."

Ishaan nodded and with a wry smile, added, "We're a team, right?" And as he hugged Jia, she sniffed his hair, sending a dopamine shot through her.

Pulling back, he said, "Mom! I know who can save us. Call Dad."

"What?"

"He'll help us. He helped me with my suspension and I'm sure he'll know what to do."

Jia sighed. "Your dad can't do anything for us from Chicago," she said. "We don't have time for this now. We've got to join the others; they'll be wondering what is taking us so long."

"Okay, but when you get the chance, can you try, please?" Ishaan said.

Jia nodded, bone-achingly tired, and staring at his eyes brimming with optimism, she saw the folly of her actions. By keeping Ishaan away from Dev and close to her, she'd transformed herself into a flawed caregiver, and him into a superhero, capable of solving Ishaan's problems from thousands of miles away.

THIRTY-FOUR

Back in the living room, they all reverted to their default seating positions, an all-night slumber party no one had asked to be a part of. They stared at the television screen on mute so as not to disturb Asha's sleep. With most of Houston underwater, the Texas National Guard had been activated, but in a do-it-yourself Texas spirit, people had stopped waiting for authorities to rescue them, instead relying on a network of volunteers who had sprung into action, responding to pleas on social media from people sharing their locations and asking for rescue. Using their personal boats, volunteers drove out into inundated areas to conduct their own rescue operations, whether it was pulling out a roomful of senior citizens trapped in a care facility, or a family trapped in an attic. In a stunning gesture of goodwill, members of the Cajun Army, a Louisiana volunteer group of private boat owners, crossed state lines to help their neighbors.

The television played a video of a girl in waist-deep water hoisting a dog onto a boat while two news anchors, likely sitting in a studio thousands of miles away from the wreckage, discussed in calm voices the path to economic recovery and rebuilding.

Rebuilding? Did that mean the worst of the storm was behind them?

"Mom, does this mean we'll be able to go home soon?" Ishaan asked.

When Jia patted his arm in agreement, Seema's eyes narrowed to slits and she crossed her arms. "You think you can walk away after everything that happened here? Should I ask Ishaan to look at the study?"

A chill gripped Jia. Lisa and Raj stared at Seema, shocked.

Was there no bottom to the depths of Seema's cruelty?

How could she sit next to her own slumbering child and suggest Jia's son experience the horror of seeing the rotting body of his dead uncle?

Jia placed her hand on Ishaan's shoulder. "My son's not going anywhere." It was one thing for her to hold a grudge against Jia, but Ishaan deserved better.

Seema had paced the hospital waiting room for hours, excited for the arrival of her first nephew. While the nurse swaddled the baby, Seema had clasped Jia's hand and said, "What do you think of the name 'Ishaan'?"

Raj pinched the bridge of his nose and squeezed his eyes shut. After opening them again, he threw his hands up. "Guys, look, we're all sleep-deprived. But if we must get through this night, it's important we stick together." He sighed and turned to Seema. "We can't turn on each other."

Seema's lips were flattened to a thin line, but after a brief pause, she gave a small nod.

Once again, the lights went out. The darkness was a blindfold, but by now, Jia's eyes quickly adjusted to the lack of light, her hand automatically reaching for Ishaan, preventing him from getting up and knocking his leg on the coffee table.

When Raj aimed his flashlight up, projecting a white beacon at the ceiling, Seema hissed, "Keep that thing away from Asha or you'll wake her up. And keep your voices down."

"Forget it," Raj said, sounding tired. "We'll just keep candles on all the time."

A click of a lighter. A flicker of a flame aglow. More clicks. Faint yellow light dispersed as Raj and Lisa lit five candles, methodically situating them around the room as if setting up a séance.

After the night she'd had, the cloying scents of rose and honeydew made Jia feel sick to her stomach.

Raj bunched his shoulders. "At least this way we won't have to worry about batteries running out."

Ishaan tapped Jia's arm. "Mom, I need to use the restroom," he whispered slowly.

In the darkness, she could see that his hands were clenched together, and from the way his face was lowered, Jia understood he wasn't ready to go alone.

Jia and Ishaan skulked down the hallway, the path illuminated by her phone's light.

Opening the door of the powder room, she positioned the phone on the basin. "I'm going to be right out here if you need anything."

Ishaan blinked rapidly, and beads of sweat popped on his upper lip.

"Hey," she said, steadying his hand. "I'll wait here till you go." She nudged him. "Go on."

While she waited outside for him to finish, a flash of realization jolted her like a lightning current.

The bathroom—not this powder room but the attached study bathroom—had two doors: one opening into the main passage and one that opened straight into the study.

An ideal location for the killer to hide.

Her teeth chattering, she waited for Ishaan to emerge, and when he did, she asked him to join the others.

Alone, she went down the hallway and doubled back toward the study. When she opened the bathroom door, a wave flowed out, drenching her feet. The bathroom was flooded, the pristine white tiles submerged in filth, a rancid stench suffusing the air.

Cold water lapped against her ankles as she pulled up the flashlight app on her phone and scanned every corner. The basin was spotless. Nothing out of the ordinary. She opened the cabinets one by one but didn't see anything.

Giving up, she set the phone on the basin, splashed cold water on her face, and wiped her skin with a soft napkin. In the dim foggy light, the image staring back at her in the mirror was wretched—disheveled hair, dark under-eye circles.

When she picked up her phone, its light passed momentarily over the door opening into the study.

Terror gripped her heart. The phone nearly slipped from her hands.

She seized it and fixed the light on the doorknob.

Her knees turned wobbly, and she had to grip the basin for support.

She must be hallucinating.

A rush of blood roared in her ears as she gaped open-mouthed at the door.

A knob enclosed in a child-safe pink cover.

But visible on the bottom of its surface, a small but clearly distinguishable spot of blood.

And within the bloodstain, clear as day, the mark of a single smudged fingerprint. An imprint of a hasty thumb.

Jia's hands flew to her mouth, and she pressed her palms tight to stop herself from making a sound.

Her head swiveled between the two bathroom doors. One door led into the hallway from which Jia had entered moments ago, while the other door opened into the study.

What if Raj had been hiding here, biding his time?

All the tension seemed to evaporate from her. The chain, the messages, none of that mattered.

Because this tiny smudge of Vipul's blood bore the killer's fingerprint.

Here was evidence that didn't incriminate her.

Here was her ticket to freedom.

Her phone blinked once, then twice before beeping with a low-battery alert.

She pulled up the camera app to take a picture of the stain.

The phone beeped again before she could focus.

A rolling thunderclap. The door flung open.

"Mom."

Ishaan grabbed her arm, maneuvering through the floodwater with ungainly steps. "Mom, come with me."

"One second," she pressed.

"No, Mom, the living room is flooding. You've got to see it."

Reluctantly, Jia depressed the power button to turn off the phone.

THIRTY-FIVE

The vivid memory of the red bloodstain, although indelible in her mind, wasn't enough. She needed *admissible evidence*, for which she would have to come back to take a picture.

They trudged back to the semi-dark living room, the carpet sodden, water levels creeping up. Raj and Lisa peered out the windows like zoo animals. Asha, now awake, nuzzled in Seema's arms.

The living room was saturated with rainwater. The retention ponds behind the backyard had steadily collected stormwater, keeping the floods at bay from that direction, but they were not built for a prolonged period of unceasing rain. Between that and the flooded study, the house would be uninhabitable within an hour.

Bursts of rain misted the windows. Although the torrential showers had reduced and daybreak was tantalizingly close, the sky remained resolutely dark.

Strong winds rattled the bay windows. The glass vibrated like it was shaking loose.

Gale-force winds struck again, and with a deafening crack the backyard wooden fence broke, a chunk of its middle portion caving under pressure. The remaining planks bent and swayed under the force of the wind, ready to buckle any moment and join their cohorts on the ground.

With a gaping hole in the fence, floodwater accumulated in the yard, turning it into a pool. Dead tree limbs bobbed in the water. Turbid waves smashed against the wall.

Another loud crack was followed by a rolling clap of thunder.

Suddenly, Seema shrieked. Asha mimicked her mother with an eardrum-splitting scream of her own. Seema gesticulated wildly at the window, and following her gaze, Jia gasped.

In the outskirts of the yard, the utility pole bent at an ominous angle. Steel wires crisscrossed at the top. Heavy gusts picked up speed, ramming into the tall structure.

Collective moans around her.

The pole was fighting the wind and losing, wires attached to it snapping like puppeteer strings as it swayed down, down, down . . .

"Run," Raj yelled. They scrambled for cover.

A second later, a deafening boom exploded through the interior.

Her ears ringing, Jia dared open her eyes. She caught her breath. They'd made it, but just barely. Ishaan's perspiring form clung to her. The lengthy pole had fallen right inside the living room, shattering the coffee table, flinging glass shards like shrapnel.

When the study had begun to flood, the water had dribbled in slowly, but now a torrent of brown floodwaters gushed in as if someone were armed with a hose on the outside.

Within seconds, freezing water filled with debris rapidly rose to their knees. The wind extinguished all but two of the candles flickering weakly on the fireplace mantel.

Sweatpants folded up to his knees, Raj stared, horrified, at a giant cylindrical box attached to the front of the pole by tangled wires. "If that thing is a transformer, this whole place is a fire hazard. We could all be electrocuted in seconds."

Jia and Ishaan scrambled up the stairs. The only person handling this turn of events remarkably well was Asha, squealing happily, perched on Seema's hip, pointing to the filthy water lashing against their skin, delighted with this "floor is lava" game brought to life.

Seema stared agape at the destroyed living room, looking devastated. "Can someone help me move the sofa upstairs, please?"

"Forget the stuff. There's no time," Raj yelled. "We need to get to higher ground now!"

He scuttled off down the corridor and reappeared carrying Grandma in his arms. He lifted her up the stairs, her wrinkled hand clenched on his arm, the loose end of her saree wet and brown as it dragged through the water. The rest followed him upstairs.

"Where's Vipul?" asked Grandma, her eyes bleary, as if she'd woken up from an unusually deep sleep.

The darkness shrouded Raj's expression, but his voice was strained. "Vipul is in the garage. He's making sure we have all the supplies we may need."

On reaching the top of the landing, Raj put Grandma on her feet, but her balance was off. She nearly slipped, and gripped Raj for support. Suppressing a yawn, she asked again, "Where's Vipul?"

Raj said, "Are you okay? Let's get you to a room where you can get some rest."

Grandma shooed Raj away. "Now go help your brother. Don't let him stay down there for long. A house can be replaced, people can't."

After settling her into the kids' bedroom, Raj said, "We can try asking for help again and hope someone from the National Guard comes out to rescue us in time."

"And if they don't?" Lisa asked softly.

Raj said, "Let's not think about that."

Jia's chest hurt. Suddenly, the house didn't feel very much like a house.

It felt like a tomb.

THIRTY-SIX

They'd seen death up close that night. Two lives taken under the most horrific of circumstances. Yet when they were faced with an imminent threat to their own lives, another emotion surpassed raw grief: determination to survive. The knowledge that multiple bodies were decomposing beneath them was stowed away like the duffel bag with passports wedged in the top shelf of the main bedroom closet.

"What's the plan? We wait this out in the attic?" Lisa asked. Her arms were wrapped tightly around herself, shoulders slouching.

Raj shook his head. "When both the floors flood completely, the attic won't be safe either."

Seema held up her hands. "We can't just sit here and wait to die." Her hair was frayed, and her voice had a hysterical edge.

Raj puffed his cheeks. "The roof is our best option."

Seema and Jia's eyes found each other. Seema's eyes bulged and her lips parted, and Jia supposed she too was picturing them with two children and an elderly person, stranded on the roof under pummeling rainfall, waiting for help.

Raj inhaled deeply, letting his breath out in a whistle. "I'm going to climb into the attic." Turning to Seema and Lisa, he said, "We need to find something to break into the roof. Like a hammer or an axe."

From her vantage point at the top of the stairs, Jia saw the swelling water rising in the living room, and her heart started beating so fast, blood pounded her ears. Soon the house would flood, the only bit of evidence in her favor, the killer's fingerprint, decimated in the incoming waves.

Raj had come up with a plan to save their present. But Jia had to safeguard her and Ishaan's future.

Kneeling beside Ishaan, Jia said, "Listen, I must go downstairs. I'll be back quickly. You stay here and promise me, if I tell you to run, you'll run outside."

Ishaan nodded; then he looked at her directly. "Are we going to die?"

His face was upturned, the morbid question posed not in fear but with simple childlike curiosity.

Jia cupped his chin in her hands. "No one is dying. Now, promise me, if anything happens, you'll try your best to swim out. You won't look for me." She gestured at his chest. "The water is deep, but you remember the swimming lessons you took?"

Ishaan bobbed his head up and down, full attention on Jia.

Jia smiled. "I know you can show everyone what a great swimmer you are."

When Ishaan replied, "I'll keep swimming not to run away, but to get help for us," Jia's limbs became light as if she were floating. She pulled him into a tight hug and wiped away her tears.

Jia whispered, "I love you. And I'm going to get us back home."

THIRTY-SEVEN

Jia snuck down the staircase, and coming closer to the bottom, she came to an abrupt halt, foot suspended midair. A gagging sensation overcame her as a pungent rotten stench hung over the air, as though the floor were a farm of decaying vegetables, the moldy stench as solid as the thick slime sticking to the bar stools.

One hand cupped firmly over her nose, she stepped in the knee-deep rainwater, cold against her body. She floundered down the hallway, feet numb, stepping over a toppled lamp, much like the character Rose in *Titanic*, if instead of the Atlantic Ocean, the *Titanic* had sunk into sewage.

Floorboards creaked in the distance. Jia jumped. A thump of metal hitting the floor. Shaking her head, she closed her eyes and pressed a palm to her thudding chest. That was only Raj lowering the ladder to the attic.

She could preserve the smudge on the bathroom knob with tape, but central to her plan was a photograph—a picture of the smeared fingerprint she would thrust in the detective's hands. *I'm not your prime suspect. I'm your main witness.*

Her nerve endings tingling with apprehension, Jia clomped down the passage. A wave of dread swelled inside her, and by the time she reached the bathroom, her thighs were immersed in flood-water.

She opened the door with a feeling of hopelessness, a part of her already knowing this wouldn't work.

No.

The bloodstain was gone. The knob itself had disappeared under liquid waste.

The edges of her vision blurry, she staggered toward the shut door.

Full-body tremors jolted through Jia. In the end she had been bested not by Vipul's killer, but by the rising waters. Jia pressed her palms against her eyes.

Her insides twisted. Vipul, dead, lying on the other side.

That's it. Vipul.

She'd dwelled on all the other family members, analyzing their motives, actions, all while neglecting the most important question.

Why was Vipul up late at night, alone in his study?

What was so important that he waited for everyone to sleep and went to the study by himself?

There was only one way to find out.

When she entered the study, Jia clamped her mouth as nausea roiled her stomach. The stench outside was nothing compared to the foul sickly odor attacking her nostrils.

Vipul was bloated, jaw stiff, one leg jutting out at an awkward angle and his body tilted to one side—he was in danger of toppling off the chair at any moment. The smell of his decay, like rotting meat left out in the sun, was stuck in her throat, as though she were inhaling a part of Vipul with every breath, and this was the last straw for her insides. Wrenching her eyes away from him, she heaved, and her vomit floated repulsively.

She didn't want to stay here a second more than she had to.

As she picked up the laptop from the desk, the silver metal chilled her fingers like the rainwater below. Jia pressed the power button and brought the screen to life. She glanced toward the hall, but if she stepped outside, someone might spot her. She had to do this under Vipul's dead gaze.

The screen was locked, instructing her to either plug in a pass code or scan a finger.

Attempts to unlock by entering Seema, Asha, and Vipul's birthdays proved futile. A part of Jia had known this wouldn't work, her guesses were too obvious, but she'd made a half-hearted effort nonetheless because the alternative terrified her.

Jia glanced at Vipul's lifeless form.

An acidic feeling rose in the back of her throat. Her teeth clenched, horrified at the prospect of what she would have to do next.

Lips pinched, breath held in one long inhale, she dragged her feet close to Vipul, and lifting his cold index finger, she pressed it on the thumbnail-sized scanner near the keyboard.

The background wallpaper disappeared. She was in.

A fibrous material scratched against her bare feet. Jia swore, the laptop slipped out of her hands, but she managed to hold onto it at the last second. An upside-down sandal emblazoned with crystals bobbed in the brown water.

Sweat beads popped on her forehead, and she slumped against the wall. Footfalls in the distance. Jia pressed her temples. This wasn't going to work. She peeked out of the study. The last thing she needed was for someone to catch her snooping through Vipul's electronics.

The document open on the laptop was a form of sorts. Vipul had filled it out halfway, typing in his email address, phone number. She looked up at Vipul, his mouth slack, and briefly felt a surge of pity for him, his last moments on earth wasted on idle paperwork.

She started to snap the laptop shut when two words on the form caught her eye.

The ground beneath her feet seemed to tilt on its axis. The words grew bigger, the weight of their implications hitting her with the force of a freight train.

Alleged Father

Jia's heart stopped.
She knew who had killed Vipul.

THIRTY-EIGHT

Jia was dizzy, adrenaline pulsing through her veins. She had to share this information with someone outside because it was too dangerous to keep to herself, and there was only one person, one person in the world, she hoped would do the right thing, if not for her, then for Ishaan.

Her phone battery on life support, she quickly pulled up their chat. He'd been nothing but mean and condescending to her all night, but the unalterable fact was: He was Ishaan's dad. She thumbed a text with madly shaking fingers.

Ishaan is in danger. Seema killed Vipul.

A slimy feeling on her left ankle. An involuntary jerk.

The slithering sensation intensified.

Lifting her leg, she saw two separate earthworms crawling on her skin.

Jia yelped and stomped her foot. The worms slipped off, but the phone dropped from her hands, falling into the dark water with a splash.

Nooooo.

Jia went on all fours, groping blindly in the dark.

A rotting stench saturated her nostrils, a floating tree branch poked into her flesh, and though her grubby hands writhed in the muck, it was useless.

Her phone, the last connection to the outside world, was severed. So close yet out of her reach. The text had gone through, right?

She had no way of knowing if Dev got her SOS, but the water was moving fast, Vipul's wheeled chair creaking with movement, his head lolling.

She had to get out of here.

Back in the living room, her elbows clutched to her sides, Jia peered out the gaping hole in the bay windows.

The house was eerily quiet. The patter of rain had become such a constant, ubiquitous sound that its absence now felt as if someone had pressed a mute button. She was unarmed, but her strongest weapon was intangible: The mechanics of Vipul's murder were a patchwork of guesses, but the *why* was incontrovertible, seared in her mind, a phrase she repeated like a mantra.

QuickTest Lab Services. Order #5462.

Jia ascended the curving stairs to the second story, where the attic stairs had been lowered onto the floor.

Raj, crouched at the entrance of the attic, hollered, "Oh, great, you're here." His hair was disheveled, face glistening with sweat, shirt discolored in spots by perspiration. "I think I'll be able to find a way through the attic space big enough for us to climb to the roof. Come upstairs and wait with Seema. I'll join you guys at the end."

He stood there expectantly, looking impatient. Jia's body started shaking uncontrollably, and she crossed her arms tightly to hide her quaking hands. "You go ahead. I . . . Ishaan and I will stay here."

Raj scratched his temple. "Stay here? What do you mean stay here? It's not safe."

He gestured to the bottom floor to prove his point, although he didn't need to. In the few seconds of their conversation, the middle steps of the curving staircase, dry when Jia had climbed them, had disappeared under roiling water. Yet being here in the open was less scary than walking into the dark hollow of the attic, entering her own coffin.

"We'll take our chances," Jia said. She glanced around. "Where's Ishaan?"

Raj blinked uncomprehendingly. "Are you afraid of closed spaces or something? Listen, we don't have time. Let me help you." He outstretched his hand, and when he descended the first steps, Jia staggered backward.

Terror seized her body like a vise grip. "Stop," she warned. "Where's Ishaan?"

Raj threw his hands up. "He's with Lisa, Asha, and Grandma. We don't have time, I need everyone upstairs. Lisa will stay back in the attic with Grandma and the kids while you, Seema, and I will fan out on the roof to flag for rescue."

Ducking his head, he went into the attic, and Jia didn't have a choice but to follow him with wobbly steps.

Inside, Seema was hunched in the back, her hair brushing against the sloping ceiling. A flashlight in her hands emitted a feeble light in the dark space. Seema's teeth chattered even though she had put on an oversized black jacket, and she fixed Jia with a cold stare.

A musky smell like that of a cave permeated the attic space. The walls were plastered with polystyrene-like foam material, and giant foil-covered pipes wound across the ceiling.

Every inch of the area screamed that this wasn't a space built for human beings.

A stray rat scuttled across the floor.

Seema yelled.

Raj said, "I've found an opening into the roof." He led them into the bowels of the attic where a ladder was set against the wall. At the ceiling a skylight was latched open, the glass pane opened upward at an angle, supported by two poles like a car hood.

Seema moved up the ladder, and Jia followed suit, her feet slippery on the wet steps.

While Seema awkwardly pulled herself out onto the roof on all fours, Jia stood on the top rung of the ladder, palms flat against the roof, and gasped.

She was awestruck. Even on this most surreal of nights, the sight took her breath away.

All the houses had relocated to the ocean, transforming the suburban street into a row of beachfront homes inundated under high tide.

The bottom halves of homes and trees were swallowed by floodwater, front yards turned into swimming pools, tree crowns protruding like giant shrubs from the surface of the ocher water.

Texas earth had silently put up with years of drilling, its soft depths plumbed again and again, all in pursuit of the release of that precious ill-begotten liquid: oil.

But tonight, nature had spoken, unleashing fury, its wrath razing decades of infrastructure.

Jia sank into despair. Floodwaters were rising, slowly but surely, and although the rain had reduced to a drizzle, it wasn't enough.

Jia strained to hear anything—the hum of a rescue chopper, a boat driving by—but there was nothing.

"You coming?" Seema called, and Jia reluctantly raised her legs out, then moved to the right of the window, struggling to gain a foothold on the slippery asphalt shingles, crouching like an animal. Looking at the wide swaths of water from this height made her head spin like she was experiencing vertigo, and she forced herself to turn away from the street toward Seema, who was sitting at the ridge joining the two sloping halves of the roof, knees pulled up, hands wrapped around the chimney for dear life.

When Seema beckoned for her to join her, Jia's heartbeats sped up, and her mind performed mental gymnastics trying to separate her inner turmoil from her physical demeanor. "I . . ." Jia forced her cadence into steadiness. "Didn't Raj say we should spread out so we have better chances for flagging rescue?"

"Is that so?" Seema said, her lips curling. "Or are you afraid I'm going to kill you?"

THIRTY-NINE

White-hot panic flooded Jia's veins. She almost lost her balance. "I don't know what you're talking about," she said, dumbstruck.

Seema arched an eyebrow. "I know you know. How did you figure it out?"

Jia was silent, scrambling for words, when Seema made a slight movement, her hand nudging closer to her coat pocket.

Jia's senses went on high alert. She had a gut feeling that the action, while subtle, was not without purpose.

"Please don't," Jia croaked just as Seema pulled out a gun.

"Sorry," Seema said, aiming it straight at Jia. "I wish it didn't have to come to this." There was a quiver in her voice, but her hand remained steady. "Now tell me how you found out."

Jia gulped. *Stay calm.*

But it was impossible to look at the black barrel and not think of Vipul's forehead obliterated by this very weapon. Everything seemed to slip away in the background, everything but the gun pointed right at her.

"Answer me!" Seema yelled.

Jia's lungs felt unbearably tight, straining to expel breaths. Behind her, a sea of floodwater. In front of her, Seema's pistol. Where was Raj?

In order to live, she knew what she had to do: keep Seema talking.

"Your forehead," Jia said. "The painkiller you took for your bump. Vipul did that to you, using his bat to try to knock you down. He hit you, but apparently not hard enough to save his life. You knew your skin would bruise, and you had to hide the marks or come up with another explanation for them. That's why you launched into that performance of slamming your head against the wall in shock and grief."

Seema's fingers absently grazed her bruised skin. Jia inched herself infinitesimally closer to the skylight that led to the attic. "You were the first one to find me in the study because you were right there in the study bathroom. All you had to do was come out the door opening into the hallway and double back into the room."

Seema scoffed, and a part of her seemed to relax. "Sounds like all you have is a bunch of guesses. I had no reason to kill Vipul. He loved me."

"Would he still love you once he found out he isn't Asha's father?" Jia said.

Seema's mouth went slack-jawed. The confident mask slipped.

"Rafael is Asha's dad," Jia said.

An ugly blotch of red flushed Seema's rain-streaked face.

"Vipul complained about finding cigarette butts on the patio, which he thought were a sign of intruders, but they were Rafael's, weren't they? I found a photo of him with a cigarette online. And Asha's spurts of Spanish. She learned that from him, right? Vipul must have figured this out at some point tonight because he had collected Rafael's hair and was trying to fill out a paternity test form." Guilt stabbed painfully at Jia. All those times Vipul had asked her if Seema was having an affair and Jia had reassured him, squelching her own doubts. Why had she been so intent on preserving Seema's sham of a marriage?

Seema's face had turned from red to a sickly, ashen hue. Her grip seemed to loosen, and for a moment, the gun lowered and was not trained on Jia, but she collected herself quickly.

A slight shift to her left, and if Jia could get a little closer, she'd make a lunge back into the attic. "Why did you do this, Seema?"

Seema's nostrils flared. "I don't owe you an explanation. This is not a movie, Jia. And I'm not an idiot villain."

"But why?" Jia repeated, and despite her dry-mouthed fear for her life, she found herself desperate to know how her sister crossed the line from an adulteress to a killer.

Seema's shoulders slumped. "I had an affair when I was in my last semester of college. Rafael was friends with one of my classmates. What could I do? Vipul and Grandma were making me miserable. I was lonely, and Rafael gave me his undivided attention, made me feel special." She gave a sad laugh. "That is, until he found out I was pregnant. Then he got cold feet and said he didn't want to break up his family. God, I was afraid my kid would pop out with his hazel eyes and Vipul would throw me out of the house. But she looked just like me. Vipul didn't suspect anything at first. And there were times even I forgot that Asha wasn't his. He loved her like his own." Seema touched her throat. "Then, a few months ago, Rafael contacted me. He told me he'd gotten divorced, and from my Insta posts, he'd guessed that Asha might be his child. He wanted to see her and even rented the house across the street. We reconnected, but then Vipul started wondering whether I was having an affair. He kept fishing for information. Asking Asha if she saw Mommy with anyone else. I knew I was running out of time."

Seema's voice broke, and Jia could tell how much her sister longed to tell her side of the story.

"I had accepted my loveless marriage. Told myself Vipul was like another kid I'd be taking care of till I died. But Rafael brought me back to life. We chatted for hours, he knew all the cool bars in the city to hang out in, and he treated me like a queen, bringing me flowers, asking me how my day went and actually listening . . . But Vipul, he wanted a maid to cook and clean after him, and if that wasn't enough, he blamed me for not giving him a son, and I was forced to keep quiet even though I knew he was the one with fertility issues, not me." Seema's eyes glazed over. "Rafael talked about all the trips we could take once we weren't meeting in secret."

Jia felt sick. "You could've left Vipul instead of . . . this."

"And live a life like you?" Seema said. Her mouth twisted into a sneer. "Some of us like to enjoy our lives, thank you very much. You think Vipul would have let me walk away into the sunset with Asha? For the rest of my life, I'd be fighting him for every alimony payment, and I couldn't bear to let my friends look at me with pity, gossiping behind my back. Don't you see? There was no way for me to live the life I deserved with Vipul alive. But there is a quiet dignity in being a widow. Did you see how Raj looked at me, like he would move mountains for his poor widowed bhabhi? Do you think he'd even talk to me if he found out I cheated on his brother?"

Her jaw tightened. "And when I heard about the hurricane, it presented a perfect opportunity. We wouldn't have to worry about nosy neighbors once everyone evacuated. Our plan was to stage a burglary. Rafael was going to kill Vipul and make it look like someone broke into the study. I had to invite family because I needed witnesses who'd take my word and support me in front of the cops. After my dear Rafael died, I had to find a way to carry on with the

292

plan. Find someone else to help me." Seema's eyes welled up. "You would've done the same thing in my position."

Jia would categorically not do any of the things Seema had described, but there was no reasoning with her sister. "It's okay," Jia said. "Just let me go and I promise I won't tell anyone about this."

"Liar!" Seema screamed, cocking the gun straight back at her heart. "Stop lying to me, *Jianna*."

FORTY

Time seemed to stop.

Seema barked a laugh, and mimed typing on her cell-phone. "'I'm coming to get Ishaan.' Yes," she said. "I was the one who sent you those messages. I had to keep you distracted. Worried about someone else."

Jia was speechless.

Seema swiped a hand across her wet face. "He really did call me to ask me to look after Ishaan when they were predicting the storm would be dangerous. That part is true. And he's even been trying to reach me all night."

Seema showed her screen to Jia.

Dev (4) Missed calls.

"But once I saw how mentioning him sent you for a loop, I figured I'd keep you distracted and torture *you* with text messages for a change. I wanted you to experience firsthand the hurt your words to Vipul inflicted on me."

Jia pinched the bridge of her nose. "I already told you, nothing—"

"Did you think I'm stupid?" Seema said. "I knew about you and Vipul months ago." Her nostrils flared. "I saw the damn texts. And I immediately checked the contact information, expecting to see a message from some sleazy coworker, but lo and behold, what do I find, a note to my sister—'Miss you. Please talk to me.'" She gritted her teeth.

"You don't understand . . ."

"I don't care," Seema said. "You had a secret rendezvous with my husband, you sat on this information for months, and I gave you multiple chances to confess tonight, but what did you do? You lied to my face. I only pretended to find Vipul's texts after his death so Raj wouldn't think I had a motive."

Jia felt dazed, like the roof would give way beneath her feet. She'd been doomed from the minute she accepted Seema's invitation, lured under the pretext of safety when all her sister had in her heart was revenge.

A movement in her peripheral vision.

"All right," Raj said, emerging from the skylight headfirst, scrabbling out one leg at a time.

Seema hid her gun back in her pocket. Her eyes wide, a barely noticeable shake of the head. A warning.

Raj planted his feet into a wide lunge and spread his arms out like a toddler learning to balance, inching over to a semi-upright position near Jia. He looked at the skies before sweeping his gaze over the houses. "Looks like we made it out in the nick of time." He patted his shirt pocket. "I figured we'd need food if we're stuck here for hours, so I was in the pantry looking for stuff. I've got some biscuits right here. Bhabhi, you'll have to head back inside. Grandma and Lisa are trying to keep her distracted, but Asha's crying for her mama."

Instantly, Seema's eyebrows were drawn together in concern, and now she looked like a normal mom rushing to a crying child.

As she started shuffling down the roof toward the ladder, Jia blurted, "She killed Vipul."

Raj blinked confusedly, like he'd emerged from a car wreck. "What?"

Seema froze. Then she kept her eyes pinned on Raj and stuffed a hand in her pocket. Waiting.

But Jia's instincts told her that Seema wouldn't pull the trigger. Her sister had had a chunk of time alone with her with a loaded gun, and yet here she was alive.

At the end of the day, they were sisters. Seema could make Jia's life hell, but she couldn't end it.

"It's true," Jia said. "Rafael is Asha's dad. I saw the DNA form on Vipul's laptop. She's trying to frame me. Ask her why she has the gun in her pocket!"

An eerie calmness settled over Seema.

Raj stared at Seema, a pleading look in his eyes. "Please, Seema, tell your sister she's lost her mind."

Seema ignored Raj completely, instead addressing Jia. "You're so ungrateful. I wasn't trying to frame you. I was simply trying to get attention away from myself. Muddy the waters. Think, Jia. Think. The cops would find the jewelry in your room, but none of it would have your fingerprints on it. I'd use Vipul's insurance money to hire the best attorneys for you to get you off."

Raj clutched his chest like he was having a cardiac arrest, and Seema, so used to Jia's gratitude, looked at her expectantly as if Jia should thank her for having a plan to secure her freedom after implicating her in a murder.

"Vipul isn't Asha's dad," Raj repeated, in the careful way of someone practicing a new language, trying to slot the words into meaning. His face blanched and he looked ill.

Jia said, "You said it had to be one of us, and I'm telling you it's her."

Raj stared at Seema in disgust as if seeing her properly for the first time.

"Oh, don't look at me that way," Seema said. "It's all Grandma's fault. That old crone has never liked me," she continued bitterly. "If she wasn't obsessed with a grandson to carry the family name, none of this would've happened. She poisoned Vipul's mind for a grandson, and devoted son that he is, he decided on my behalf that we should have a second child. Not that he would ever think of consulting me on these important decisions. If we hadn't started trying for another child, Vipul may never have suspected Asha wasn't his."

"Are you trying to pin this on an eighty-year-old woman?" Raj asked. "Do you have any idea how she's going to feel once she finds out about Vipul? I don't know how she'll be able to handle it, I'm afraid this will kill her. She's not feeling well as it is. I've been worried about her, she's never seemed so out of sorts . . ."

A blush crept up Seema's cheeks, and Jia remembered Grandma's unsarcastically confused demeanor when Raj woke her. The pills Seema had pushed on Jia.

A fresh horror whipped through Jia. "Did you drug her?"

"Relax. I just slipped some melatonin in her milk so she would stay asleep."

Raj looked aghast. "What? You asked me to bring her the milk." His face contorted as though he had been poisoned. "Vipul dying was bad enough. And now this—" His face was twisted in genuine anguish, his horror in contrast with Seema's calmness.

Her sister's unflappable appearance discomfited Jia, and even as things were becoming clearer, Jia felt like she was still missing something, blinded to something obvious right in front of her. She directed her gaze back at Seema. She hadn't wasted a second defending herself in front of Raj.

Seema was outnumbered, two to one. But her lack of fear terrified Jia.

Her sister hadn't even bothered to pull out the gun.

Like she didn't need to, as if she still had an ace up her sleeve. Something to silence both Raj and Jia.

In a flash of burning panic, her memory fished out Seema's words: *Find a way to carry on with the plan. Find someone else to help me . . .*

Someone else.

Jia's spine went rigid.

"Whoa . . . so much water . . ."

Jia's tongue felt thick. She knew that voice better than her own. And even before she jerked to her left, she knew her worst nightmare was coming true.

Ishaan climbed out onto the roof, and right behind him, Lisa.

FORTY-ONE

shaan," Jia cried, and Ishaan tried to wriggle his hand out of Lisa's, but she held onto his arm and took a step backward, away from the skylight, closer to the water. Ishaan sat slanted, one palm on the roof panel, his other hand in Lisa's clutches.

Seema said, "Not so fast."

"Stay here, Ishaan," Lisa said. She turned to Jia. "Tell him."

Her chin trembling, Jia said, "Ishaan, listen to Lisa Auntie. Stay there." Her lungs hurt as if she couldn't breathe.

"Lisa?" Raj said, his breaths coming out in rasps. He started to speak, but only groaning sounds emerged from his mouth, as though his vocal cords were malfunctioning. "You? . . . No . . . That's not possible. Have you lost your mind?" he croaked.

Lisa flinched like she had been slapped. "Just let me explain, Raj. I did this for us. I was just trying to get enough money for one last round of IVF treatments. My mom almost gave up before she had me, and I didn't want to make the same mistake."

The black circles on Lisa's waist flashed in Jia's mind; the bruises were not signs of abuse but side effects of multiple injections.

"So, we ran out of money," Raj said, his voice rising. "And you . . ." He glanced at Ishaan, swallowed.

Jia pleaded with Lisa, clasping her hands. "Please let Ishaan go."

"I don't understand," Raj said. "I thought Seema hated you."

"That's exactly why I chose her," Seema said. "After Rafael died, I had to kill Vipul myself and find someone to establish my alibi. No one would suspect us of working together. Honestly, I've never been a big fan of Lisa ever since she became Grandma's favorite. No offense."

"None taken," Lisa said.

"When Lisa came to me after Vipul refused to loan her money, I asked her to be my alibi. In turn, I would help her." Seema looked at Raj. "Help you *both* out."

"Don't hurt Ishaan," Jia begged.

Raj stared in shock at his wife as if she were an alien. "Do you see yourself? Saying you did all this for us to have children. You're literally holding a child hostage." He winced. "Do you even like kids?"

"No!" Lisa blurted. "But I was still willing to go all this way, for you. Don't you see how much I love you?"

"This isn't love," Raj said, disgusted. "If you'd been honest with me, I'd have happily adopted a dog and lived the rest of my life with you. I don't care about that stuff. But this . . ."

Seema said briskly, "All right. Someone's gonna rescue us eventually. Now, we're family and families don't turn on one another. There's only one way out of this. We all have to stick to a story of an intrusion. A burglar killed Vipul. All the evidence is going to be wiped out anyway."

"Family?" Raj spat. "You're talking about family after killing my brother? Don't think for a second that I'm going to let you get away with this."

"Really?" Seema snapped. "Think of your mother. What will you tell her?" She counted on her fingers. "Her son is dead. His wife did it. Her favorite daughter-in-law helped her. Her beloved grand-daughter is not hers. Do you think her ancient heart will be able to handle all of that? Once the drugs wear off, she'll have questions, none of which you'll have any answers for."

Raj turned speechless. He covered his face in his hands, repeating "This cannot be happening."

Seema flicked her gaze to Jia. "You have to understand. I'm just looking out for my kid, the same way you are. Don't I have the right to start a new life?" She gestured toward Lisa. "And doesn't she deserve a chance to keep her marriage intact?"

Jia took deep breaths. Two women both using marriage as a shield for their despicable acts. They'd colluded in the murder, and while Seema had done it to end her marriage and reinvent herself, Lisa had done it to keep her marriage alive.

"Don't you need my signature on your character statement?" Seema said. "I'll help you keep custody of Ishaan."

Ishaan squirmed in Lisa's grip.

"We'll need one more thing, a confession from you," added Seema, all businesslike. "For backup. In case you have a change of heart."

Raj said, "Don't let her bully you."

Jia put on a show, furrowing her brows in concentration as if contemplating Seema's offer, but she'd spotted something else out of the corner of her eye.

Shriveled fingers wrapped around the window frame on a corner of the skylight. A sliver of a familiar bronze handle.

A beat. Then the window was shrouded in dark once more.

Was that a mirage?

There was only one way to find out.

"I'll do it," she said over Raj's protests. "Let's all go back inside and I'll sign wherever you say."

Seema smiled, triumphant. Raj lowered his head in crushing disappointment, but it was only Lisa whom Jia cared about. Lisa, who held onto Ishaan but who had now moved toward the attic, placing herself directly in line with the skylight opening.

"Grandma, now!" Jia yelled hoarsely.

Nothing happened. Lisa, alarmed, started to step back.

The next instant, a blur of wood thrust out. Grandma's walking cane sliced through the air, its shaft whomping Lisa's leg.

A cry of pain. Lisa doubled over. Ishaan wrested himself free from her grip and clambered toward Jia. At the same time, Raj lunged at Lisa, pinning her down.

"Stop," Seema warned from her position at the rooftop.

Ishaan hobbled in her direction. He was close now. Jia held out her arm, their hands grazed—but then his steps faltered on the slippery roof.

"Slow down!" Jia screamed.

But Ishaan lost his balance, stumbling on the wet shingles.

She made a grab for him, and her fingertips brushed his shirt. But it was no use; he went tumbling down.

Her mouth dry, stomach twisted in sheer terror, she watched her boy slide like a ragdoll down the roof. Then he fell off the edge with a gut-wrenching splash, instantly swallowed up by the opaque water.

At the edge, she screamed Ishaan's name till she was hoarse, casting her eyes about wildly, looking for a ripple, trying to see in which direction to jump.

"Raj, help!" Jia yelled. He started moving toward Jia, but Lisa punched him in the back. Raj whipped around, grabbing her throat.

"Raj, stop," Seema yelled. "This is your last warning."

A single gunshot pierced the air.

"Oh Goddd . . ." Seema's anguished scream filled her ears, and simultaneously a searing pain spread through Jia. Her limbs went loose.

Rolling down the roof, she crashed off, free-falling into the water, and by this time her arm was in such a blinding agony that the last thought she had before going completely underwater, before cold water filled her lungs and obscured her sight, was quite simple: Death wouldn't be so bad after all.

FORTY-TWO

Jia's nose broke the surface of water, and she was grateful for a
miniscule intake of oxygen. Contrary to her mental resignation, her physical faculties weren't ready to give up just yet,
her body reduced to a molecular mass desperately seeking air. Her
eardrums burst with frigid water, tongue tasted metallic as a stream
of her own blood fanned out in the water, her windpipe burning in
anguish.

Thrashing upward, she emerged for a millisecond before going
underwater again, but in this short span, her watery retinas registered something.

Limbs wrapped around a tree bough.

Ishaan.

She worked her own limbs into a frenzy, sheer panic for survival
bolstered by a desire to see him again.

She flailed desperately, willing her body to float up, and this
time when she resurfaced, he waved.

He'd seen her.

She pushed herself to flap forward before coming up again,

coughed up water. She had to be getting closer because she saw him clearly now, torso parallel with the mossy tree trunk.

But then her heart sank.

She wasn't getting closer. He was on the move, lowering himself down.

Abandoning his safety to get to her.

"No," she screamed, but her voice was too frail. Her bleeding arm was limp. She was going to pass out.

A hum of a motor in the distance. Ishaan cocked his head in that direction. He'd heard it too.

Jia pushed past her pain, projecting herself upward, and her and Ishaan's mouths opened simultaneously in perfect harmony, like they were sharing a body once again, their voices merging into a unified scream.

"*Helppppp* . . ." Their shrieks ricocheted across the air.

The drone of the boat got progressively louder, Jia's throat closed up, but Ishaan kept screaming.

Help was here. Ishaan was safe.

Her arm felt like it was on fire. Exhaustion pulled her under. The pain was too much to bear, and this time Jia closed her eyes because it was easier to submit to the waiting void.

FORTY-THREE

When she came to, the first thing she discerned was a man's beard and a flash of orange, and for a brief hallucinatory second, she thought she'd died. She tried to focus. A hard, wet seat vibrating beneath her legs, the whirr of a motor. Houses flying by in a blur. The smell of perspiration hitting her nostrils.

She was in a boat crammed with people. Some of them had backpacks on; some sat empty-handed, likely having hurried out at a moment's notice.

Ishaan tugged at her elbow. "Mom, you're okay." He had a warm towel on his shoulders, and when he hugged her, Jia winced and noticed her right arm was wrapped in a tourniquet. They'd made it.

Shafts of light parted the cloudy sky.

Mom said that Surya, the sun god, was humanity's true savior.

The bearded man came over to her, clad in a bright life jacket. He said, "You're lucky, the bullet only grazed your skin, and we happened to have a vet on board. But we need to get you to a hospital. I have some Tylenol on hand for the pain." Jia heartily gulped down the medication, shutting her eyes, waiting for it to work its way through her bloodstream, numbing her.

Through the haze, she felt a jolt of alarm. "Wait," she said, snapping her eyes open. "Please, you have to go back," she urged them. "We have people stranded in that house."

"Ma'am, don't worry," said the man patiently. "Your kid already told us about your situation. But our boat is full. I've made a call and another boat is on its way."

Jia's breathing steadied. "Are you with the National Guard?"

"Nope," he said. "Cajun Army, ma'am. From Louisiana. We're local volunteers with boats of our own. A buddy of ours sent us an alert. Your ex-husband contacted a friend of his cousin asking for help. He said he saw on the news how badly houses were flooded in the suburb, and when he couldn't reach your sister, he panicked. We added your name to the list of neighborhoods we drove by and then we heard your son shouting for help."

"I told you," Ishaan said, beaming. "Dad found a way. Like always."

Jia squeezed her eyes shut, pictured Dev in Chicago. Watching the horrific images on the news. Doing everything in his power to protect his son, just like she would have.

Jia nodded. "Yes, he did." She was so tired. She wanted to go to sleep, but her mind snagged on "like always."

"What did you mean back in the house when you said that Dad helped you with your suspension?"

Ishaan side-eyed her. "For one, he didn't automatically assume it was my fault." He continued, "Dad said he'd been bullied too. He had to wear braces and the other kids teased him about it. But he never confided in Grandpa because he said only weak people get bullied. Dad didn't want me to feel the same. He said I had one advantage. Unlike when he was young, these days everyone has cell phones and someone or the other would've recorded something. He gave me an idea. Even if my classmates didn't want to go on record, someone could drop a video of what had happened. And thanks to Dad, I got it yesterday, before everything went crazy. Now I have proof."

"Proof?"

"Gimme your phone."

"I lost it," Jia said ruefully.

Ishaan asked to borrow one of the other passengers' phones and brought up the Facebook app.

He hit play on a video clip and from the first frame, Jia's insides fizzed with unease. Ishaan was situated on a seat in his school cafeteria, eating his sandwich, when a boy with a heavyset build came up behind him.

"That's Sam," Ishaan said.

Sam commanded Ishaan to vacate his seat, but Ishaan ignored him and continued eating his lunch, at which point Sam, towering over him, came close to Ishaan's ear and said loudly, "I said, get up, Apu." Around them other kids were starting to notice, but no one said anything.

On the screen, Ishaan swallowed, then glanced back at him. "No. And the '90s called, they want their insult back."

There were a few snickers in the background. Ishaan smiled briefly, triumphant at this small win, but the very next minute, his smile slipped as Sam rolled his sleeves up and put him in a chokehold, dragging him away from the bench.

No. No. No. Jia's lungs tightened as though she herself were being assaulted, and all she wanted to do was go inside the pixelated screen and prize away the heavy hand and remove Ishaan from the headlock.

In the video, Ishaan gulped, struggling to free himself, and someone else in the background whipped out a phone to record too, but no one—*no one*—stepped up to help him. Then Sam leaned in again and whispered something in Ishaan's ear. Ishaan's face twisted before he stood up, and suddenly he pushed Sam back with force, sending him toppling. A loud clatter was followed by an even louder moan of pain. The frame jumped and went out of focus at the end.

Rendered completely speechless, Jia stared at Ishaan, tears running down her cheeks. "What did he say to you?" she whispered.

Ishaan lowered his head and his left foot rubbed at a spot on the carpet. "He said 'Your mom has a fat ass.'" Ishaan looked up, hands balled into fists. "I didn't want him to get a concussion, but I had no choice."

Her chest burned with indignation. How dare the school punish Ishaan and not Sam? All these students witnessing the horror, but no one had told her the truth. "Why didn't you tell me?" she asked, but she knew the answer already. Jia had accepted the school's version of events and interrogated Ishaan instead of giving him a chance to explain.

Jia was dejected. Dev had come to Ishaan's rescue and given him the benefit of the doubt, whereas she'd treated her son with suspicion. She looked back at the video again. Fast-forwarded to the last few seconds. There was a boy just out of the frame who looked awfully familiar. Where had she seen him?

Then she remembered.

"Wasn't this boy talking to you at the candy store?"

Ishaan nodded. "He's part of Sam's group. They dared me to steal the candy from the store." He shrugged. "I thought if I did it, it would get them off my back."

Jia sucked in a breath. How could she have been so wrong about her son?

Instead of protecting her son from bullies, she'd suspected him. Her mind leapt to the Nerf gun. She'd assumed it was further evidence of his stealing, but she now realized that it was most likely exactly what it seemed: simply a toy misplaced by a kid.

They looked up as another motorboat powered through, heading back the way they'd come, parting the water into foamy waves.

The house would be completely flooded by now. Jia prayed it was not too late.

AFTER DISEMBARKING THE BOAT, THEY WERE HERDED TO A HIGH school gym packed with other evacuees. Donated blankets carpeted the waxed floors; some people slept on inflatable mattresses, and volunteers distributed cold sandwiches and bottled water. The makeshift shelter was stuffy, the air musty and humid.

Next to a few senior citizens awaiting transfer to a hospital, Grandma hunched on a foldable chair, Raj sitting cross-legged on the floor next to her. He jumped to his feet and hugged Ishaan.

"Where's Seema and Asha?" Jia asked. As much as she never wanted to see her sister again, she had a burning desire to confirm that Seema and Asha had been rescued safely. Raj's expression turned dark. "Bhabhi . . . Seema thought you'd died and kept saying she deserved to die too." He spoke in a flat, affectless voice as if he were talking about a stranger, not someone he'd known for years. "She and Asha, along with Lisa, were sent to a different shelter in a separate boat because ours was full."

"It's my fault," Grandma croaked, her gray eyes clouded with tears. "I waited too long."

It was the first time Jia had seen her cry.

They were interrupted by a woman with a clipboard noting

down everyone's names, and Jia wondered what Seema was doing right now. Did she truly regret her actions?

Jia wouldn't see her sister again for four months, their encounter a stark departure from their old homey visits, a clock ticking down the number of minutes they were allowed to talk, Seema dressed in an orange jumpsuit, her hands cuffed.

FORTY-FOUR

SIX MONTHS LATER

Meet the Author!

TRAGEDY IN SUGAR LAND,
by Raj Joshi

Reading by Jia Shah

Every last chair, arranged in rows in the center of the library, was occupied. When Jia entered, she felt everyone's eyes on her, murmurs rising, chairs scraping as people tried to get a better look. Jia and Raj stood in a corner next to a table piled with copies, each jacketed with a glossy image of an imposing mansion in the throes of a storm, titled *Tragedy in Sugar Land.*

Raj approached the lectern and unfurled a copy of the *Houston*

Chronicle, crisp as his cotton shirt. "'Grisly Killings in Sugar Land,'" he read from the newspaper. "You all know me as the surviving brother from the tragedy that occurred in a suburban house in Sugar Land . . ."

Jia scanned the room and saw the onlookers hanging on Raj's every word. The murders had made national headlines because they hit all the lurid notes of a sensationalist story: a wealthy family, a suburb where homicide was unheard of, and two beautiful women conspiring together.

Seema and Lisa's involvement had also sparked a spate of feminist articles condemning the sensationalist coverage focusing on Seema's affair, the articles' tones almost in awe of the damage women could wreak when they put aside racial and other differences to work together. Jia had been worried that the negative attention would make Ishaan's life even more difficult, but he had been universally lauded as the boy who saved his mother.

The video of Sam assaulting Ishaan probably would have vindicated him anyway, but with Ishaan's newfound fame, it went viral, shared millions of times on social media, and the school couldn't possibly ignore it. The principal did an about-face, opening an internal investigation into the incident and the wrestling team's curriculum, from which Sam had learned the choking technique. Sam's parents, hounded by media and barraged by virtual hate posts, dropped the lawsuit.

Jia was amazed at how humbly Ishaan took this remarkable turn of events in stride.

And she'd forever be in debt of one person for saving their lives: Dev.

He flew in from Chicago as soon as flights resumed operations, and he and Ishaan had a teary reunion at George Bush Airport. Seeing them dissolve into high-fives and fist bumps, Jia bubbled with happiness. She now understood that Dev didn't need to be a good husband to be a great father. They agreed to have Ishaan spend the winter break with him till they figured out a long-term shared-parenting arrangement that would work for both of them, no lawyers arbitrating on their behalf.

Seema was currently in prison awaiting trial, but the prosecutor's case against her was entirely built on circumstantial evidence since the hurricane had decimated the house, even making it difficult to pin down the time of Vipul's death. The focus on Seema turned Rafael's death into a mere footnote in the case, used only as proof of Seema's motive. After a dribble of media leaks, a theory gained traction: Vipul, enraged by his wife's affair, had taken advantage of Rafael's deathly allergy. But with both the initial victim and his presumed killer dead, the cops directed their energy on Seema, casting her as a scheming wife who murdered her husband in cold blood.

Initially, Jia gave a lengthy statement to the investigators detailing Seema's confession, eager to see her pay for putting Ishaan's life in danger, her words damning enough for a grand jury to issue a swift indictment.

But as the months dragged on, her parents' absence took a toll on Asha. She ran in Raj's house, searching all the rooms for her mom and dad, didn't sleep well, lost weight, became fussy and irritable, and her condition deteriorated after a bout of pneumonia, which culminated in hospitalization due to Grandma's obstinate insistence on home remedies.

Jia was crushed when she went to visit Asha. Her delicate arm was hooked to an IV, matted hair stuck to her sickly skin, and she mumbled "Mama" in her sleep. Raj, officially her godparent, was clearly in over his head.

As soon as Asha was released from the hospital, Jia requested a visit to the facility where Seema was imprisoned.

Prison life did not suit Seema. Her hair was unkempt, oily like it hadn't been washed in weeks. Crusty flakes sat in the corners of her eyes, and her left cheek had a hazy bruise.

But her face lit up as soon as Asha ran into her arms, and when they hugged each other tightly, Jia knew there was only one way forward.

Recant her testimony to secure Seema's release.

After everything Seema had put her through, she'd never see eye to eye with her. But Jia couldn't let her words consign her innocent niece to the fate of an orphan.

While it wasn't easy to get Raj and Grandma on board, they relented if Seema agreed to place Vipul's assets in a trust set up for Asha. Jia and Seema's own mother wanted nothing to do with her eldest daughter anymore, and if Seema thought gossip after a divorce was bad, she had no idea what waited for her in the Indian community after a stint in prison. Seema would get her freedom, but not her same life back.

/'/'/'/'

RAJ LOOKED AROUND THE LIBRARY. "MY BROTHER USED TO TAKE ME to libraries in my childhood. He was always supportive of my interests even though he didn't think they were particularly useful. While some of you may think of this as a cheap attempt to cash in on my brother's death, if Vipul is watching from above, I'm certain he's thinking, *Finally, finally my writer brother found a way to make some money.*"

Faint chortles rippled through the room.

Jia suppressed a smile looking at the people in the front rows, some of them flipping through the hardcover copies, eager to dive deep into a sensational account of the case.

They were in for a surprise.

Jia had read an early copy and it wasn't about the murders at all, rather a nuanced examination of a brother's love for a sibling and regrets for things unsaid. The real tragedy, Raj conveyed lyrically over the course of two-hundred-odd pages was that we took our closest relationships for granted.

Raj gazed sideways at Jia before continuing, "Even though I lost so much that night, I got more than I could've ever asked for. I found a lifelong friend. And today I would like to request my friend Jia to read an excerpt from this book."

Jia stood up and walked slowly to the podium, rubbing the side of her arm out of habit. Seema had fired the gun aiming for Raj, hitting Jia by accident, but Jia was fortunate that the bullet had only grazed her arm, allowing her to make a full recovery. Lisa was handed a fate worse than a prison sentence. Raj had filed for divorce, ending their marriage.

"Thank you, Raj. I owe a debt of gratitude to the volunteers who rescued us. I learned many lessons that night. I used to think that without the support of family, I couldn't raise a kid because I wasn't a good mother. But all moms need help, especially single mothers." She smiled at Raj. "That's why I have partnered with Raj to start an NGO exclusively dedicated to assisting mothers looking to end their marriages. We will focus on helping women through the logistics of divorce, from securing an apartment to setting up new bank accounts. We have enough wedding planners in this country, I think we could use some divorce planners."

Laughter trickled through the room. Jia smiled at Raj. "Raj has been kind enough to donate one percent from every sale of his book for my endeavor. Single mothers need all the support they can get."

Later, as she drove off, for the first time, the rows of impressive houses she passed didn't evoke the slightest envy, and instead she felt relief, even a bit of pride. Finally, she could see the people in pretty houses living perfect lives for the mirages they really were.

Bright sunlight refracted off the windshield, poking her eyes, and she lowered the car visor. It was a perfectly warm sunny day, as if the city too was eager to move on from the events of that fateful night, ready to hoodwink visitors with promises of pleasant weather.

The city had finally grown on her. Nothing life had in store for her could outmatch what she'd experienced. A new Jia had emerged from the wreckage of that night. The news articles sometimes called her a survivor, sometimes a victim, but she was more than that.

She was a fighter.

FORTY-FIVE

GRANDMA

SIX MONTHS BEFORE THE STORM

The handsome neighbor was back. She'd known it in her bones when she saw Seema cleaning out a vase for a fresh set of roses, humming a tune under her breath. Seema had a predictable routine on his visits: an hour in the beauty parlor in the morning, a spring in her step, offers to make different health juices for Grandma. Inside her room, Grandma hobbled to the shut door and pressed her ear against it. Seema laughed, a full-throated sound she never heard around her dear son Vipul.

Grandma eyed the glass of orange juice by her bedside. Seema assumed she was very clever, trying to put Grandma to sleep with her foreign drugs, but Grandma was one step ahead, and ever since that afternoon when she'd woken up from a wonderful four-hour nap after drinking lemonade prepared by Seema, Grandma had learned not to take anything her daughter-in-law had made unsupervised.

Grandma thought of the three velvet boxes safely tucked beneath her blouses in the cupboard. When Grandma had generously suggested she wear the necklace with the beautiful green emerald for her baby shower, Seema's mouth twisted into disgust. It didn't matter anymore. Seema didn't deserve to touch her family heirlooms with her dishonest hands. She'd taken enough. Whenever Raj came to visit next, she would ask him to take it all for Lisa. The white girl had surprised her with her respect for Grandma and for her traditions, showing Grandma pictures of herself doing perfect yoga poses.

The neighbor said something in a low voice Grandma didn't understand. But whatever it was, it made Seema very unhappy because she said, "You don't get it, I can't just walk away from Vipul . . ."

"We should make a plan," he said.

Grandma stepped back; her frail chest heaved. Did he mean what she thought he meant?

Maybe the man was pressuring her to divorce Vipul. Grandma cursed the day he'd moved into the neighborhood three months ago; had known he was trouble the first time he walked into the house asking about the solar panels. His visits had become frequent, drop-ins in the morning while Vipul was at work, always carrying a box of sweets for Asha. She felt sick thinking how brazen Seema was, cavorting with her lover in a house her dear son worked hard to pay for.

Grandma shook her head. Who would marry Vipul at his age? He wasn't the best looker even in his youth, and girls these days had no appreciation for the stability he brought to a relationship.

She licked her chapped, permanently dry lips. Seema would leave Vipul, just like her sister, Jia, had left her own husband; would drain Vipul of all his hard-earned money, keep this big house, and walk away with Asha. Neither of the sisters had a scintilla of good values.

How could Grandma live without Asha? She wanted a grandson, yes, but still, she was used to Asha's sunny presence, her granddaughter a permanent fixture of her life just like her backache.

No. She had to intervene.

Seema and Rafael appeared to have moved on to a discussion of the weather. They were talking about a coming storm, a storm that would trap them. Grandma didn't understand. Were they planning to confront Vipul together? That must be it, she reasoned.

She couldn't afford to let that happen. A mother would do anything for her child. And Vipul might be a grown-up, but for her, he would always be her little boy.

Grandma listened for the lock in the front door and, once convinced their rendezvous had ended, ventured out to the kitchen. People assumed age was a weakness. But underestimation was the best gift.

Despite her arthritis, Grandma's movements were fluid. This was her domain. She knew every inch of the pantry; not a jar was removed without her noticing it.

In the sink, Grandma saw a plate with smudges of curry. Curious, she noticed two separate potato curries emptied into different fancy bowls on the countertop, and again a flash of anger rose in her, that this daughter-in-law who complained all day about cooking for her husband didn't mind taking special requests from a neighbor.

She tasted both with a spoon, and slowly, a smile spread across her lips.

This was it. His fatal flaw.

He must be like one of Asha's asthmatic friends. Grandma had suggested the child's mom try herbal homeopathic treatments instead of keeping him chained to these small pumps full of drugs.

Let this man come, thought Grandma, her body shaking with

righteous anger. She'd take care of the problem before they had a chance to talk to Vipul. If they had a perfect plan, she had an even better one, and because age had taught her to be patient, she would wait.

Wait for the night of the storm.

ACKNOWLEDGMENTS

Thank you to agent extraordinaire Lori Galvin. I'm so lucky she represents me. I can draw a straight line from signing with her to all the good things happening in my publishing career. She is fantastic at her job and just an awesome person to work with.

Thank you to my wonderful editor, Lindsey Rose, for helping me write the story I was meant to tell. It's been a dream working with you. Big thanks to the team at Dutton: Charlotte Peters, Jamie Knapp, Amanda Walker, Isabel DaSilva, Alice Dalrymple, Tiffany Estreicher, Mary Beth Constant, Juli Meinz, and Sarah Oberrender.

Thanks to Kellye Garrett, for adding me to Crime Writers of Color, a supportive community of rock stars! Thank you to my mentor June Hur, for your support and encouragement. Thank you to Miranda Darrow for selecting me in the RevPit contest. Thank you to Kushal, my wonderful husband. None of this would happen without you supporting my dreams. You and Avi are the best things to happen to me. Thank you to my in-laws, because of whom my son has known endless love from the time of his birth.

Mom, thank you for a life of unconditional love, warm hugs, and laughter. You are my rock. Thank you, Dad, for all your sacrifices, for all the books you brought for us to read, and for never making me feel like my career was any less important because I'm a girl. To my brother, Dhumil, thank you for giving me the best gift, the gift of education.

Thank you, Dimple, my forever best friend. Thanks also to my friend Swapna, who read a (very) rough draft of this book. I will always seek your counsel, for my stories and my life.

Last, but not the least, thank you dear reader for reading this book.

ABOUT THE AUTHOR

Nishita Parekh immigrated to the US from Mumbai in her teens and now resides in Texas with her family. She is a software programmer but a writer at heart. She is an active member of Crime Writers of Color, Sisters of Crime, a #RevPit contest winner, and loves writing about her experiences as a woman and immigrant. *The Night of the Storm* is her first novel.